FuTure
washingTon

Other books by WSFA Press:

The Father of Stones
Lucius Shepard

Through Darkest Resnick with Gun and Camera
Mike Resnick

The Edges of Things
Lewis Shiner

Home by the Sea
Pat Cadigan

FUTURE washington

Edited by Ernest Lilley

Washington Science Fiction Association
(WSFA)

About The Editor

Ernest Lilley has been publishing SFRevu
(www.sfrevu.com), an online science fiction review
magazine since 1997. He is currently living in Alexandria,
Virginia and is a member of the Washington Science
Fiction Association (WSFA). *Future Washington* is the first
anthology he has edited.

Printed by Thomson-Shore, Inc. 7300 West Joy Road,
Dexter, MI 48120-9701.

Trade Paperback ISBN: 0-9621725-4-5
Hard Cover ISBN: 0-9621725-5-3

Cover illustration by Mike Clarke

This book printed on acid-free paper

Acknowledgements

First and foremost, thanks must go to the Washington Science Fiction Association for letting me try my hand at anthologizing, as well as welcoming me to the area and the local SF community. They're a terrific bunch, and if you're in the area some first or third Friday of the month, you should look up their website (www.wsfa.org) and stop by for a meeting.

Second, but in no lesser way, the authors and artists who signed on for this venture. Having a chance to edit my first anthology was great . . . but to do it with many of my favorite authors was really a treat.

The WSFA crew that worked on this project deserves special recognition. Without their support, I never could have gotten this all done, and it certainly wouldn't have been half as much fun.

Special Mention goes to:

Gayle Surrette–Copyediting and Layout
Michael Walsh–Sage Publishing Wisdom
Drew Bittner–Publicity
Cathy Green–Contracts Coordination
Sam Lubell–Surfactant
Robert Garcia—Design Consultant & Production

And lastly, my deepest thanks go to the gal who dragged me to DC in the first place–

E.J. McClure (CDR, USN)

290 2689

Contents

INTRODUCTION
Ernest Lilley

Though I'm a new DC resident, I've always been impressed by the feel of the place—I love the tourists coming to check up on how their tax dollars are being spent, people from all over the world coming to see this locus of power . . . and to try and get a piece of it.

I'm a child of the space age. I started reading SF in the early '60s, when the future was a place full of promise, and the charge was for us to make something wonderful happen. In truth, a lot of wonderful things have happened in the span of nearly half a century, but not necessarily the ones we expected.

I've been to the National Air & Space Museum at regular intervals throughout my life, and recently reflected that everything I've ever thought of as an advanced air or space-craft is collected there . . . and retired. The face of the imagined future changes as a reflection of the present, no matter how tightly we may want to hold onto the future we grew up with. The real challenge is to embrace that change and to make the most of what comes.

As John Lennon pointed out, "Life is what happens to you while you're making other plans."

When I turned this collection of writers loose on a Washingtonian world of tomorrow, I hoped I'd get stories back showing how we had cleverly figured out how to get along, used technology to make representative democracy work, and either solved or adapted to the challenges posed by a changing planet. I'd hoped that someone would

1

address the inequity of power in DC, where the population is mostly Black and without legislative representation, and the power is mostly White and without any stake in the city, coming and going with changes in administration.

What I got back was a collection of terrific stories, but not necessarily of the kinds of futures I wanted. In reality, SF has never been much of a predictor of things to come, so maybe that's just as well. Maybe we've been better at forestalling the future than foretelling it. Maybe the stories I got back will serve best not in the answers they provide, but in the questions they raise.

It's a beautiful spring day here just five miles south of the Washington monument, and it's a short walk to the banks of the Potomac from here, where I can see it clearly. From this distance, it looks serene and stately, the monument and the capitol building rising up to set the height limits for the city. The view from the distance often hides important details though, and you can't really see a place until you've arrived, whether in space or time.

Will the Washington of tomorrow be a beacon of democracy, a monument to the adage about the dangers of absolute power, or a nearly forgotten footnote in humanity's history?

Time will surely tell.

Ernest Lilley
May 1, 2005
Alexandria, Virginia

Introduction to
Mr. Zmith Goes to Washington
Ernest Lilley

"No aliens," I said to everyone I asked for stories from. And still I got several submissions that included, inevitably, the line: "Take us to your leader." The alien as observer is one of SF's favorite ideas, and these stories were all pretty good . . . good enough so that I broke down and took a few in despite myself.

Steve Sawicki's story is actually an exception. I was familiar with (and fond of) his ongoing series of short stories about a group of aliens that live in his basement and spirit him off on adventures that tend to leave you scratching your head and chuckling at the same time and thought one might set up the anthology nicely. If you know Steve, you'll recognize his laconic self as the main character, and I'm not completely sure that these stories are actually fiction. Though to the best of my knowledge, he didn't have a basement when he started writing them. Which only means I never found one.

Anyway, "Mr. Zmith Goes To Washington" is the alien story I asked for to frame the book, and it's just what I wanted.

MR. ZMITH GOES TO WASHINGTON

STEVEN SAWICKI

We landed the mothership on the narrow swath of Mall fronting the National Air and Space Museum.

"I hope we will have time after the hearing to visit," Hummer said, his tenstacles waving more or less in that direction.

"I understand they have ICBM inside," Warr said, his shape shifting through a dozen forms, one or two of which would seem hauntingly familiar, especially if you were a country bumpkin.

"Will they have both the chocolate and the vanilla?" Klaarg slithered along behind, trailing a pseudopodded mouth in the dirt, tasting whatever he came across.

"Chocolate and vanilla?" I said. It wasn't always easy to be with the aliens. They often seemed more confused about things than I was. And I was *from* here.

"ICBM," Warr said. "I like mine in a big cup. Klaarg likes his in a crunchy cone."

"You're thinking of ICBY, I Can't Believe it's Yogurt," I said.

"Oh," Hummer said. "Was that not one of the points of contention of your cold war?"

"Um, no," I said.

Klaarg sucked up a large piece of debris, or possibly a squirrel. "We were wondering why your world spent so many years being concerned and afraid of frozen desserts."

"Hey," I said as we continued to walk towards the Capitol building. "How come no one really sees you?"

"They don't want to," Warr said. "You Earthers tend to see only what you want to see."

"It can't be that simple," I said.

"It's not," said Hummer. "We resonate on the 148th band of the spectral equation. Your retina sends a confused signal to your brain, which struggles to interpret the data as a waffle in the fabric of the spatial/dimensional vortex. We just give it a small push in the right direction with some pre-hypnotic suggestions. We have an abstract if you are truly interested."

"No," I said. "You've told me enough." Which meant they'd really told me nothing at all, their superior technology and science being pretty much incomprehensible to me.

We reached the Capitol steps and started to maneuver around the concrete security barriers.

"How do you plan on getting past them?" I nodded toward the pair of armed guards stationed before the metal detectors just inside the doors.

"We have passes," Klaarg said, waving a laminated badge in front of my face.

Hummer was already through and Warr was just clearing the detector. The guards turned to me: the me without a badge or alien technology and with a two-dollar pocketknife in his pocket. Klaarg was pushing me forward, just enough for the knife to set off the detectors. The guards dropped their hands to their guns and took a step toward me.

Klaarg started waving his tentacles. "This is not the one you want," he said.

"He's not the one we want," one guard said to the other.

"Let him go," Klaarg waved his tentacles in a figure eight pattern.

"Get out of here," the guard said to me.

Klaarg pushed me the rest of the way through and we were off down the corridor.

"Wow," I said, "just like *Star Wars*."

Hummer swung four eye-tipped pseudopods toward me.

"Lucas got that from you?" I said, recognizing the superior patronizing look I was getting.

"We gave him many things," Klaarg said.

"The cantina?" I said.

"Took him there for lunch," Hummer said.

"Land speeders?"

"Pollution free, anti-gravity wave propulsion is the standard transport on every planet," Warr said. "Except this one, of course."

"Light sabers?"

"Package opener. One comes with every Galactic Express delivery," Klaarg said.

"The Death Star?"

The aliens looked at one another, pseudopodded eyestalks swinging in all directions.

"We had things to drop off, we really had no choice," Hummer finally said.

"The mothership was filling up," Klaarg said.

"Filling up?" I said.

"If you are going to keep repeating everything we say we are going to stop talking to you," Hummer said, twitching two of his tenstacles from left to right. "It is embarrassing for a superior species to have to admit this but we needed someplace to put the things that have been used to completion."

"Garbage?" I said. "I'm surprised such an advanced, as you keep telling me, superior species hasn't managed to find a way to recycle everything."

"Not everything can be remade," Warr said. "For example, drained gravity-less crystals, anything made from one of the invisible elements, stellar dust composite materials and all of the transmolecular striation fusions."

"Bloog," Klaarg added.

"Yes, Bloog." Warr whipped his tenstacles in affirmation.

"So you take all this stuff and stick it in a big spaceship?"

"Moons," Hummer said. "We make moons."

"Wow, Lucas sure got that wrong."

"He would not listen," Warr said.

"That would explain episode one," I said.

"And the haircut," Hummer said.

We reached a set of sturdy walnut doors and stopped. A placard set to one side read, Select Committee to Resolve Extraterrestrial and Alien Meetings.

"Isn't Alien and Extraterrestrial the same thing?" I said.

"Not all Aliens are Extraterrestrials," Hummer noted.

"No?" I scratched my head.

"Canadians," Klaarg said.

"Ah," I said. "Right."

We entered.

The room was square, rows of seats facing a raised dais behind which a half a dozen senators sat. A row of tables occupied the space fronting and below the dais. The aliens made their way to the table. I followed. No one seemed to notice, not that there were all that many people in the room in the first place, maybe a dozen spectators and the obligatory pair of aides for each senator. The press was conspicuously absent.

The aliens took seats at the table, or rather just shifted their forms in place so that they occupied chairs. I sat on the end. Hummer stretched forth a tenstacle and tapped the microphone in front of him. No one noticed. He tapped again. Finally one of the senators glanced over. Senator McArther, from Arkansas, according to the nameplate before him. His eyes widened and his mouth dropped open. This was repeated throughout the room as everyone slowly became aware of the aliens.

"What . . . what is this?" Senator Brooks, ranking Republican from Nevada was the first to actually make a coherent sound.

"We took you up on your invitation," Hummer said.

The senators regained their faculties all at the same time, more or less, and the room erupted in voiced confusion.

"Order, order," Senator Ranowski, Democrat from Minnesota and committee chair, banged a gavel repeatedly. The small, round block of wood he pounded on danced after each strike. "Order."

The room slowly subsided to a whispered murmur. I noticed that some of the aides were trying to leave but couldn't seem to manage opening the doors.

"This is a closed Senate hearing," Ranowski said, "and I will not let it become a farce. Jenkins," he said over his shoulder to one of his staff, "get security and have these costumed invaders removed."

As the aide scrambled toward the door, Senator Rollins, a Democrat and the lowest ranking member of the committee, leaned forward looking directly at Hummer. "What did you mean when you said you were invited?"

"Senator Ranowski said, on the eighth passing of the lunar cycle plus three solar twirls," Hummer's voice dropped and a perfect imitation of Ranowski came from one of his mouthed pseudopods, "if the Extraterrestrials are out there we certainly invite them to come and testify."

The room returned to silence and Ranowski's aide scurried from the still unopened door to whisper to the senator.

"Use the phone, dammit," Ranowski's reaction was immediate.

"Your telecommunications devices have been put on delay," Warr said. "We did not think you would want to be interrupted."

Some of the younger senators were making the connection that this might not be a hoax.

"How did you get here?" Rollins leaned into the microphone.

"Mark VI mothership," Hummer said.

"And I suppose you parked in front of the White House?" Ranowski voiced his disbelief.

"No," Warr said. "We landed in the green space just outside." A tenstacle waved in the direction of the Mall. "We crushed a bush. Sorry. He didn't survive the meeting. We did try to miss him."

"Him?" Senator Chang, Republican from California said. "Do you mean to say you landed on the . . ."

"No, no, no . . ." I interrupted. "The aliens tell me that all things are alive and at least one of the six sexes. They landed on an actual bush."

"Who are you?" Senator Asperger, Democrat, New York, asked.

"Me?" I said. "Um, nobody, really."

"Are you a prisoner?" Rollins leaned forward again.

"Have they performed devilish experiments on you?" Chang said before I could respond.

"How were you captured?" McArther said.

"How are they treating you?" Brooks added.

"Have you been probed?" Boothe, Republican from Maine softly breathed into the mike.

"Order," Ranowksi banged his gavel. "Order."

The questions died down.

"Were we invited just to watch or did you have something else in mind?" Hummer swung multiple eyestalks toward the seated legislators while two of his tenstacles wrapped themselves around the microphone.

Warr flipped a mouth-tipped pseudopod at Hummer. "It is an interesting experience."

"But not as much fun as baseball," Klaarg added.

"Can you come back tomorrow?" Chang looked at Ranowski to confirm the possibility.

"Possibly next week," Ranowksi fixed a steady gaze on Hummer.

"No," Hummer said. "Tomorrow we're looking at grain elevators."

"And next week we're going for ice cream," Klaarg said.

"Chair," Senator Rollins spoke to Ranowski. "I motion we recess for 30 minutes and then reconvene for a period of questions and, I hope, answers."

"We only have this much rotation," Hummer said,

holding up two pseudopods. "Then we have to be some-where else."

The Senators looked at one another, Ranowski glared at his staff member who could only respond with a shrug.

"Twenty minutes," I said.

"Yes," Hummer said, "we're sharing podling stories on Altair IV. It's parsecs and parsecs from here."

"You can travel parsecs?" Asperger's eyebrows dipped and rose.

"In minutes?" Boothe said softly into the mike.

"Well, yes," Klaarg let his tenstacles twist around the microphone first in one direction and then in the other. "Of course if there is traffic it will take us longer."

"Parsecs," Ranowski said. "Doesn't that mean you travel faster than light?"

"Doesn't everybody?" Hummer said.

"How do you do that?" Rollins' eyes moved nervously from alien to alien.

"I pull the switch that locks the doors, Klaarg enters the stop place numbers and Warr pushes the dark button," Hummer said.

"But how does it work?" Asperger's voice rose with each word.

Hummer's pseudopodded eyes dropped. "We don't really know."

"You must have documents," Chang said.

"We did," Klaarg said, "but we lost them when we stopped to pull on some cosmic strings."

"Strings," Boothe said. "The future, yes?"

Hummer grew uncomfortable. One thing I had learned was that the aliens didn't know how to lie. Forgot how they told me one time. Of course you still had to know how to ask them questions in the right way to get them to give you a straight answer.

"I'll take that as a yes," Boothe said. "You have seen our future, have you not?"

"Not," Klaarg said.

"Futures then," Boothe seemed to be catching on. "Cosmic strings can show you alternate futures, what has not yet happened but could, the lines that radiate out from major decisions."

Warr sucked a microphone into a pseudopodded mouth. The speaker made some interesting sounds before he spit it out.

"What have you seen?" Rollins caught on to Boothe's line of questioning.

"We have seen many things," Hummer said.

"Of our future?" Boothe abruptly leaned forward in a familiar move meant to intimidate.

"We have looked at possibilities," Klaarg said. "There are many."

"And not all of them are dystopian," Hummer said, "regardless of your inability to see that yourselves."

"What happens to the United States?" Chang wanted to know.

"Who wins the next election?" Asperger spoke before any of the aliens could answer.

"Does it take another hundred years for the Red Sox to win the World Series again?" Rollins asked.

"These are not the kinds of questions we expected you to ask us," Hummer said.

Ranowski leaned forward after listening to a quick whisper from his aide. "We've spent billions of dollars listening for evidence of intelligent life and we haven't heard a thing. Why not?"

Hummer let his pseudopodded eyes swing up to the Senator. "Most intelligent species get cable."

"What about time travel?" Brooks asked.

"What about it?" Klaarg let a pseudopodded mouth run along the carpet looking for interesting things to ingest.

"Do you have it?" Brooks let some exasperation slip into his voice.

"It works best with small bugs," Klaarg said, "at least

that's what the temporal manipulagists tell us. Everything else comes out kind of squishy on the other side."

"You must have something you can share with us," Ranowski said, "something you've learned from your travels, some knowledge that we can benefit from."

"No," Warr said.

"Not really," Klaarg added.

"It's against the code," Hummer said.

"The code?" Boothe almost whispered.

An aide leaned into Ranowski

"You mean like the prime directive?" Ranowski said.

"You mean like Star Trek?" Klaarg said.

Ranowski checked with the aide before nodding.

"No," said Klaarg. "We have no prime directive. I was referring to the acclimation code of the empty distances passage. There is a part near the end which prohibits voyagers from giving any primitive race a thing they might use to hurt themselves."

"Have you heard of the Klinzintu?" Hummer said.

The senators looked to one another blankly.

"The Hurunga? The Aoalaoapoa? The Splanafanafor?" Hummer went through a short list of alien races.

The senators continued their blank stares.

"They are all congregates of beings who no longer are," Warr said.

"The Aoalaoapoa were given the recipe for Gort, kla-tu necto-barada," Hummer said, dropping his pseudopods to the table. "It took less than five star twists for them to destroy themselves."

"This Gort, klepto . . ." Rollins could not finish. "It was some kind of weapon?"

"Dessert topping," Klaarg said.

"This is absurd," Ranowski snapped, slapping a palm against the smooth walnut of the dais. "These answers are meaningless."

"You're not asking very good questions," Hummer said.

"Can't you tell us something?" Chang glared at me.

"Me?" I sputtered. "No, I didn't even know we were coming here. We were just supposed to pop out for some eggs and flour so they could try a new spooze recipe."

"Spooze?" Ranowski said.

"It's a food," I said, "sort of."

"Would you like some?" Klaarg changed most of his mouthed and eyed pseudopods into manipulators and quickly deposited a lump of shining goo in front of each senator.

"It's organic," Hummer said.

"Perhaps," Ranowski said eyeing the spreading goo, "later."

"It won't last," I said.

"It's organic," Klaarg said.

"Surely," Boothe's voice barely came through the speakers, "there is something you can tell us."

Hummer sent pseudopodded eyes toward Klaarg and Warr who did the same until the area around the table was filled with writhing pseudopods and tenstacles. A moment later the space was clear.

"It is true that we have journeyed out to the cosmic strings and watched your future," Klaarg said.

"But this was mostly because you are going through a period of not good TV," Warr said.

"You should make better shows in the very near future," Hummer said.

"Unless, of course," Warr added, "you don't"

"There are things we have seen that are disturbing," Klaarg swished his tenstacles across the table.

"There are things we have seen that are full of pain and remorse," Hummer moved his mouthed pseudopod closer to the microphone.

"There are moments of joy and exhilaration," Warr said.

"Perhaps there are a few things we can show you," Hummer let his eyed pseudopods run to Warr and Klaarg.

"Tell us," Ranowksi, along with the rest of the senators hunched forward.

"Be good to yourselves," Hummer said.

"Be good to others," Klaarg said.

"Don't clone until you know all the sequences," Hummer said.

"Remember to look up," Klaarg retracted all of his pseudopodded mouths.

"The future is like oxygen," Hummer said. "It is there for all of you but can be ruined by a very few."

"The new strike zone is bad for baseball," Warr said.

The senators all looked at me.

"I don't really have any advice," I said. "Although I do wish you would finally get around to. . . ."

They were all asleep, or mimicking some state that looked remarkably like it.

"It is time for us to leave," Hummer said.

"I don't think you accomplished much," I said.

"The longest trip begins with the smallest bit of cold fusion," Klaarg said.

"You are slow beings who are quick to go nowhere," Warr said.

"I guess," I said, as we left the room and turned to head down the corridor back to the outside.

"It will take many such meetings in many different places and even then you may never be ready," Hummer said.

We passed the guards and started down the stairs.

"Oh," I said. "Are we really going to Altair IV?"

"Since we have not left yet it becomes impossible to answer," Klaarg, ever the literalist, flung a number of mouthed pseudopods behind him.

"We would be open to possibilities," Hummer said. The mothership loomed before us.

"Well," I said, "I was thinking we could go to Vermont and look for Ben and Jerry. I think they'd be interested in that frozen cow idea you were telling me about."

"It is more than an idea," Warr said, moving up the ramp. "We have a number of prototypes."

"Yes," Klaarg entered the ship last as he always did, "we expanded your subterranean living quarters to make space."

"Look," I said, "you can't keep making the basement bigger every time you need more space."

The aliens all stopped and focused an array of pseudopodded eyes on me.

"Yes we can," Hummer said, pulling the switch that locked the doors.

INTRODUCTION TO IGNITION
Ernest Lilley

I had dreams of the Washingtonian World of Tomorrow getting some airtime in this collection, but Global Warming and Theocracy was the more popular vision of things to come. Separately, or as here in a very nice little piece, hand in hand.

What I like about this story, besides the writing, which is excellent, is the cyclic nature of things that lurks in the background. If you don't recognize the fragmented quote that gets unearthed early on, Google it after you've finished and read a bit about the context that it was first said in to see just how fitting it is. See . . . reading SF can be fun, thought provoking, and educational . . . all at the same time.

IGNITION

JACK MCDEVITT

I saw no sign of a devil.

We'd been working on an extension of the Holy Journey subway when we ran into large blocks of concrete, stacked one atop the other, buried in the earth. The blocks weren't supposed to be there, but they were. The extension, when finished, would cross the river south into St. Andrew's Parish, taking substantial pressure off the bridges. They lay directly in our way. So I kept my crew drilling, and eventually we broke through—into a large space.

I pointed my light up. The ceiling must have been more than a hundred feet.

Now the truth is I hadn't given any thought to devils and demons until I flashed my light into the darkness and saw, first, broken columns scattered around the place, as if it had once been a temple. Then there was the statue.

The statue was gigantic, maybe three times as high as I was. Or it would have been had the base not been buried in earth, broken stone, and assorted debris.

"What happened here?" demanded a voice behind me. Cort Benson, my number one guy. He pushed in and immediately locked on the giant figure rising out of the earth floor. "My Lord," he said, his voice suddenly very low. "What is *that*?"

I had never seen a statue before. I'd heard of them. Knew about them. But I'd never actually seen one. Nor, I suspected, had anyone else on the work crew. It was a man. I moved a few steps closer and held up my lamp. He was dressed oddly, loose-fitting clothes from another age. Odd-looking coat or vest. Hard to tell which. The statue was sunk into the ground to a point midway between knees and hips. There was something clasped in his left hand. A rolled sheet of paper, looked like.

My crew stayed near the door. One of them called for a blessing. Another said it was devil's work.

Elsewhere around the space, some columns were still standing. They connected to a curved wall, forming a boundary around the statue. Beyond the wall and the columns were more concrete blocks like the ones we'd had to cut through to get in.

Okay. Let me tell you straight out I never believed in evil spirits. I said prayers against them every Sunday, like everybody else, and sometimes during midweek services. But I didn't really buy into it. You know what I mean? Although that's easy to say, sitting in the sunlight.

But here was this *thing*.

The air was thick, and somehow smelled of other days. I played the light against the wall. Several rows of arcane symbols were engraved in it. They were filled with dirt and clay, so it was hard to make them out. I picked at them with a crowbar, pulled some earth loose, and saw what they were: ancient English. The language still showed up occasionally around the parish, and over in Seven Crosses, and even as far north as St. Thomas. The characters were usually engraved on chunks of rock that must once have been cornerstones and arches and front entrances and even occasionally, as here, on walls. The world was filled with rubble from the civilization that God in His wrath had brought down.

I thought about that for a minute. Wages of sin. Then I pointed the lamp up and saw a second group of characters on a narrow strip circling the ceiling.

Cort grumbled something I couldn't make out and walked past me toward the statue.

Three or four lamps were now playing across its face,

from the guys who stood back at the entrance. They showed no inclination though to come any closer.

The lights gave life to the features. His eyes tracked me, the lips curved into a smile. It gave me chills; I'll admit that.

His features radiated power. And superiority. Though any guy twenty feet tall is going to look superior. The sculptor, if indeed there had been a sculptor, had given him an aura of the supernatural.

⌐━╾╌╌╌╾━⌐

I checked in with the office, let them know what I'd found, and at their instruction, told my crew they could take the rest of the morning off or until a decision was made what to do about the discovery.

Cort waited until I got off the circuit. Then he said, "Eddie would be interested in this."

"Who's Eddie?" I wished Cort would follow the others outside. Get some fresh air. Do something constructive. Just please don't hang around and make suggestions.

"Come on, Blinky," said Cort. "Eddie Trexler. My cousin. You know him." Since he'd come back from prison, Cort seemed to have trouble breathing. You could always hear it, always knew when he was nearby. He probably shouldn't have been working down in the subways, but he was on the bishop's list and we couldn't get permission to transfer him.

I vaguely remembered once getting introduced to Trexler, a long time ago. But I couldn't recall anything about him. Or why he would possibly be interested in the chamber.

"I'll be back in a little while," said Cort. He was always ready to skate at the edges of the law. It was what had gotten him in trouble in the first place.

"Wait a minute," I said. "You know the rules."

"All they say is we have to report something like this. You've done that. Did they tell you to keep everybody out?"

"No."

"There you are, then."

"That's what they want, though."

"Hellfire, Andy, if that's what they want they ought to *say* it." He fished a phone out of his pocket. "I'm going to give him a yell."

Then he was gone. It wasn't worth a confrontation. Cort thought I got in line too easily, and sometimes I had to rein him in. But this didn't seem like one of those times. If he got himself and his cousin in trouble, so be it.

The giant gazed down at me. I went over and touched him, touched his thigh, brushed away some of the accumulated dust. He was bronze.

The lights were gone now, save the one I was carrying. I felt alone.

⸺✦⸺

You'd never have known Eddie Trexler was a relative of Cort's. Where Cort was heavy and unkempt and probably indestructible, the cousin was tall and reedy and pressed. He owned a high-pitched voice and wore thick glasses, and he walked like a duck.

But there was no doubting his enthusiasm when he shook my hand and, without waiting for permission, climbed past me into the space. Trexler was a clerk at the Department of Theological Studies, but his hobby was ancient history. He'd brought one of those large lanterns that will light up a city block. He was two steps inside when he switched it on and put the beam on the statue. "Magnificent," he said. His voice had gone a notch higher.

Cort chuckled. "He asked me to say thanks for asking him over."

"Sure," I said. "My pleasure." We followed him in.

He stood gawking at the figure, at the wall, at the columns. Even at the concrete blocks. "I never thought I'd live to see anything like this." And, "You know what this is, Cort?" And, "Lovely."

"It's a statue," I said. I could have added that it desperately needed to be washed, that it was chipped in more than a few places, that it was half-buried. That it was blasphemous.

Thou shalt not make unto thyself any graven image.

But I let it go.

"Do *you* know what it is?" Cort asked him.

"I have an idea." He plunged into the space, climbed over the debris, studied the statue, touched one of the standing columns, and closed in on the wall—on the inscription. Then he went behind the wall and looked at the blocks. "Nicely fitted," he said. "Seamless."

"Yes," we both replied, though I doubt either of us had noticed.

"This is big news," he said. "If it's what I think it is."

"Why, Ed?" I asked. "What do you think it is?"

"Look at the writing on the walls. This place is prediluvian. *Before* the flood."

"Okay. And your point . . .?"

"Look at the blocks."

"What about them?"

"Think why they're there."

"Why are they there?"

"They tried to save it," he said, as much to himself as us. "God help them, they tried to save it."

"Yes," I said, not sure what I was agreeing to.

"It must have sunk during the flooding. Too heavy. It was more than thirty thousand tons. Add all that concrete—." He shook his head. "And here it is."

"I guess so," I said.

"That means—." His eyes gleamed with a light of their own. "They knew the flood was coming."

"The Great Flood?"

"Yes. Official doctrine is. . ."

"That it happened without warning," said Cort.

"Correct." He pressed his palms against the stone, as if to read a message hidden within the cold gray surface.

"That's going to stir the pot a bit." He pulled a camera from a sweater pocket and began taking pictures.

Cort stayed at his side, fascinated. "Can you read any of it, Ed?"

"Not really. If we can get it clean, we should be able to figure it out." He turned back to me. "Cort tells me you've alerted the authorities."

"Of course," I said. "It's a requirement."

"Yeah," he said. "I know. Pity."

I couldn't miss the implied accusation. "Hey," I said. "I didn't have a choice. We're law-abiding."

He told me it wasn't my fault. "How long will it take them to get here?"

"No way to know," Cort rumbled, raising an eyebrow in my direction.

Trexler began trying to clear the symbols. Cort and I joined in. But it was hard going and we didn't make much progress. He stepped back and took more pictures, and frowned. "*Publish*," he said, finally.

"What? Publish what?"

"This word means *publish*." It was about nine lines down. And, four lines below that: "*Reliance*."

He shook his head and glanced at me again. "I don't suppose there's any chance you could go out and head them off when they get here."

"You mean the police?"

"Yes."

"What would I tell them?"

"Anything you can think of."

"No," I said. "I don't think I could get away with that."

He rolled his eyes. And in that moment noticed the overhead inscription. "What's that?"

"More letters," said Cort. "I'll try to slow down the police."

"Thank you." He threw a withering glance in my direction. Then he returned his attention to the roof. "That's in better condition up there," he said.

"Yes," I said. I was trying to decide what to do. I kept seeing the police hauling off all three of us.

"*. . . Have sworn . . .*"

"What?"

He was still looking up. "It says *have sworn*, and there's *alert* off to the right."

"Okay."

"No. Wait. It's *altar*."

I watched him change his angle and stand on his toes as if getting an inch closer would help.

"*Mind of man* at the end."

I heard the sound of arriving vehicles.

He jerked his head around. Stared toward the hole we'd cut through the blocks. "So soon?" He looked dismayed.

"I guess."

He went back to the inscription. "The last three words are *mind of man*. No question about it."

Doors slammed. From the main tunnel came the rumble of a passing train. Dust drifted down on us.

"*. . . Have sworn . . . altar . . . mind of man.*"

"Makes no sense," I said.

"I can't make out the rest of it." He changed his angle again. "I need to get closer to it. You have a ladder handy?"

"Not high enough to reach *that*," I said.

"Damn. We need a little time."

"Maybe it's something this guy said," I suggested, indicating the statue.

He sighed. "Of course it is. Said or wrote. What else would it be?"

I didn't much like the attitude he was taking. "The statue's blasphemous," I reminded him. There was a line from the *Divine Handbook*: You don't make statues of people because that implies they are godlike.

"Don't be stupid," he said. Then he went back to the inscription. "The first word is only a single letter. Probably a pronoun. Has to be *I*."

There were voices outside now.

"*Hostility.* Some kind of *hostility.* Maybe *extraordinary.*"
The voices became loud.

"I think it's *hostility against.* Has to be. And *tyrant.* Yes.
. . . *Hostility against something something tyrant.*"

There was a scuffle outside. Mercifully short.

"No. It's not *tyrant.* It's, I think it's *tyranny.* Yes. That's
it. *Tyranny.*"

People were crowding into the chamber. Five men, four
in police uniforms.

"I'm Inspector Valensky," said the one in plain clothes.
He flashed an ID toward Trexler, as if I weren't there. He
was middle-aged, bearded, and very official. Cort trailed in
behind them, hands apparently secured behind his back.

"Good afternoon, Inspector," said Trexler, at which
point Valensky saw the statue.

"The Lord is my keeper, sir," he said. "We *do* have devil's
spawn here, don't we?"

Trexler's light fell on the police officers and I saw they
were carrying bags of explosives. "Don't come in here with
that," he warned. "What are you doing? Get that out of
here."

The inspector drew himself up straight, and tugged at
his beard. "Sir," he said, "gentlemen, I think who comes and
who goes is our decision. And the fact is, I must ask *you* to
leave."

Trexler didn't budge.

"This thing is blasphemous," said Valensky, sounding
as if he were struggling to keep his voice level. "We'll have
to get rid of it."

"What do you mean, 'get rid of it'?"

"I meant exactly what I said, sir. We're going to send it
back where it belongs. Meantime, you'd be prudent to mind
your manners." He turned to me. "I take it you're Blinkman
Baylor."

I winced. I never understood what my folks were thinking when they gave me that name. "That's correct."

"Good. You did the right thing, Mr. Baylor, although it

might have been a good idea to keep these two out of here." He raised his voice so we could all hear. "I hope none of you touched this abomination."

"No," I said, trying to sound reassuring. "Of course not."

He looked dead at me. "You *do* know not to touch any of these relics, don't you?"

"Oh, yes," I said. "I keep my hands off."

"Good, Mr. Baylor. Very prudent."

"*I* touched it," said Trexler.

"It renders you unclean, sir. You'll want to come with us when we're finished here."

"What for?"

"We'll have to take you to All-Sorrows for a ceremonial cleansing."

Trexler glared back with contempt. They'd have to carry him.

Valensky managed to look both annoyed and disappointed. "I do wish you'd cooperate, sir." He turned to Cort. "What about you?"

"Me?" Cort said. "I haven't been anywhere near it."

"Good." Two of the officers put on white gloves. They carried the charges across the chamber, picking their way through the debris, and laid them against the statue.

When Trexler tried to intervene, a third officer, a woman, headed him off. "Just stay calm, sir," she said, "if you will."

We watched while they made adjustments and connections.

Trexler glared at Valensky. "You blockhead," he said. "Do you have any idea what this place is worth? What it *is*?"

Valensky looked unmoved. "I know exactly what it is. Thank God one of us does." He turned to me. "I suggest you get him out of here."

The two who were setting the explosives stood up and brushed off their knees. "All set," one of them said. The other knelt back down and tugged at something. "Ready to go," he added.

Valensky took a remote from his pocket. "Everybody out, please," he said. He moved toward the exit, walking slowly while he waited for the rest of us to file out. Trexler stayed where he was.

"Come on, Eddie," said Cort.

Trexler shook his head. "I'm not going anywhere."

A signal passed between the inspector and the officers. They filed past Trexler. The woman touched her cap and said goodbye.

"I do wish you'd be reasonable," said Valensky.

Trexler moved closer to the statue. "Go ahead," he said. "Do what you have to."

"You leave me no choice, sir."

"Idiot."

The officers left, taking a struggling Cort with them. All except Valensky. "I'll set off the charge in one minute," he said. "That gives you time to change your mind and get out."

Trexler did not move. "Blow it up and be damned."

"Eddie." I felt helpless. "Getting yourself killed won't help anything."

"Listen to him," said Valensky. Then he looked my way. Time to go.

I waited a few seconds, watched Valensky disappear. "Ed," I said, "for God's sake . . ."

"He won't do it," said Trexler. "Too much paperwork if he kills somebody."

⁕

When the rebellion started, two months later, with the coordinated robberies of two banks and the looting of a parish arms warehouse, the authorities were slow to recognize it for what it was. And that cost them everything.

The two historians of the revolution, the two I know of, both believe Edward Trexler's death was the spark that started it all. There's some truth to that. But of course a lot of other people had died before he did, charged with heresy, or blasphemy, or various other attitudinal felonies.

God knows, though, Trexler's death motivated *me*. Who would ever have believed that conservative old Blinky Baylor would pick up a gun and go to war? But there was something else that stuck in my mind. That, for a lot of us, eventually became the engine that drove the revolution.

"(I?) . . . Have sworn . . . altar . . . hostility (against?) . . . tyranny . . . mind of man."

It wasn't hard to fill in the blanks. And sometimes, during the dark times, it kept me going. I think it kept a lot of us going. You want to make a revolution work, you need more than a taste for vengeance.

INTRODUCTION TO INDIANA WANTS ME
Ernest Lilley

Brenda delighted me by coming up with an absolutely appropriate story about something that never occurred to me. Intrigue among Realtors. This story comes very close to being eclipsed by actual events as many DC offices are now relocating outside the Beltway in order to comply with new anti-terrorism regulations, where there's room to keep cars away from buildings. Brenda's scenario will no doubt send security types scurrying to check out a whole new group of possible subversives. . . .

INDIANA WANTS ME

BRENDA W. CLOUGH

You wouldn't think it, but being a hedge witch meshes beautifully with a career in real estate. Both jobs are on-and-off dead ends, neither pays very much, and revolve around the concept of *home*. On Thursday I was wearing the realty hat, writing up a deal to sell this fellow's house.

"Anything," he said like they all do. "Get me anything you can."

I didn't look up from my keyboard. "I can't make any promises, Mr. Macateer. You read the papers."

No need to say more. When a pocket nuke was found in a men's room at the Department of Agriculture downtown, it didn't even need to detonate. Washington DC became radioactive anyway. The following week the yellow-bellied chicken hawks in Congress voted unanimously to move the legislative branch to Indiana. A new White House was built north of Fargo, North Dakota. Without the enormous engine of the federal government behind it, the real estate market in the greater Washington metro area went into free fall. And guess who was behind the eight ball? Real estate agents, that's who. More hopefully I added, "Have you found a place in Indianapolis yet?"

Mr. Macateer nodded with a sigh. "Had to pay through the teeth for a condo. God, I'm going to miss my house. Those vultures out there, they have you over a barrel."

"A bunch of sidewinders," I agreed. There went the prospect of a small referral fee–the Indiana Realtors had agreed to throw us a bone every now and then. No bone

29

today! Mr. Macateer signed, and I shuffled all the copies into his stack and my stack. It was hard not to feel like the last rat on the sinking Titanic.

It wasn't quite the end of the day but I turned off the photocopier and powered down the computers. The sign on the door says very clearly, "NO listings accepted after 3 P.M.!" Even so a couple of women came up as I wrestled with the lock of the door.

"I need to sell my townhouse right away!" the first one wailed.

"Is it in Arlington or Alexandria?"

"No, Manassas."

I shook my head. Nobody is ever going to buy a town-house in the outer burbs ever again, not with big houses close in going for a song. "Quit paying on the mortgage and walk away," I suggested. "It's a dead loss."

She wrung her hands in despair and turned away. The second woman, who had been hanging politely back, came forward. "Now, Susan–when was the last time you passed up a listing?"

I glared at her, and gave the key a futile twist. "How nice to see you, Lynn. In fact I have several thousand unsold houses on the books right this minute. Would you like to see one?"

Lynn laughed heartily. "Transplant them to Hamilton County Indiana, and it's a deal!" Then she hiccuped. She must have started happy hour early.

"What are you in town for, Lynn? Too many sales in Indiana?" Oops, mustn't be bitter, not with an Indianapolis Realtor who could throw business my way. "Maybe we can go have a drink."

"I haven't time, dear! I just dropped by to make you a little proposition. A group of us are meeting in an hour with some high-level DoD officials, with a new plan. You thought I was joking, didn't you? But we really are going to try transplanting. Dig up some entire houses and truck them on flatbeds from DC to Indiana. If we do ten or twelve at once economies of scale come into play. I wanted to know if you want in–help at this end, maybe."

"By selecting homes?" I broke in, excited. Those thousands of unsold homes!

"Well no, dear. The customers already *have* their houses here. We're just moving them. We'll need some feet on the ground at this end, to set up paperwork and do the regulatory hoops . . ."

What a depressing prospect! But I couldn't afford to say no. I gave the office door a vicious jerk and the stiff bolt finally dropped into place. "I'm in, Lynn. But I have to run. Places to go and people to be."

"Delighted to hear it, darling! Once we've finalized it at our end I'll email you. Now run along!"

She blew me an air kiss and turned away. I did my best not to hate the sight of her slim toned tush in the fashionable tight skirt. In my own hippie-ish long peasant skirt I looked exactly like the 'local help' I was going to be. Then I noticed the briefcase–buttery pink leather, the exact color of Lynn's suit, leaning against the wall where she had been waiting for me. It had her business card ("Selling Big in West Indianapolis since 2009!") in the luggage tag, and it was very heavy. Obviously I had to get it back to her. I tossed it into my car with all my other stuff and forgot about it. Time for my other hat!

The upside of the federal government moving away is rush hour. There's none now. Ten minutes trundling along deserted streets, past dark windows and overgrown lawns, and I was pulling into my own driveway. The yard is fenced with chain link, easy to climb. But the cats know the boundary. Hammy and John-cat came up purring as soon as I was through the gate. "Oh, you are a fatso," I told Hammy. "When are those kittens coming, huh? Tonight or tomorrow, I guess."

No supernatural household should be without a coven of cats as guards, companions, and all-around help. The spell can only be set up among an odd number of cats that are closely related, ideally of the same color. My nine are orange-tabby and white, and if I do say so myself I am the go-to gal if you want a set of your own. Problem is, this is an even smaller market than Washington real estate, so Hammy and her sister Pat were carrying my financial future. The sorcerer in Delaware who was going to buy those kittens would probably be my only sale this year. Of course Hammy didn't understand her importance and was not going to fail to greet me. I scratched her head, gave Madison perched on the roof guttering a wave, and stroked Georgie on the porch. But Mason, who had already hopped up onto the hood of my car, gave a warning meow.

"Right, the bag," I recalled. "Good kitty, Mason. Lynn owes you a catnip mouse."

Four or five cats surged around me, purring and nudging for attention, as I delved into Lynn's bag. There was her tiny sexy cell phone in a shiny case, so I couldn't call her. But with luck there'd be a card from her hotel or something about where her evening meeting was going to be. Or perhaps she'd have the sense to phone her own number. A fat sheaf of Indianapolis realty listings. A folder of stuff about the transplant scheme, labeled "Operation Rosebud." Roses, grafting–get it? They had a dramatist over there in the Indiana Association of Realtors. That was everything in the main section of the bag. I unsnapped the back section.

"This leather is sooo gorgeous," I told the cats. Did I mention they're great to talk to? "I bet this bag cost her a couple thousand bucks. She's as rich as Midas. You know it's really unhealthy to be envious like this. I'll get an ulcer . . ."

A red folder, labeled Operation Booster. Another cute real estate scheme. They have some creative marketing minds over in Indiana, you had to give them that. Maybe there'd be a concept I could use here? I flipped through the contents, puzzled. They seemed to be in chronological order, but some of these documents were not in English and all of them seemed very complicated. Did Lynn really read stuff like this? At junior college she was never known as the sharpest knife in the drawer.

But when I got to the last paper, the oldest document in the folder, it was perfectly comprehensible: "A Plan to Increase Sales 1000%." I read it once, twice, and then slammed the folder down.

"They planned this!" I shouted at the cats. "Those Realtors in the heartland planned to steal the federal bureaucracy from us!" The size of the concept took your breath away—scaring Congress into the hinterlands. But how did a bunch of hick salesmen get their hands on a pocket nuke? That had been a genuine terrorist armament, not something you can pick up at the Wal-mart in Brownsburg or Beech Grove. Besides, they had caught the bomb-maker shortly after–he had been escaping through Canada.

Flipping madly back and forth through the folder, I thought I understood. Someone had set Osama bin Laden's cousin up, played him like a fish on the line–helped him to bring in the bomb, and then sold him out to the FBI before it could be detonated. All fair and square–if a member of al Qaeda is scammed, nobody will shed a tear–but what breadth! What a grand scheme! Nobody hurt, a terrorist in jail, and billions of dollars in real estate sales. The only real losers were. . . . "Us," I said out loud. "People in the DC metro area."

"This is beyond me," I told Ben, the nearest cat. "I have to pass this to someone who knows what this is about."

At that moment the sexy little cell phone began to play the theme from Beethoven's Fifth. "So tasteful," I muttered, struggling with the tiny pill-shaped buttons. Finally I was able to say into it, "Hello, Lynn–is that you?"

"Susan? Oh thank heaven, you have my briefcase!"

"I sure do, and you owe me one, honey. You ought to be more careful with it. There are some important things in here."

"Susan! You didn't root around in my papers, did you?"

"Of course–I had to get your cell phone out. And excuse me if I say that you Hoosier Realtors are so twisty, they could use your spinal cords to pull corks."

"Oh Susan," she said sadly. "You should not have done that."

"I don't see why not," I said. "I–Lynn? Hello?" I shook the little phone with irritation. Maybe Lynn had moved out of range? Well, she could darn well call back. In the meantime, it came to me who to consult. That sorcerer in Delaware–Solomon had retired from the NSA just before the big scare. Without relocation funding, he had been trapped here with his worthless house like so many other home-owners. He had a sideline in minor magic like me, but unlike me his really was profitable–a way to conjure blue crab out of deeper channels in the Chesapeake. Maybe he still kept up with his old friends at the Agency. I phoned him right away, on my own line. "Hello, Solomon?"

"Susie, doll, how are ya, bloomin'? And my kitties, are they still in the oven?"

"They'll probably be born this week, maybe even the next couple days," I reported. "Both mothers are healthy and happy."

"Good, good. When they're weaned I'll come down with a couple cat carriers. Borrowing one from my daughter."

"Have you chosen a set of names yet?"

"Oh yeah. You used the Founding Fathers, right? I was thinking of naming mine after wines. Cabernet, Pinot, Syrah, that kind of thing. Chablis."

"Very clever! They'll be so cute. Solomon, I have a bunch of mysterious papers here. I'd like to show them to you and get an opinion."

"Are they business?" He meant magical business.

"No, they really are mysterious. I think your security expertise might be helpful here. Do you have a fax?"

"You could scan 'em and send 'em as a zip file," he grumbled.

"Realtors like to fax," I said. "Because of the signatures.

Let me have your fax number. . . . Okay. There's a bunch of them, so it'll take a while."

"I'll call you when I look 'em over," he said. "Say hi to the kitties for me."

I hung up. "Solomon says hi," I told the nearest cat, who happened to be Jeffy. It's important to keep a cat coven up to date on magical contacts. I tapped the sheaf of papers from the Booster file to even up the edges, and slid them into the hopper of the fax machine. My home machine was old, and the sheets fed through slowly.

Again that annoying Beethoven's Fifth. I answered it, saying, "So how about that drink, Lynn?"

Actually it sounded like she didn't need any more. "I'm so sorry, Susan." She was almost whispering. "This is bigger than both of us. They're coming."

"You mean to pick up your briefcase? No need to make a special trip, Lynn–we could meet up somewhere."

"No, I'm not coming. They're coming."

And blip! Suddenly she was cut off again. These cheap little phones! "Oh well. Time for all expectant mommies to rest," I told Hammie and Patty. I could leave the fax to slowly digest its stack of papers all night.

I led the troupe of felines up the stairs to my bedroom. Some of them are always outside, keeping an eye on the perimeter. They're always popping in through the cat flap and cycling back out again. The two expectant females I meant to shut into the spare bathroom, so they wouldn't go and have their kittens out under a bush or something. Their gestalt allows all the cats to know what any cat in the coven knows, but only about my security and that of the house. The rest of the time they are just cats.

I changed into pajamas, brushed my teeth, and was just about to climb into bed when I noticed there were no cats in the bedroom any more. "Guys?" I looked out into the hall. All five of the indoor animals were standing at the top of the stairs, glaring down into the dark. "Hey, kitties. What's up?"

The others continued to watch, but Georgy came back
to wind briefly around my ankles. Something outside, perhaps. I went back into the bedroom and peeked out past
the blind. Sure enough, a car at the curb. I couldn't see any
of the outdoor cats, but they would stay under cover.
Felines aren't combat animals–they're useful for reconnais-
sance and guard duty. "I'm not expecting visitors at this
hour of the night," I told Georgy. "They must be visiting
next door. . . ."

Suddenly a piercing yowl rose from below. Good heavens, was that Mason? I hauled the window sash up and
leaned out. Lit by the dim driveway lamp, three pale faces
looked up at me. "Ms. Keatley?" a male voice asked. "Susan
Keatley? Lynn Shipper sent us over to pick up her briefcase."

I didn't answer. I was staring open-mouthed down at
Mason, Jeffy, Georgy, John-Cat and Madison. They were
standing on the walk just below me, turned sideways to the
visitors outside the fence. Each cat was puffed up, every
hair on end. Their backs were arched like Halloween cats,
and low savage snarls rose to my ears, alternating every
now and then with a savage hiss. They are *so* not supposed
to do this!

But I can take a hint. "Sorry," I called down to my visitors. "I'm not dressed to receive visitors. And . . ." time for
some inventive lying, "my husband is asleep after line-
backer practice today with the Redskins. Come back tomorrow."

"Ms. Keatley, we need the papers in that case tonight."
He opened the gate and John-Cat positively screamed, a
howl of furious rage. "Could you, um, call off your cat?"

"I don't think so," I said firmly. Had my molasses-slow
fax machine finished sending the Booster file yet? If they
got into the house . . .

"Oh come on, they're just pets." Another of the men
pushed forward, swinging the raincoat draped over his
arm. "Yow!"

Jeffy had leaped in, ripped out a chunk of pants and leg, and darted out again. "They're in a bad mood," I said. "Please go away!"

"I'm bleeding," the victim moaned.

"I can see the briefcase on the table inside," the third one reported, craning his neck. "It's pink, right?" Damn, I had forgotten to turn off the living room light again. "Come on, Sammy–you got your Realtor master keys, right?"

"What are you going to do," I yelled. "Take me back to Indiana?"

They stared up at me. "Shit," one of them said. "She knows."

"Hold them off, guys!" I whispered. Scuttling back from the window I grabbed the phone and dialed 911. "I'm a single older woman living alone," I gabbled to the person who answered. "And three strange men are kicking down my front door! Yes, 4501 Clarendon Street. No, I don't know them. Yes, they know I'm home. Guns, that's right–they have guns." Well, they *could* have. Who knew what was under those raincoats? That should get the police over here fast.

I tiptoed out into the hall and picked up Hammie. She growled at me but didn't bite as I pushed her into the spare bedroom and shut the door. Pat immediately saw what was going on. In spite of her pregnant bulk she dived under the hall cupboard like greased lightning, and glared at me out of furious green eyes. How dare you interrupt when we're trying to defend you, she seemed to be saying.

I was on my hands and knees, trying to poke her loose with a rolled-up newspaper, when I heard the sirens. I dashed to the window and was in time to see two police cars, one from each end of the street. Between the cops and the felines, my visitors had nowhere to hide. "That's them!" I called down.

"We're real estate agents," the limping one protested. "We thought this house was for sale."

"And you're inspecting the property at midnight, right,"

I said. But I didn't really care if charges would stick. Once that fax was finished, their fangs would be drawn.

"Aagh!" a cop exclaimed. "That cat bit me!"

"Oh, I'm so sorry," I said. "It's nothing to fret about—they've all had rabies shots. Let me come down and get them into the house." The cats absolutely refused to do this, however. They sat eight in a row on the porch rail—Hammy was still stuck in the bedroom–oozing malice from every whisker, as the Hoosier Realtors were loaded into police cars. I filled out forms and answered police questions for what seemed like hours, but the felines didn't budge.

"You sure have a lot of pets," one cop remarked.

"Nine, with more on the way," I said with dignity. "I'm the weird cat lady."

"I can see that." Finally it was all over and they went away. I went inside, but only three cats came in with me. The others took up the patrol outdoors, in case of another invasion. The fax machine was silent. It was probably too late to resurrect the Washington real estate market, or move all the federal agencies back. "But at least the cat is out of the bag," I told Jeffy.

INTRODUCTION TO PRIMATE IN FOREST
Ernest Lilley

Kim Stanley Robinson's *Forty Signs of Rain* came out a little while before I started working on this anthology, and about the same time that the really bad *The Day After Tomorrow* appeared in theaters. Kim's book is written in very near future DC and surrounding environs and watches scientists and politicians come to grips with, or try to ignore, radical weather changes as the waters rise. The first book ends with the Washington Mall flooded after a superstorm, the animals from the National Zoo released and settling into new habitats . . . and the central character, Frank, settling into a new habitat of his own, living in a car on the street while maintaining a high visibility position at the National Science Foundation. This may sound odd, and I guess it is, but friends of mine are probably shaking their heads about now remembering that I lived out of my station wagon for a few months, while photographing Route 66 in 2001, so it doesn't seem that odd to me. Opting out of the whole home ownership thing is a lifestyle that we may see more of in the future, and DC's homeless population may well be in the vanguard. Frank is looking for humanity to reconnect with its primal self without giving up what we've learned about the universe and this story does reach down to pluck some pretty deep strings in the reader.

Primate in the Forest is the first chapter of his next book: *Fifty Degrees Below*. Thanks to the timing of these things the novel should come out pretty soon after the publication of this anthology, so readers won't be unduly frustrated waiting for the continuance.

PRIMATE IN FOREST

(FROM CHAPTER ONE: *FIFTY DEGREES BELOW*)
KIM STANLEY ROBINSON

Frank returned to his office, collecting his thoughts. A workman was there, installing a power strip on the newly exposed wall behind his desk, and he waited patiently until the man left. He sat at the desk, swiveled and looked out the window at the mobile in the atrium.

He had spent the night in his car and then lunched with the director of the National Science Foundation, and no one was the wiser. He did feel a little spacey. But when appearances were maintained, no one could tell. Nothing obvious gave it away. One retained a certain privacy.

Remembering a resolution he had made that morning, he picked up the phone and called the National Zoo.

"Hi, I'm calling to ask about zoo animals that might still be at large?"

"Sure, let me pass you to Nancy."

Nancy came on and said hi in a friendly voice, and Frank told her about hearing what seemed like a big animal, near the edge of the park at night.

"Do you have a list of zoo animals still on the loose?"

"Sure, it's on our website. Do you want to join our group?"

"What do you mean?"

"There's a committee of the volunteer group, FONZ, Friends of the National Zoo. You can join that, it's called the Feral Observation Group."

"The FOG?"

"Yes. We're all in the FOG now, right?"

"Yes."

She gave him the website address, and he checked it out. It turned out to be a good one. Some 1500 Fonzies already. There was a page devoted to the Khembalis' swimming tigers. On the FOG page was a list of the animals that had been spotted, as well as a separate list for animals missing since the flood and not yet seen. There was a jaguar on this list. And gibbons had been seen, eight of them, white-cheeked gibbons, along with three siamangs. Almost always in Rock Creek Park.

"Hmmm." Frank recalled the cry he had heard at dawn and pursued the creatures through the web pages. Gibbons and siamangs hooted in a regular dawn chorus; siamangs were even louder than gibbons, being larger. Could be heard six miles rather than one.

It looked like being in FOG might confer permission to go into Rock Creek Park. You couldn't observe animals in a park you were forbidden to enter. He called Nancy back. "Do FOG members get to go into Rock Creek Park?"

"Some do. We usually go in groups, but we have some individual permits you can check out."

"Cool. Tell me how I do that."

⚹

He left the building and walked down Wilson and up a side street, to the Optimodal Health Club. Diane had said it was within easy walking distance, and it was. That was good; and the place looked okay.

Actually he had always preferred getting his exercise outdoors, by doing something challenging. Up until now he had felt that clubs like these were mostly just another way to commodify leisure time, in this case changing things people used to do outdoors, for free, into things they paid to do inside. Silly as such; but if you needed to rent a bathroom, they were great.

So he did his best to remain expressionless (resulting in a visage unusually grim) while he gave the young woman at the desk a credit card, and signed the forms. Full membership, no. Personal trainer ready to take over his thinking about his body but without incurring any legal liability, no way. He did pay extra for a permanent locker in which to store some of his stuff. Another bathroom kit there, another change of clothes; it would all come in useful.

He followed his guide around the rooms of the place, keeping his expressionless expression firmly in place. By the time he was done, the poor girl looked thoroughly unsettled.

⟨≈≈≈⟩

Back at NSF he went into the basement to his Honda, a great little car. But now it did not serve the purpose. He drove west on Wilson for a long time, until he came to the Honda/Ford/Lexus dealer where he had leased this car a year before. In this one aspect of the fiasco that was remaining in DC, his timing was good; he needed to re-up for another year. The eager salesman handling him was happy to hear that this time he wanted to lease an Odyssey van. One of the best vans on the road, the man told him as they walked out to view one. Also one of the smallest, Frank didn't say.

Dull silver, the most anonymous color around, like a cloak of invisibility. Rear seat removal, yes; therefore room in back for his single mattress, now in storage. Tinted windows all around the back created a pretty high degree of privacy. It was almost as good as the VW van he had lived in for a couple of Yosemite summers, parked in the Camp Four parking lot enjoying the stove and refrigerator and pop-top in his tiny motor home. Culturally the notion of small vehicle as home had crashed since then, having been based on a beat/hippie idea of frugality that had lost out to the usual American excess, to the point of being made illegal by a Congress bought by the auto industry. No stoves allowed in little vans, of course! Had to house them in giant RVs.

But this Odyssey would serve the purpose. Frank skimmed the lease terms, signed the forms. He saw that he might need to rent a post office box. But maybe the NSF address would do.

Walking back out to take possession of his new bedroom, he and the salesman passed a line of parked SUVs— tall fat station wagons, in effect, called Expedition or Explorer, absurdities for the generations to come to shake their heads at in the way they once marveled at the finned cars of the fifties.

"Do people still buy these?" Frank asked despite himself.

"Sure. Although now you mention it, there is some surplus here at the end of the year." It was May. "Long story short, gas is getting too expensive. I drive one of these," tapping a Lincoln Navigator. "They're great. They've got a couple of TVs in the back."

But they're stupid, Frank didn't say. In prisoner's dilemma terms, they were always-defective. They were America saying Fuck Off to the rest of the world. Deliberate waste, in a kind of ritual desecration. Not just denial but defiance, a Götterdämmerung gesture that said: If we're going down we're going to take the whole world with us. And the roads were full of them. And the Gulf Stream had stopped.

"Amazing," Frank said.

He drove his new Odyssey directly to the storage place in Arlington where he had rented a unit. He liked the feel of the van; it drove like a car. In front of his storage unit he took out its back seats, put them in the oversized metal-and-concrete closet, less than half full with his stuff; took his single mattress out and laid it in the back of the van. Perfect fit. He could use the same sheets and pillows he had been using in his apartment.

"Home—less, home—less. Ha ha ha, ha ha ha, ho ho ho."

He could sort through the rest of his stored stuff later on. Possibly very little of it would ever come out of boxes again.

He locked up and drove to the Beltway, around in the jam to Wisconsin Avenue, down into the city. The newly ritualized pass by the elevator kiosk at Bethesda. Now he could have dropped in on the Quiblers without feeling pitiful, even though in most respects his circumstances had not changed since the night before; but now he had a plan. And a van. And this time he didn't want to stop. Over to Connecticut, down to the neighborhood north of the zoo, turn onto the same street he had the night before. He noted how the establishing of habits was part of the homing instinct.

Most streets in this neighborhood were permit parking by day and open parking by night, except for the one night a week they were cleaned. Once parked, the van became perfectly nondescript. Equidistant from two driveways; streetlight near but not too near. He would learn the full drill only by practicing it, but this street looked to be a good one.

Out and up Connecticut. An Edward Hopper tableaux depicting the end of the day–streetworker waiting on the sidewalk for rush hour to be over and the night work to begin. It was mostly retail on this part of Connecticut, with upscale apartments and offices behind, then the residential neighborhood. No doubt extremely expensive even though the houses were not big.

Like anywhere else in DC, there were restaurants from all over the world. It wasn't just that one could get Ethiopian or Azeri, but that there would be choices: Hari food from southern Ethiopia, or Sudanese style from the north? Good, bad or superb Lebanese?

Having grown up in southern California, Frank could never get used to this array. These days he was fondest of the Middle Eastern and Mediterranean cuisines, and this area of Northwest was rich in both, so he had to think about which one he wanted, and whether to eat in or do take-out. Eating alone in a restaurant he would have to have something to read. Funny how reading in a restaurant was okay, while watching a laptop or talking on a cell phone was not. Actually, judging by the number of laptops visible in the taverna at the corner of Connecticut and Brandywine, that custom had already changed. Maybe they were reading from their laptops. That might be okay. He would have to try it and see how it felt.

He decided to do take-out. It was dinnertime but there was still lots of light left to the day; he could take a meal out into the park and enjoy the sunset. He walked on Connecticut until he came on a Greek restaurant that would put dolmades and calamari in paper boxes, with a dill yogurt sauce in a tiny plastic container. Too bad about the ouzo and retsina, only sold in the restaurant; he liked those tastes. He ordered an ouzo to drink while waiting for his food, downing it before the ice cubes even got a chance to turn it milky.

Back on the street, the taste of licorice enveloped him like a key signature, black and sweet. Steamy dusk of spring, hazed with blossom dust. Sweat slipping past two women; something in their sudden shared laughter set him to thinking about his woman from the elevator. Would she call? And if so, when? And what would she say, and what would he say? A licorish mood an anticipation of lust, like a wolf whistle in his mind. Vegetable smell of the flood. The two women had been so beautiful. Washington was like that.

The food in his paper sack was making him hungry, so he turned east and walked into Rock Creek Park, following a path that eventually brought him to a pair of picnic tables, bunched at one end of a small bedraggled lawn. A stone fireplace like a little charcoal oven anchored the ensemble. The muddy grass was uncut. Birch and sycamore trees overhung the area. There had been lots of picnic areas in the park, but most had been located down near the creek and so presumably had been washed away. This one was set higher, in a little hollow next to Ross Drive. All of them, Frank recalled, used to be marked by big signs saying CLOSED AT DUSK. Nothing like that remained now. He sat at one of the tables, opened up his food.

He was about halfway through the calamari when several men tromped into the glade and sat at the other table or stood before the stone fireplace, bringing with them a heavy waft of stale sweat, smoke, and beer. Worn jackets, plastic bags: homeless guys.

Two of them pulled beer cans out of a paper grocery bag. A grizzled one in fatigues saluted Frank with a can. "Hey man."

Frank nodded politely. "Evening."

"Want a beer?"

"No thanks."

"What's a matter?"

Frank shrugged. "Sure, why not."

"Yar. There ya go."

Frank finished his calamari and drank the offered Pabst Blue Ribbon, watching the men settle around him. His benefactor and two of the others were dressed in the khaki camouflage fatigues that signified Vietnam Vet Down On Luck (Your Fault, Give Money). Sure enough, a cardboard sign with a long story scrawled in felt-tip on it protruded from one of their bags.

Next to the three vets, a slight man with a dark red beard and ponytail sat on the table. The other three men were black, one of these a youth or even a boy. They sat down at Frank's table. The youngster unpacked a box that contained a chess set, chessboard, and timer. The man who had offered Frank a beer came over and sat down across from the youth as he set the board. The pieces were cheap plastic, but the timer looked more expensive. The two started a game, the kid slapping the plunger on his side of the timer down after pauses averaging about fifteen seconds, while the vet usually depressed his with a slow touch, after a minute or more had passed, always declaring "Ah fuck."

"Want to play next?" the boy asked Frank. "Bet you five dollars."

"I'm not good enough to play for money."

"Bet you that box of squid there."

"No way." Frank ate on while they continued. "You guys aren't playing for money," he observed.

"He already took all I got," the vet said. "Now I'm like pitching him batting practice. He's dancing on my body, the little fucker."

The boy shook his head. "You just ain't paying attention."

"You wore me out, Chessman. You're beating me when I'm down. You're a fucking menace. I'm setting up my sneak attack."

"Checkmate."

The other guys laughed.

Then three men ran into their little clearing. "Hi guys!" they shouted as they hustled to the far end of the site.

"What the hell?" Frank said.

The big vet guffawed. "It's the frisbee players!"

"They're always running," one of the other vets explained. He wore a VFW baseball cap and his face was dissolute and whiskery. He shouted to the runners: "Hey who's winning!"

"The wind!" one of them replied.

"Evening, gentlemen," another said. "Happy Thursday."

"Is that what it is?"

"Hey who's winning? Who's winning?"

"The wind is winning. We're all winning."

"That's what you say! I got my money on you now! Don't you let me down now!"

The players faced a fairway of mostly open air to the north.

"What's your target?" Frank called.

The tallest of them had blue eyes, gold-red dreadlocks, mostly gathered under a bandana, and a scraggly red-gold beard. He was the one who had greeted the homeless guys first. Now he paused and said to Frank, "The trashcan, down there by that light. Par four, little dogleg." He took a step and made his throw, a smooth uncoiling motion, and then the others threw and they were off into the dusk.

"They run," the second vet explained.

"Running frisbee golf?"

"Yeah some people do it that way. Rolfing they call it, running golf. Not these guys though! They just run without no name for it. They don't always use the regular targets either. There's some baskets out here, they're metal things with chains hanging from them. You got to hit the chains and the Frisbees fall in a basket."

"Except they don't," the first vet scoffed.

"Yeah it's a finicky sport. Like fucking golf, you know."

Down the path Frank could see the runners picking up their Frisbees and stopping for only a moment before throwing again.

"How often do they come here?"

"A lot!"

"You can ask them, they'll be back in a while. They run the course forward and back."

They sat there, once or twice hearing the runners call out. Fifteen minutes later the men did indeed return, on the path they had left.

Frank said to the dreadlocked one, "Hey, can I follow you and learn the course?"

"Well sure, but we do run it, as you see."

"Oh yeah that's fine, I'll keep up."

"Sure then. You want a Frisbee to throw?"

"I'd probably lose it."

"Always possible out here, but try this one. I found it today, so it must be meant for you."

"Okay."

Like any other climber, Frank had spent a fair amount

of camp time tossing a Frisbee back and forth. He much preferred it to hacky sack, which he was no good at. Now he took the disk they gave him and followed them to their next tee, and threw it last, conservatively, as his main desire was to keep it going straight up the narrow fairway. His shot only went half as far as theirs, but he could see where it had crashed into the overgrown grass, so he considered it a success, and ran after the others. They were pretty fast, not sprinting but moving right along, at what Frank guessed was about a seven-minute mile pace if they kept it up; and they slowed only briefly to pick up their Frisbees and throw them again. It quickly became apparent that the slowing down, throwing, and starting up again cost more energy than running straight through would have, and Frank had to focus on the work of it. The players pointed out the next target, and trusted he would not clock them in the backs of their heads after they threw and ran off. And in fact if he shot immediately after them he could fire it over their heads and keep his shot straight.

Some of the targets were trash cans, tree trunks, or big rocks, but most were metal baskets on metal poles, the poles standing chest high and supporting chains that hung from a ring at the top. Frank had never seen such a thing before. The Frisbee had to hit the chains in such a way that its momentum was stopped and it fell in the basket. If it bounced out it was like a rimmer in golf or basketball, and a put-in shot had to be added to one's score.

One of the players made a putt from about twenty yards away, and they all hooted. Frank saw no sign they were keeping score or competing. The dreadlocked player threw and his Frisbee too hit the chains, but fell to the ground. "Shit." Off they ran to pick them up and start the next hole. Frank threw an easy approach shot, then tossed his Frisbee in.

"What was par there?" he asked as he ran with them.

"Three. They're all threes but three, which is a two, and nine, which is a four."

"There are nine holes?"

"Yes, but we play the course backward too, so we have eighteen. Backward they're totally different."

"I see."

So they ran, stopped, stooped, threw, and took off again, chasing the shots like dogs. Frank got into his running rhythm, and realized their pace was more the equivalent of an eight or nine-minute mile. He could run with these guys, then. Throwing was another matter, they were amazingly strong and accurate; their shots had a miraculous quality, flying right to the baskets and often crashing into the chains from quite a distance.

"You guys are good!" he said at one tee.

"It's just practice," the dreadlocked one said. "We play a lot."

"It's our religion," one of the others said, and his companions cackled as they made their next drives.

Then one of Frank's own approach shots clanged into the chains and dropped straight in, from about thirty yards out. The others hooted loudly in congratulation.

On his next approach he focused on throwing at the basket, let go, watched it fly straight there and hit with a resounding clash of the chains. A miracle! A glow filled him, and he ran with an extra bounce in his step.

At the end of their round they stood steaming in the dusk, not far from the picnic area and the homeless guys. The players compared numbers, "twenty-eight," "thirty-three," which turned out to be how many strokes under par they were for the day. Then high fives and handshakes, and they began to move off in different directions.

"I want to do that again," Frank said to the dreadlocked guy.

"Any time, you were keeping right with us. We're here most days around this time." He headed off in the direction of the homeless guys, and Frank accompanied him, thinking to return to his dinner site and clear away his trash.

The homeless guys were still there, nattering at each

other like Laurel and Hardy: "I did not! You did. I did not, you did." Something in the intonation revealed to Frank that these were the two he had heard the night before, passing him in the dark.

"Now you wanna play?" the chess player said when he saw Frank.

"Oh, I don't know."

He sat across from the boy, sweating, still feeling the glow of his miracle shot. Throwing on the run; no doubt it was a very old thing, a hunter thing. His whole brain and body had been working out there. Hunting, sure, and the finding and picking up of the Frisbees in the dusk was like gathering. Hunting and gathering; and maybe these were no longer the same activities if one were hunting for explanations, or gathering data. Maybe only physical hunting and gathering would do.

The homeless guys droned on, bickering over their half-assed efforts to get a fire started in the stone fireplace. A piece of shit, as one called it.

"Who built that?" Frank asked.

"National Park. Yeah, look at it. It's got a *roof.*"

"It looks like a smoker."

"They were idiots."

"It was the WPA, probably."

Frank said, "Isn't this place closed at dusk?"

"Yeah right."

"The whole fucking park is closed, man. Twenty-four seven."

"Closed for the duration."

"Yeah right."

"Closed until further notice."

"Five dollar game?" the youngster said to Frank, rattling the box of pieces.

Frank sighed. "I don't want to bet. I'll play you for free." Frank waved at the first vet. "I'll be more batting practice for you, like him."

"Zeno ain't never just batting practice!"

The boy's frown was different. "Well, okay."

Frank hadn't played since a long-ago climbing expedition to the Cirque of the Unclimbables, a setting in which chess had always seemed as inconsequential as tiddlywinks. Now he quickly found that using the timer actually helped his game, by making him give up analyzing the situation in depth in favor of just going with the flow of things, with the shape or pattern. In the literature they called this approach a "good-enough decision heuristic," although in this case it wasn't even close to good enough; he attacked on the left side, had both knights out and a great push going, and then suddenly it was all revealed as hollow, and he was looking at the wrong end of the end game.

"Shit," he said, obscurely pleased.

"Told ya," Zeno scolded him.

The night was warm and full of spring smells, mixing with the mud stench. Frank was still hot from the frisbee run. Some distant gawking cries wafted up from the ravine, as if peacocks were on the loose.

The guys at the next table were laughing hard. The third vet was sitting on the ground, trying to read a *Post* by laying it on the ground in front of the fitful fire. "You can only see the fire if you lie on the ground, or look right down the smoke hole. How stupid is that?" They rained curses on their miserable fire. Chessman finished boxing his chess pieces and took off.

Zeno said to Frank, "Why didn't you play him for money, man? Take him five blow jobs to make up for that."

"Whoah," Frank said, startled.

Zeno laughed, a harsh ragged bray, mocking and aggressive, tobacco-raspy. "Ha ha ha." A kind of rebuke or slap. He had the handsome face of a movie villain, a sidekick to someone like Charles Bronson or Jack Palance. "Ha ha—what you think, man?"

Frank bagged his dinner boxes and stood. "What if I had beat him?"

"You ain't gonna beat him," with a twist of the mouth that added, asshole.

"Next time," Frank promised, and took off.

Primate in forest. Warm and sweaty, full of food, beer and ouzo; still fully endorphined from running with the frisbee guys. It was dark now, although the park wore the same nightcap of noctilucent cloud it had the night before, close over the trees. It provided enough light to see by, just barely. The tree trunks were obvious in some somatic sense; Frank slipped between them as if dodging furniture in a dark house he knew very well. He felt alert, relaxed. Exfoliating in the vegetable night, in the background hum of the city, the click of twigs under his feet. He swam through the park.

An orange flicker glimpsed in the distance caused him to slow down, change direction, and approach it at an angle. He hid behind trees as he approached. He sidled closer, like a spy or a hunter. It felt good. Like the frisbee run, but different. He got close enough to be sure it was a campfire, at the center of another brace of picnic tables. Here they had a normal fire ring to work with. Faces in the firelight: bearded, dirty, ruddy. Homeless guys like the ones behind him, like the ones on the street corners around the city, sitting by signs asking for money. Mostly men, but there was one woman sitting at this fire, knitting. She gave the whole scene a domestic look, like something out of Hogarth.

After a while Frank moved on, descending in darkness through the trees. The gash of the torn ravine appeared below him, white in the darkness. A broad canyon of sandstone, brilliant under the luminous cloud. The creek was a black ribbon cutting through it. Probably the moon was near full, somewhere up above the clouds; there was more light than the city alone could account for. Both the cloud ceiling and the newly torn ravine glowed, the sandstone like sinuous naked flesh.

A truck, rumbling in the distance. The sound of the creek burbling over stones. Distant laughter, a car starting; tinkle of broken glass; something like a dumpster lid slamming down. And always the hum of the city, a million noises blended together, like the light caught in the cloud. It was neither quiet, nor dark, nor empty. It definitely was not wilderness. It was city and forest simultaneously. It was hard to characterize how it felt.

Where would one sleep out here?

Immediately the question organized his walk. He had been wandering before, but now he was on the hunt again. He saw that many things were a hunt. It did not have to be a hunt to kill and eat animals. Any search on foot was a kind of hunt. As now.

He ranged up and away from the ravine. First in importance would be seclusion. A flat dry spot, tucked out of the way. There, for instance, a tree had been knocked over in the flood, its big tangle of roots raised to the sky, creating a partial cave under it—but too damp, too closed in.

Cobwebs caught his face and he wiped them away. He looked up into the network of black branches. Being up in a tree would solve so many problems. That was a prehominid thought, perhaps caused merely by craning his neck back. No doubt there was an arboreal complex in the brain crying out: Go home. Go home!

He ranged uphill, moving mostly northward. A hilltop was another option. He looked at one of the knolls that divided Rock Creek's vestigial western tributaries. Nice in some ways; flat; but as with root hollows, these were places where all manner of creatures might take refuge. The truth was that the best nooks were best for everything out there. A distant crash in the brush reminded him that this might include the zoo's jaguar.

He would need to make some daytime explorations, that was clear. He could always stay in his van, of course, but this felt more real. Scouting trips for the Feral Observation Group. We're all in the fog now, Nancy had said. He would spend some of his time hunting for animals. A kind of return to the paleolithic, right here in Washington DC. Re-paleolithization: it sounded very scientific, like the engineers who spoke of amishization when they meant to simplify a design. Landscape restoration inside the brain. The pursuit of happiness; and the happiness was in the pursuit.

Frank smiled briefly. He realized he had been tense ever since leaving the rented apartment. Now he was more relaxed, watchful but relaxed, moving about easily. It was late; he was getting tired. Another branch across the face and he decided to call it a night.

He made his way west to Connecticut, hit it at Fessenden, walked south on the sidewalk blinking in the flood of light. It might as well have been Las Vegas or Miami to him now; everything blazing neon colors in the warm spring night. People were out. He strolled along among them. The city too was a habitat, and as such a riot of sensation. He would have to think about how that fit in with the re-paleolithization project, because the city was a big part of contemporary society, and people were obviously addicted to it. Frank was himself, at least to parts of it. The technological sublime made everything magical, as if they were all tripping with the shaman—but all the time, which was too much. They had therefore lost touch with reality, gone mad as a collective.

And yet this street was reality too. He would have to think about all this.

When he came to his van no one was in sight, and he slipped inside and locked the doors. It was dark, quiet, and comfortable. Very much like a room. A bit stuffy; he turned on the power, cracked the windows. He could start the engine and power the air conditioner for a while if he really needed to.

He set his wristwatch alarm for 4:30 a.m.; afraid he might sleep through the dawn in such a room. Then he lay down on his familiar old mattress, and felt his body start to relax even further. Home sweet home! It made him laugh.

❦

At 4:30 his alarm beeped. He squeezed it quiet and slipped on his running shoes and got out of the van before his sleepiness knocked him back down. Out into the dawn, the world of grays. This was how cats must see, all the grays so finely gradated. A different kind of seeing altogether.

Into the forest again. The leafy venation of the forest air was a masterpiece of three-dimensionality, the precise spacing of everything suggesting some kind of vast sculpture, as in an Ansel Adams photo. The human eye had an astonishing depth of field.

He stood over the tawny sandstone of Rock Creek's newly burnished ravine, hearing his breathing. It was barely cool. The sky was shifting from a flat gray to a curved pale blue.

"Ooooooooooop!"

He shivered deep in his flesh, like a horse.

The sound came from overhead; a rising "*ooooooooooo*" that then suddenly fell. Something like the cooing of a dove, or the call of a coyote. A voice or a kind of siren—musical, unearthly, bizarre. Glissandos up and down. Voices, yes. Gibbons and/or siamangs. Frank had heard such calls long ago, at the San Diego Zoo.

It sounded like there were several of them now. "*Ooooop! Oooooooooooop! Oooooooooooop!*" Lows to highs, penetrating and pure. The hair on Frank's neck was standing up.

He tried it himself. "Ooooooop!" he sang, softly. It seemed to fit in. He could do a fair imitation of one part of their range. His voice wasn't as fluid, or as clear in tone, and yet still, it was somewhat the same. Close enough to join in unobtrusively.

So he sang with them, and stepped ever so slowly between the trees, looking up trying to catch a glimpse of them. They were feeding off each other's energy, sounding more and more rambunctious. Wild animals! And they were celebrating the new day; there was no doubt about it. Maybe even celebrating their freedom. There was no way to tell, but to Frank it sounded like it.

Certainly it was true for him—the sound filled him, the morning filled him, spring and all, and he bellowed "Ooooooopee oop oop!" voice cracking at its highest. He longed to sing higher; he hooted as loudly as he could. The gibbons didn't care. It wasn't at all clear they had even noticed him. He tried to imitate all the calls he was hearing, failed at most of them. Up, down, crescendo, decrescendo, pianissimo, fortissimo. An intoxicating music. Had any composer ever heard this, ever used this? What were people doing, thinking they knew what music was?

The chorus grew louder and more agitated as the sky lightened. When sunlight pierced the forest they all went crazy together.

Then he saw three of them in the trees, sitting on high branches. He saw their long arms and longer tails, their broad shoulders and skinny butts. One swung away on arms that were as long as its body, to land on a branch by another, accept a cuff and hoot some more. Again their raucous noise buffeted Frank. When they finally quieted down, after an earsplitting climax, the green day was upon them.

Introduction to Hallowe'en Party
Ernest Lilley

Nancy Jane Moore's story has the distinction of being the only unsolicited story I included in the anthology. I got a number of them, even though I hadn't asked, and the worst of them wasn't at all bad . . . just not quite what I wanted. No, I take that back. I rejected her unsolicited submission and asked if she had anything without aliens in it. She did. So I guess I asked for it.

What I wanted was a look at the future overlain on the present . . . and it would be hard to come up with a better fulfillment of that than this little story. While New York City is often described as an amalgamation of neighborhoods, or something like that, this DC to come is closer to a collection of countries, and not necessarily first world ones at that. What's scary, or amusing, is that it doesn't seem all that different from the directions to parties we get now. . . .

HALLOWE'EN PARTY

NANCY JANE MOORE

Hi Friends! It's time for the annual Somerset Place Hallowe'en Block Party. Mark your calendars now: Saturday, October 31, 2015, 800 Block of Somerset Place N.W., Washington, D.C., from noon until the last person leaves or falls asleep.

Come hungry: we've got major food plans. Sam Killebrew will be in charge of the barbeque again. (We have to let him do it, because he won't give out his special sauce recipe.) In addition to the usual pork ribs, beef and chicken, we're going to have some venison this year. Some of the teenagers took part in the Rock Creek Park deer hunt to thin the herd that lives on everyone's azaleas.

The beer promises to be great, even if we can't import any Old Dominion from Virginia. Several neighbors have gone in for serious home brew operations and we'll have everything from lager to stout. We'll even have some dandelion wine. Hey, if you can't get rid of the damn things, might as well use them for something.

The neighbors who just bought 813 will do the haunted house–they're about to start renovations, so they don't mind if someone goes through a screen trying to get away from the evil witch. We'll get a small bonfire going about dark and even have some trick or treating for the kids (this will happen in our block only, with plenty of supervision, so it won't violate the D.C. law against such activities). Bring a costume if you've got one, but in case you don't, we've got plenty stashed away from earlier bashes.

For those of you who still remember the police raid of 2011, don't worry. We've got permits to close the street, build the bonfire, and run the barbeque. We all did our share of standing in line at the District Building, the police station, and the Environmental Protection Agency (approval of the environment permit took six months and a threatened lawsuit, but we got it). Amelia Jones from 829 is a retired D.C. cop, so she's rounding up some off-duty cops who will provide security in exchange for venison and beer. They'll be able to settle things if some over-enthusiastic rookie wants to shut us down.

That said, remember that the police will be out in force on Hallowe'en. Come sober and stay until you can leave the same way. And don't forget your passports and citizen IDs. You're very likely to hit one or more checkpoints on your way here. In addition to cops, the Shepherd Park/Takoma Park/North Brightwood (SPITNOB) Citizens' Patrol will be on the job. We're active in SPITNOB and have a couple of members on the patrol, so you shouldn't have any trouble if you show your invite. Be very polite to these people–everyone on the patrol has a black belt.

As everyone knows, October weather is very unpredictable. Last year we got hit with a freak snowstorm and the year before we passed on the bonfire because we were sweating too much in the high-nineties temp. And it can always rain. Remember that the forecast can change drastically these days–dress in layers and plan for extremes.

Specific directions are set out below:

Directions Using Metro:
The Metro Police have done an excellent job of retaking the system and it is now quite safe to use the subway if you can get to it. For "Inside the Beltway" residents, this will be the best way to get here. However, since the subway closes at midnight, bring your sleeping bag and plan to spend the night.

Take the subway to the Takoma Station. This station is in D.C., so you won't have to cross any state lines once you leave the Metro. Walk west to Fifth Street, then south to Somerset Place, and then west again to our block. Don't be alarmed by the big complex surrounded by the barbed-wire-topped fence–it's just the high school. This should be a very safe walk, due to the SPITNOB patrols.

<u>Driving Directions from West of Rock Creek Park</u>

If you live in the part of Washington that's west of Rock Creek Park and prefer to drive, please remember that you can't use Rock Creek Parkway. The various tribes that have established camps in the park control the road and won't let cars on it. On Hallowe'en, most of the cross points will be blocked as well; the only safe way to drive across the Park will be Military Road, which will be kept open by the D.C. police (we hope). We don't recommend walking or biking through the park on Hallowe'en; things tend to get crazy in there. Women in particular should be advised that there is at least one group of men doing the drumming thing and "getting in touch with their feelings" in the Park and sometimes they decide to touch something besides themselves.

You should remember that the local citizens' patrols in your neighborhoods, especially Chevy Chase and George-town, are very suspicious of traffic coming from east of the Park. Don't plan to go home until you're sober and don't forget your IDs.

<u>Directions from Southeast/Southwest D.C.</u>

The Sousa Bridge hasn't been repaired since the 2014 floods washed it out. If you must drive, your best bet will be the Anacostia ferry, which lands you near Eighth Street S.E. (You might even see the Anacostia River Monster, if you're lucky or if you start drinking early.) You'll need to come through Northeast Washington after that, since you must avoid the federal enclave and North Capitol Street is too dangerous to use. We recommend that you avoid driving through the Capitol Hill neighborhood, as their citizens' patrol is noted for being unkind to people from Anacostia and points south.

Directions from Maryland

First off, don't forget your passports. You will need them to enter D.C. We haven't heard of any major problems at any Maryland/District border checkpoints lately, but don't push your luck by standing on your rights. Most of you will probably need to come through the People's Republic of Takoma Park. SPITNOB has a good relationship with the PRTP—they'd love to annex us—so show this invite and you shouldn't have any difficulties getting through.

Coming from Baltimore, do not use Interstate 95 or the Baltimore-Washington Parkway. They are still rebuilding the parts of 95 that were blown up in the 12/12/12 terrorist attacks and most of the work is done on weekends to avoid making rush hour worse than usual. As for the parkway, another bridge collapsed last week. The contractor is claiming an Act of God, but rumor has it that he outsourced all the design work to Southeast Asia and sent them the wrong specs. Only adventure junkies use the Parkway.

Directions from Virginia

Alas for the red state/blue state divide–getting into the District from Virginia is much harder than coming in from Maryland. You might as well plan to come for several days –bring your sleeping bags and we'll put you up for as long as you'd like.

Leave your guns at home. Your carry permit is no good in D.C. and the border patrol will confiscate your gun and maybe even arrest you if they're feeling cranky. Don't trust your ability to hide things–these people will search your car thoroughly.

The ferry across the Potomac is faster than the bridges, where traffic creeps along at a snail's pace. Take the back roads, if you can: both Interstate 66 and 95 get bombed regularly. I've heard that 66 is completely rebuilt, but we wouldn't be surprised if the New South Patriots staged another attack on Hallowe'en. They seem to like holidays.

Virginians should make a point of avoiding the People's Republic of Takoma Park. Virginia will throw you in jail if you come back with a visa stamp from the PRTP and you can't count on the border guards. Some will "forget" to stamp your passport but others will stamp it twice just to be nasty.

❧

If those directions don't cover you, give us a call and we'll let you know what we've heard lately. When you get to our part of town, drive slowly—don't run over our pets and children playing in the street and our neighbors stopping to chat. So long as you drive carefully, you can ignore the one-way signs; it's impossible to get onto Somerset Place without going the wrong way down a one-way. Show your invite if you get stopped.

We look forward to seeing you at Hallowe'en.

Introduction to Hothouse
Ernest Lilley

Though Thomas Harlan has been around as a wargame designer and Fantasy writer for a while now, I only discovered him with his SF novel *Wasteland of Flint*, followed by *House of Reeds*, an alternate "science-fiction / archaeological-mystery/ space warfare epic set in a far-future dominated by the México (Aztec) Empire." Though I'm not a tremendous fan of Alt Fic, these are set far enough along so that the point is somewhat moot, and they're excellent stories. I had just finished interviewing Thomas for SFRevu.com when it occurred to me that his take on this future might be interesting as well . . . and he didn't let me down.

HOTHOUSE

Thomas Harlan

Arlington Island, 2046 AD

Sleet spat around the pilothouse cowling as Gundarsen turned the patrol launch into the Glebe Road dock. The *Skjold*'s nose bumped gently along old Michelins as the Norwegian idled down the turbines, letting the jet-boat settle. The dock itself was deserted, overshadowed by lightless buildings. At the prow, Sanchez turned up the woolen collar of his jacket, spat into the oily water and adjusted his gun belt.

"We need another muddy," the senior officer grumbled, "to watch the boat."

"Don't have one," Gund answered, tucking the boat keys into his jacket pocket. "Too cold for your thin southern blood?"

Sanchez' face wrinkled at the mocking tone. "Viking gangs run loose in the tidewater. They'd like this boat . . . so we'll clear this alarm and get back on the water as fast as possible."

Gund said nothing, flicking on a portable spot and digging out his gsat. The screen showed a maze of streets around a single blue star. "Map says . . . up Walter Reed and around to Sixteenth. A house, I'd say. Not an apartment."

"Squatters don't subscribe to Globalert," Sanchez grunted. "It'll be abandoned by the crabs, like all the rest." He lifted his shotgun, indicating the crumbling, half-submerged rows of red brick apartments. "But it won't be empty. You loaded, noob?"

Gund patted the Sig automatic in his gun rig. "I'm ready."

Under the clouds, Sixteenth Street was pitchy black by the time the two officers slogged up the hill. The eastern sky was lit by an eerie red, white and blue glow from the searchlights surrounding the Washington Obelisk. Both men moved cautiously, attention drawn tight by every stray sound. Rusted cars choking the street earned a wide berth. Feral dogs were endemic to the abandoned tidewater cities.

"This one?" Sanchez tilted his head at a vine-encrusted gate, gunstock snug against his shoulder. Somewhere out beyond the houses, dogs were yapping at oncoming night.

Gund pushed the gate open. "Not locked, as usual."

Arlington had been abandoned in a hurry. The Norwegian stepped into the yard and paused. The spotlight revealed an eerily flat lawn, throwing hard-edged shadows across glassed-in windows, a door, and a tight box of rosebushes. "*Knullen hel . . .*"

"Move it," Sanchez growled, pushing in behind him. "Let's find the alarm and . . ."

Gund shook his head. "Snacks, someone *has* been home." The spot had steadied, beam fixed on the half-open doorway. "This lawn's been *mown*," he whispered.

"*No one . . .*" Sanchez lowered his voice. "No one out here has a *gardener.*"

"Someone does." Gund's pale fingers brushed across evenly cut stems. "You cover, I'll get the door."

They were across the turf in four long strides. Gund led, automatic leveled over the spotlight, Sanchez behind, shotgun raised and ready. A little atrium led to a second door, and then wet boots were sinking into deep-pile carpet. The Norwegian froze again, stunned by the smell of hot yeast hanging in the air. The air felt warm and thick. The spot exposed rows of paintings, a high ceiling, and the gleam of crystal.

"Break-in," Sanchez whispered. "Kill the light."

The halogen glare faded as Sanchez scuttled forward. His shotgun eased the next door open and Sanchez stepped into a brightly-lit passageway between stairs to the left, and a dining room on his right. There was a woman kneeling on the floor, pale hair tied up behind her head. Sanchez' boot came down, grinding into broken glass. The woman's head snapped around, eyes wide in alarm. Her hands were poised over a Pyrex cylinder. The floor around her was littered with glass slivers, white powder and water.

"Easy now," Sanchez barked. "Stand up!"

"Your boots are wet," she said in a strangled voice. "Watch where you walk!" She stood, hands muddy. "You will ruin–you will soil the carpet!"

"Sorry!" Sanchez jumped back, startling Gund. The big man blinked in surprise, staring at the woman. Her eyes were very pale and azure, like winter sunlight on lake ice. *A Finn?* He thought, taking in her angular features. *Not an apple-cheeked Bergen-city girl, for sure.*

"What happened?" Gundarsen blurted, cutting off Sanchez's "Who are . . ."

They both stopped, eyeing each other in irritation.

"Policemen?" The girl was astonished. "Where did you two *juntti* spring from?"

"There was an alarm . . ." Sanchez took in the dining room with a slow, deliberate survey. Gund lowered his automatic, distracted by the mouth-watering smell in the air. "Is that bread baking?"

"Yes," the woman said, raising her broom threateningly. "You go away! I have work to do."

"Who broke in?" Gundarsen said, stepping in front of the girl. "Someone tripped a Globalarm trigger, little mouse. Where's the owner?"

She met his eyes with a cold, flat stare. Gund's lips started to sneer in response, two strays meeting for the first time. "There were men," The woman said. "They took the professor. I am cleaning up the mess they made."

"Professor?" Sanchez circled the dining room table, frowning at the stacks of papers, books, diagrams and odd objects he saw in the adjoining rooms. The library drew his steps; a big, high-ceilinged room stuffed with magazines, vidpaks, a sofa and two comfortable looking chairs squeezed in amongst the bookcases. The chair nearest the door had magazines and books draped over the velvet arms. Sanchez turned the topmost book over. Bold yellow letters jumped up at him, framing a faded painting of an oared warship sailing across a star-filled sky.

"Emil Petaja's *Kalevala*?" The Latino officer made a disgusted face. *Euronorse propaganda. Why don't they accept they're not going home?* "Why did he stay when everyone else evacuated?"

"This is his house," the girl said back stiff. "He has always owned it."

Gund stepped around the mess on the floor, and pushed open the kitchen door. A meal tray holding dinner for one sat on a meticulously clean sideboard. "Professor lives by himself, does he?"

He turned, eyeing the girl again. "You sleep under the stairs?"

"I have a room," she said, a sharp edge in her voice.

"No one else around?" Gundarsen moved through the kitchen, feeling an odd sense of disassociation. The rest of Arlington was a wilderness of overgrown golf-courses, burned-out buildings, drowned streets . . . most of old Washington metro had been abandoned when the Chesapeake tidal barriers collapsed in '32 and the chill Atlantic rushed in on supercane winds to drown the city. Parts of Arlington and Alexandria remained above the floodwaters, but the residential neighborhoods couldn't support themselves when the government moved south, away from the steadily encroaching ice. Not when no one built new causeways into the dead cities.

"Anyone ever bothered you before?" Sanchez stood at the far wall of the library, staring up at a wall of heavy glass tubes. "In all this time?"

"No one comes up here," the girl said, carefully brushing sand into the dustpan. "The garden wall keeps the dogs out, and groceries are delivered from Fort Myer on Tuesdays."

"No one lives around here? No squatters, no gangs?" Sanchez stopped at an empty space. The wooden paneling was damaged. "Did these 'men' take something besides the professor?"

The library itself was a wreck, stacks of old paperbound periodicals piled on the floor, sheaves of printouts stacked under the tables, framed pictures lying askew. Sanchez leaned in to read a faded label.

"They took a . . . an *ice core*? From Camp Century, on . . . Greenland? From 1956 . . . these things are damned old!"

"Stay away from those," the girl growled. "They are valuable scientific evidence! Not to be touched, not to be played with!"

"Someone tore this one right off the wall," Sanchez said, suspicious. "Are they really worth something?"

"He said so," the girl said, sliding into the room, her hands nervous. She started to tidy up. "They are the first of their kind and irreplaceable."

"Sure." Sanchez ventured a chuckle. "No ice on Greenland these days . . ."

The girl stiffened, thin little shoulders hunching up. The officer caught a glimpse of unadulterated fury pinching her face, and his shotgun up swung up in a blur. "Hands behind your head, señorita. Vamanos!"

Gund stepped into the room, chewing on a lamb-chop. "This is excellent. What's on now?"

"Cuff her," Sanchez snarled. "Got a temper, this one. Might have fallen out with her boss . . ."

"Surely," Gund grinned, and kicked the girl behind the knees. A pair of sticky-cuffs were on her wrists before she could rise. "That wasn't so hard, was it?"

Sanchez lowered the shotgun, relieved. "Sit her down in

the dining room while I check the house. And see if you can get us some backup."

Ten minutes later, Sanchez clattered down the stairs. Gund was finishing off the Professor's dinner. "Find anything?"

"She has a room, so does the Professor." Sanchez tossed an ID pak on the table. "J. C. Dye, University of Houston. A geophysicist and paleoclimatologist. His pak says *el profesor* is over a hundred-and-ten years old. Amazing. You get a hold of anyone?"

"No. The usual atmospheric crap is junking up the band."

"Great." Sanchez frowned. "He can't walk, so we'll need to helo him out."

Gund sniffed, looking back at the girl. "Century plus, huh? Guess he kept his hands off you, mouse. Too bad." He flashed a toothy grin. "Why drag *him* off, anyway, if these core-things are so valuable? Someone going to pay to get him back?"

Sanchez sorted through the pictures on the desk. He picked up one and showed it to the girl. "Is this Professor Dye?"

She grimaced. "He does not look like that anymore."

"I'd imagine not." Sanchez handed the snapshot to Gund. Four men in parkas stood in front of an airplane with long skis. One of them was young, with glasses and a beard. Behind them stretched a limitless expanse of white emptiness.

"Doesn't look like much," Gundarsen said. "Big brain though, right?"

"He is a genius," the girl snarled. "Are you going to rescue him? You are policemen?"

"True . . ." Gund looked at Sanchez. "Should we kick this upstairs? Not really our job, now is it? Not smuggling, not illegals, not looters . . . sounds like Bureau business."

Sanchez shook his head. "We're first on the scene, so we

do our part." He turned to the girl. "Where's your ID pak, señorita?"

The girl stared at the floor. Sanchez raised an eyebrow. "Illegal, huh? You have a name?"

"Aila," she said, giving them both a flinty stare. "He will die if you do not do *something*. They will not be gentle!"

"Ah-huh." Gund licked butter from his fingers. "Bet not. But they were gentle with you, weren't they? Left you here alive, with a broom and a mop to clean up. Very nice. I mean, if these *men* existed at all. What if you got tired of this old geek and decided to . . . smother him? Cut his throat? See what you could get for yourself?"

Sanchez turned Aila's hands over in the sticky-cuffs. "Let go of me!"

He ignored the noise. Her fingers were dusty with flour and specked with water. "No, she didn't do him in . . . not directly. Get her up and we'll find the professor's wheel-chair."

"What do we need that for?" Gund dragged Aila to her feet. "You think he's still around?"

"We'll see." Sanchez quartered the floor. "This way." Wheel tracks, with sand and water spattered over them, led out of the library towards the back of the house. "You keep hold of her, Gund. She's a slippery one."

The tracks led them out through a laundry room and into a huge, dark room with walls of glass and steel, filled with the damp, heady odor of flowers and vines. The glow of the flashlight gleamed back from thick fronds and spatulate leaves.

"Goddamn, but it stinks!" Gund twisted Aila's arm, making her squeak. "What *is* this, mouse?"

"The solarium," she muttered. "The professor's last, great work."

"Right . . ." Sanchez kicked something metallic with his boot. There was a rattling sound as an empty wheelchair rolled away across gravel. Sanchez dodged automatically to the left. Gund reacted too, slapping a hand across the girl's mouth and went right. The wheelchair rolled into a door-frame with a heavy clank.

Nothing happened.

Sanchez played the flashlight over the opening. Like the front door, this one stood ajar, leading into an airlock-like entryway. Inside the threshold, a slipper lay on the ground.

"Got 'im," the officer whispered. "Gund, let the girl breathe, huh?"

Sanchez turned off his flashlight and waited for his eyes to adjust. "Ok, Aila, to help the professor, you need to help us. What's the yard like . . . is there a wall, trees, what? A helo-deck or a garage?"

There was a long pause, but then she said: "A little yard with grass and then yes, a gardening shed and the rear wall."

"But a gate, right? Onto an alleyway? For a car?"

"No, no alley. Beyond the wall are woods."

"Right." Sanchez slid through the entryway, hand reaching for the latch. . . .

As the outer door swung open, letting in a chill wave of night air. A cigarette was burning in someone's mouth. Sanchez saw that as he swung up the shotgun–and a voice said, "Hurry up, you stupid *pillu—*"

Sanchez reversed the shotgun and slammed the stock forward. The cigarette made an excellent aiming point. Rubber slammed into bone and there was a choked cry. The man pitched backwards onto a graveled walkway. His cry was met by answering shouts and Sanchez glimpsed men running. *Too many!*

"Eyes!" He rasped at Gund. His thumb rolled the ammo-selector to *flash* and the shotgun pounded his shoulder. The entire yard lit with a rippling flare of hot white light. Someone shrieked in terrible pain, but Sanchez had no time to see why. He was out the door and rolling to the left. Gund threw the girl through the doorway, sending her crashing into the man moaning on the gravel. The big Norwegian came out low and darted to the right. Sanchez bounced up, saw one of the running men had stopped a flashbang with his chest and was rolling on the ground, clothing on fire, wailing like a broke-legged dog.

There were four or five others–scattering–and the fading glare shone hard from bared steel. Sanchez fired twice, the shotgun booming loud. The nearest two men punched back, taking knockems straight in the chest.

Off to the right, Gund's automatic vented propellant in a bright tongue of flame and a shrill *crack-crack*. A figure trying to throw a jacket on the burning man staggered, flipped around and sprawled lifelessly on the grass. The last man out of the trees charged in, throwing himself under the blast of the automatic. Gund skipped to one side, cursing, as the man rolled up and the Norwegian gasped, feeling something cold graze his out flung arm.

Sanchez twisted to get a square aim and the shotgun hammered again. Propellant flare yielded a snapshot of the girl flat on the gravel before the knockem hit the last man square in the back. He staggered forward, colliding with Gund. They grappled, a long wave-bladed knife glittering in the beam of the flashlight. The Norwegian grunted, feeling an icicle bite into his shoulder. He clipped the man across the forehead. Stunned, the attacker slumped away.

Gasping, Gund nearly fainted, feeling a wet, oozy wound spurt under his fingers. "Ah God, I need a medic."

"You're not the only one," Sanchez said, scuttling forward. He paused, helping the girl sit up. "Are you hurt?"

"No," Aila whispered, staring around. "That was so swift."

"It is, sometimes." Sanchez rolled the knife-man face down and trussed him expertly with more sticky-cuff. "Gund, get off your ass. Work to do."

The Norwegian swayed, but managed to get both hands on his automatic, covering the rest of the bodies. "Got it. I've got it."

Sanchez made a quick circuit, picking up knives and throwing them into the bushes, cuffing the other assailants. The storm finally decided to drop some snow, swallowing up the glow of the Obelisk, leaving the yard entirely dark.

In the flashlight's beam, Sanchez could see the robbers had thin features, pasty blonde hair and the usual assortment of tattoos. Their jackets and caps were covered with embroidery, most of it obscene, and well suited to the everlasting winter.

"Vikings," he muttered, dragging the two unconscious thugs back to where Gund was sitting on the step, fumbling with a bandage pak. "Señorita, will you help Officer Gundarsen if I release you?"

Aila gave Sanchez an opaque stare for a moment, but then nodded. Gund hissed when she pulled the jacket aside.

"You're quite a bleeder," Sanchez commented, surveying the garden. "Got stuck good, too."

"He had a *knullen* sword!" Gund snarled, keeping a close eye on the girl. She got the bandage on the wound, though her numb hands were clumsy. "Went straight through my jacket. . . ."

"Armor in the jacket is for bullets," Sanchez said absently. Someone was missing. "You keep an eye on things here." He thumbed the shotgun to flashbang again and paced along the path, shining the flashlight into the bushes and under the trees. Fifty feet back from the house, the path turned left and the vague shape of a garage appeared. There was something on the ground beside the door, something in white. . ..

"Professor Dye?" Sanchez circled the huddled shape on the ground. The academic's eyes were closed, his lips parted by a faint breath. "Now we do need a medic."

Dye was very light, barely a hundred pounds. Cradling the man in his arms, Sanchez returned to the house. Aila was sitting on the grass, the Norwegian's jacket draped over her shoulders, staring down blankly at one of the dead vikings. She had the boy's hand in hers.

"Let's get him inside," Sanchez said, motioning for Gund to get up. "Señora, you too."

"What about these cuckoos?" Gund waved his automatic at the robbers.

"We'll round them up," Sanchez said, turning to get the professor through the door. "After the doc is back in bed where he belongs."

Under electric lights, Dye's face was wrinkled parchment. Sanchez tipped a Service flask against the thin blue lips. Dye's face scrunched up as he took the draught and then coughed weakly. "What. . . . Who are you?"

"Federal Maritime Police." Sanchez showed the old man his pak. "We were the nearest unit to respond to your Globalert call."

Dye squinted at the badge. "You should not have been called. Special Operations at Fort Myer is responsible for my safety."

"No one else here, *oldefar*," Gund interjected. "You'd be dead and dumped if we hadn't come along."

Sanchez suddenly wondered why the robbers had waited in the rear yard. "Professor, did your assailants say anything about why they took you? Were they going to ask for ransom?"

"No," the old man coughed. "Where is Aila? Has she been hurt?"

"She's fine." Sanchez eyed the girl standing silently beside one of the chairs. "Though she still has questions to answer."

"Not to you, she doesn't." The professor rasped. "Major Besson will handle all of this. Child, where is my dinner?"

Aila stirred. She bared her teeth at Gundarsen, saying, "Someone ate it, professor. I'll . . ."

"We'll get you something," Sanchez interrupted. "Professor, the men who broke in, they took one of these ice cores from your wall. Why would they do that?"

"What happened?" Dye didn't have the strength to sit up. "Someone disturbed one of my rares?"

"Here on the wall." Sanchez stepped to the empty space. "There were six; but the one at the end is gone." He looked back at the professor. "Aila said they were irreplaceable – but they just seem to be filled with sand. . . ."

"Sand?" Dye said, dismissively. "Only number six contains grit from the drill-bit hitting bedrock. The others . . . they are ice, officer. Ice and particulate matter. Dust, to you. As for their value . . . They are a reminder of foolish youth. Beyond that, they are entirely useless."

Aila made a choked growling sound, drawing the attention of all three men.

"He is lying," she hissed. "He told Mikael they were beyond price!"

Dye laughed weakly. "What would the gardener know about such things?"

Sanchez didn't like what he saw on the girl's face. "Gund, you'd better cuff her again."

"I will be good." Aila sat down in the chair. "But he is still lying. They are precious."

"They are *not*," Dye sounded confident. "They are only old climatological samples. I kept them because they were unique." Sanchez caught a flash of pride in the old man's voice. "They are the basal cut from the very first deep core at the Century site. It is sad one was broken, for the *sand* you see spilled on the floor represents the world climate of nearly a hundred-fifty thousand years ago." He managed to lift his hand. "We drilled a three kilometer bore through the ice, down to bedrock which had not seen the sun since the Pleistocene. A cross-section, you see, of the earth's weather and climate for an age. Many other samples have been taken since then, you understand, and some of them deeper – like the Vostok-B core from Antarctica – but these . . . these were the first."

"You took them?" Sanchez remembered the men standing in the snow. "You were just a kid. . . ."

"Fresh out of graduate school. The youngest post-doc to ever graduate from UH. My drill design–well, that's what caught the eye of the Air Force. They wanted to see under the glacier, making sure the radar station reactors wouldn't be subsumed by ice shifting in summertime . . . they needn't have worried! The Thule ice sheet was stable for . . . for thirty-five thousand years."

The professor's voice trailed off.

Sanchez glanced at Gund to make sure he was keeping an eye on the girl, and then turned back to Dye. "Greenland melted forty years ago, doc. Did you see that coming?"

"It had happened before," the professor said, closing his eyes. "Down at the bottom of the core . . . there were pine needles. Plain as day. Such things move in cycles, you must understand. The earth's path around the sun oscillates–the world tips back and forth over the millennia–and sometimes the world is choked by ice, and sometimes not."

"Heard all that in school," Sanchez tracing the clear surface with his fingertips. The glass was cold to the touch. "Guess our civilization ran out of time, huh? Nature's pendulum swung and . . . pow! The seas rise; drowning entire nations . . . the ice advances, crushing the rest. What are these dark bands?" Striations in the ice were visible to the naked eye in cylinder number four.

"Vulcanism," Dye whispered. "Ash-fall from eruptions a world away, or changes in the acidity of the snow. . . ."

"Huh." Sanchez's eyes narrowed, peering at the core. "And you can tell when that happened? Just from where the line is in the cylinder?" He spread his arms. "Like a chart–a timeline of the earth–but this isn't the whole thing, right? You said it was thousands of meters long?"

"Yes. Far too long to keep. The rest were disposed of years ago. No space to keep them, you see, and no trucks to move them. Things got too hectic. . . ."

Sanchez squatted in front of the professor. "Gotta question, doc. I'm just a muddy working the tidewater in a thir-ty-footer, chasing water rats and killing stray dogs, but . . . how quick did you figure out the pendulum was swinging, after you pulled this soda-straw from the ice? Because it must have been pretty clear which way things were going. I mean, sixty or seventy years is *nothing* compared to this timeline! Nothing!"

The officer jolted to his feet. "Shit, *viejo*, it must have looked like the cap was *already* melting!" Sanchez turned violently, measuring the remaining core sections by eye. "This is like . . . maybe thirty-six feet of the sample. Out of nine *thousand!* That's close to a year per inch for your hundred-fifty large. That's data you can see with the naked eye!"

Dye said nothing. It seemed he'd stopped breathing.

"Professor?" Sanchez looked at the girl. "He pass out?"

"He does not want to say," she said, voice flat. "He does not want to admit what he did."

"What he did?" Gund stirred, obviously bored. "Pissed his pants is what he did. Come on, let's find a helo to lift him out of here." The Norwegian checked his chrono. "We've only got another thirty minutes on shift anyway."

"Shut up, Gund. Señorita, what do you mean?"

Aila pointed at the papers stacked on the desk. "He told lies, when they asked him what was written in the ice. If you read those old magazines, you will see."

"I didn't lie," Dye groaned. "I should not have taught you to read, child. You do not understand how things were. . . ."

"He *lied.*" Aila almost leapt at the old man, but Gund interposed himself. At gunpoint she sat down, but her voice got sharper and sharper. "It was his fault. *His.* Those other men helped, but *he* was the one that . . ."

"I did not lie!" The professor's eyes flew open. "This was only one sample! One! By the time the pattern was confirmed; from the Campito chronologies, from the Vostok core, it was *too late.* The CO_2 balance in the atmosphere had already shifted and . . . and the caps were melting. Far too late to do anything. . . ."

Sanchez stared at Dye and even Gund finally caught on.

"You. . . ." The Norwegian's face drained white. "You knew the Flood was coming? This thing on the wall–it said the Ice was coming? The great cold? In nineteen-*knullen*-fifty-six? *And you didn't tell anyone?* You dicked around for sixty years until it was too *knullen* late?"

Dye slumped back, utterly drained. "It was only a guess. Some papers were published. But no one listened. Who could conceive the atmospheric balance could shift so quickly?"

Sanchez tapped core number four. "Did this . . . the abrupt change, the onset of the Ice, the weather. . . . Could you see a change like that here?"

"Four times," Dye whispered. "Do you understand punctuated equilibrium? A long slow build to some critical point and then. . .then it is so abrupt. Only decades, perhaps a century and then thousands of years to swing back again. . . ."

"Goddamn." Gund stared at the professor, fists clenching and unclenching. His voice was tight with rage. "Goddamn. Sanchez, you know how it was. Millions of people crammed into the boats . . . couldn't take anything, couldn't save anything, everyone lost and confused. Goddamn. Tens of thousands of us died just getting here, to America, or to Africa, or . . ." He stopped, his eyes going dead. "All I remember is the roar of machine guns, and screaming. That's all. That's all I have left. Just the sound of the guns."

"You're wrong, *juntti,*" Aila said, so softly the three men could barely hear her. "It was not thousands who died when summer failed. It was millions. Tens of millions." Her gaze fixed on the old man. "Some nations have simply disappeared. Perhaps there are only one or two of their people left."

Suddenly Sanchez realized she didn't look like the other Norse refugees he'd ever seen. Her eyes were wrong–almost slanted–and her cheekbones were sharper.

"You're not a Finn," he blurted.

Her lips peeled back from glittering white teeth, eyes narrowing to bare slits.

"Of course not," Dye coughed in amusement. "She is *Saami.* A Lapplander. Like her brother, my idiot gardener. I took them in after the Flood. They were only toddlers."

Sanchez lifted his chin. "Where *is* the gardener?"

"He is outside," Aila replied tonelessly. "His face was burned away."

"I see." The Latino officer frowned, thinking. "He thought the core was money. He met some vikings prowling for a flop, and decided they should rob this old man living on a hill. So they came in and broke things up a bit." Sanchez looked down at the Professor. "Took you too, just in case."

"That doesn't make any sense," Gund growled. "No one will believe *ice* is worth anything. . . ."

"It is *not worthless*," Aila hissed, jerking up from the chair. The old book fell to the floor. "Stop telling these lies! Louhi's blood is more precious than any gold or jewel!"

"Louhi?" Dye blinked owlishly at her. "Oh, you poor child–the Witch of Pohjola is only a monster in a fairy tale. A figment out of an old . . ."

"She is *real*, you old liar!" Aila snatched up the book. "The Ice Mother holds winter's chill in her heart, keeping the people safe; in olden times winter came when she slept and frost-spirits escaped from her nostrils. But *you*, stupid *oldefar*, you wounded her, you drank her blood, *you ruined the world!*"

"Stop it, Aila," Sanchez moved, automatic leveled. "Those books aren't *real*. That looks like a . . ."

Gund grabbed the girl's arm, spinning her around. The old book flew off in a flutter of pages and Sanchez was distracted for just an instant. There was a choked cry, and when he looked back Aila had stabbed Gundarsen in the throat with a knife. With a howl, she drove the choking officer back, thin arms straining as the big man slammed into the wall. There was a squeaking sound of metal digging deep into wood.

Sanchez fired wildly, trying to miss his partner.

The girl ducked, snatched up a stack of magazines from the floor and threw them at his face. Sanchez threw out an arm, knocking the pulps away and fired again. The trip-hammer *bang-bang-bang* of the Sig rattled the heavy glass cylinders, but Aila had already fled.

"Madre de dios," Sanchez swore. "That one is quick."

He ducked into the dining area, both hands on the Sig, quartering the room for the girl. *Nothing.*

"Shit!" Sanchez ducked back into the library.

Gund was stiff against the wall, fingers pressed against his throat. The knife-hilt was flush to the skin and Sanchez was shocked the man still breathed. The Latino officer stepped close.

"Damn . . . she missed both trachea and arteries . . . this thing must be crazy sharp."

"It's a Marttiini *Kondor*," Dye rasped from the sofa. "With an edge like diamond wire."

Gund tried not to swallow, breathing shallowly through both nostrils. Sanchez patted his good shoulder gently. "Don't worry, I'll get a medivac here in thirty minutes with the big radio on the boat. You just hold still. Real still. OK?"

The Norwegian blinked, making the tiniest possible nod.

Sanchez took off at a run.

Sanchez was puffing hard when he staggered to a halt on the Glebe Road dock. Over the wind, he barely caught the sound of two Pratt & Whitney gas turbines firing up. "What th . . . Goddamit, Gund, you gave her your fucking jacket!"

Sanchez sprinted towards the end of the pier, the Sig out in his hand. The launch was turning nose to the storm when he ran out of concrete.

"Stop!" His shout seemed feeble. "Aila, Gund and the Professor will die if they don't get medical help! I need the radio. . . ."

Sanchez raised the Sig again, listening for the targeting tone, gauging the distance between the moving boat and the dock. *Not more than ten, twelve meters. An easy shot if I could see a single damn thing.*

"They *should* die," came her faint response. "*Him* most of all, for dooming so many innocents. I owe him nothing, though he gave me a great gift. I tried to spare him, but such kindness only cost me Mikael." The turbines kicked up a notch and the boat slewed sideways, dancing on the heavy, dark water. Sanchez felt his heart leap into his throat. Even Gund, who'd grown up with boats, treated the *Skjold* diffidently. "I understand your duty, officer. But I am Pohjola's last fair daughter, and my doom is to see Mother's wound healed. *His* death will pay a little of a great weregeld, I think. The rest is in my hands."

A light came on the pilothouse, shining through an open hatchway. In that moment, Sanchez glimpsed pale gold and heavy glass shining under the running lights. There was a sharp, insistent chime from his automatic. Snow was blowing past. Aila was silhouetted against the lamp.

Then the hatch closed, and Sanchez dropped the Sig, thumbing back the safety. The airjets kicked up a glossy plume and then the launch was gone, gliding out the estuary towards Potomac Sound and the open sea.

The library was growing cold when Sanchez returned. Gund was lying face down on the floor in a huge, dark pool; the side of his throat cut neatly open. The Marttiini remained embedded in the wall, blade filmed with blood. Dye was still on the sofa, eyes closed.

"Oh Gund . . ." Sanchez knelt beside his partner. "You couldn't hold still, could you? Stupid Viking . . ."

"I believe," came Dye's old, rasping voice. "His carotid artery was nicked by the blow. He started to choke, then fell. As you see," the professor coughed weakly, "there was nothing I could do."

Sanchez rose up on his knees, his round face tight with disgust. "You didn't give a shit, did you? All you wanted was the big house in a nice neighborhood and a fat pension . . . the rest of the world could slide right down to icy hell for all you cared."

He touched Gund's limp arm. "Just like you let him die. And that boy who kept your *lawn*, and the girl . . ." Sanchez paused. He looked around the library again, this time with new eyes. "You are a disgusting old shit, aren't you? You didn't adopt two orphans out of kindness. You *collected* them. Like you've collected everything in the hothouse. . . ."

The Professor scowled. "My solarium holds a sample of every native plant, flower and herb growing in Greater Washington – everything obliterated by the climate change. Mankind will outlast the ice, and when the Atlantic conveyor restarts, my legacy will be waiting. Many rare things will survive, which might have been lost! This much, I can give back."

"Aila didn't think much of your great project," Sanchez replied.

Dye laughed mockingly. "Can you believe that rubbish? Witches' blood indeed! I hope you caught her, officer. She needs to be locked up, or shot, or sent to a penal battalion to do national service."

"I didn't catch her or shoot her," Sanchez said, turning Gundarsen's body over. He retrieved the man's pak, his Sig, the gunrig and gearbelt. The Norwegian's features were already slack with death. "I let her go."

"What? Why would you do such an idiotic thing?"

The corners of Sanchez' eyes tightened and his lips drew back in a tight, feral grin.

"Because," the officer said, "nothing Man's science could devise brought an end to winter, nor have our prayers, or the intercession of the saints, or the swing of your goddamn pendulum. But *I* will spot a girl who *believes* this chance, no matter how small, to see summer come again. Comprende?"

"You're a fool!" Dye spat on the floor. "You'll be disciplined. In these times, the Provisional Authority is strict with traitors or incompetents. I'm a National Resource, and I won't be—where, where are you going?"

Sanchez halted in the doorway. "I was going down to Fort Myer to get a recovery team for you and Gund." He tapped his chrono. "But my shift is over."

"Officer, you can't. Officer! You have to . . ."

Sanchez left the doors open as he left, and his boots were wet with blood, leaving a long red track through the snow as he trudged across the lawn and through the garden gate, which he made sure stood wide.

I'm sorry, Gund, I know how much you hate those dogs.

Introduction to The Day of the RFIDs
Ernest Lilley

I'd just finished Ed's book *Moonstruck*, which takes place in and around DC, so I knew he was a shoe-in for area knowledge. It turns out that he knows a lot more than how to get to Reagan (or for die-hards, National) Airport in this tale of technology five seconds from now. And it turns out (says a usually reliable source) that he's got his facts right.

THE DAY OF THE RFIDS

EDWARD M. LERNER

The way into the **Homeland Security Bureau** seldom runs through mom & pop grocery stores and the **Internet Movie Data Base**. Even less often does that route continue onto the **Ten Most Wanted Fugitives list**.

Chalk me up as one to take the road (lane, alley, trail, deer path) less traveled.

I'm not blogging this for your sympathy—but I hope, at the least, to establish credibility and get your attention. I'm posting this, in fact, for your own good. And, while I am being direct, one more thing. . . .

I'm not the only one being watched.

❦

At one level, I would like to blog my story under that grand old pseudonym "Publius." As patriotic, though, as I believe my goals to be, my role model is someone far removed from Madison or Hamilton or Jay. There is, in any event, nothing to be gained from a pen name: The feds know exactly who I am. The challenge lies not in anonymity, but in elusiveness . . . at least long enough to spread the word. Maybe personal details will make this all a bit more credible.

So who am I? The family name has always been a point of obscure pride to my parents: Boyer. "Like the suave actor, my boy," Dad would say, as though I had any idea whom he meant. "You could be like him." Despite my cool

87

attempts at disinterest, I eventually absorbed that the long-gone thespian was **Charles Boyer**, with whom I identified about as much as with Bela Lugosi or Fred Flintstone.

Oddly omitted from this bit of cinematic trivia was how the black-and-white era actor pronounced his name: boy-YEA. Grandpa had Americanized the name, so that it came out boy-ER—from which it was a short step to boy-ARE. As in: Boy, are you a geek. The family business being a small grocery, it was only a small step further to the leitmotif of my youth: Geek Boy are dee.

The grocery wasn't all bad. It supported the family, and I had a built-in after-school job, which didn't help the Boyardee jokes. Dad, fortunately, wanted me out of the store as much as did I. Owning a grocery store means hard work and long hours. "If you follow in my foot steps, Zach," he would volunteer more or less weekly, "I will personally break your ankles." Not that there was ever any chance I would make such a career choice: The geek taunts were reasonably well-founded. I'm good with computers and better with microelectronics. I went to college to become an EE and meant never to look back.

Easier said than done.

It's not that I ever thought the store did *well*, but pitching in every day after high school I had believed the place did okay. Going away to college gave me a whole new perspective. Seeing the store only every few months, on holidays and at breaks, the place looked different to me: dated, fewer shoppers each time, an ever-older clientele, brands that—now that my friends regularly shopped at Wal-mart and Costco and Big Bob's—seemed oh so dated.

Throughout high school I had argued with Dad about upgrading to checkout stations with barcode scanners. (I'm sure you know the advantages: fast, efficient checkout and machine-readable data on what was selling.) It wasn't like I was pushing new technology. I had lost the argument, of course. Tech was never Dad's thing, so you can imagine how he felt about putting serious money into it.

By the time I had finished college, I had seen at the big-box stores the technology that was fast replacing barcodes—and there were Mom and Dad still punching prices into old cash registers, still walking the aisles to decide what to reorder and when. They were doomed . . . without my help, anyway.

<hr />

Through These Portals
Pass the Best-Fed Mortals

Growing up, the carefully hand-lettered sign on the store's entrance seemed clever. It might even have been true once. But time marched on and "portal" came to mean Yahoo! and AOL. As the sign faded, the clientele, looking progressively *too* well-fed, gained paunches and lost hair. And outside of the undertaking business, an ever-aging clientele is bad news.

That's how, new-and-fascinating EE day job notwithstanding, I came to spend hours each week in big-box emporia. On weekends, their cavernous aisles echoed with a chittering, droning, buzzing sound that would make seventeen-year cicadas proud. But it was for a good cause.

The barcode technology Mom and Dad had yet to accept was fast being replaced by radio frequency ID tags: RFIDs. That's "are-fids," if you prefer to speak your acronyms (and like triffids, if you favor the classics). While a barcode can be read only when in line of sight—you've seen the red laser beams at checkouts—the coded microwave pulses to which an **RFID** tag responds are omni-directional. One invisible, inaudible, electromagnetic *ping* and the whole jumbled contents of a cartful of books or CDs—or groceries—declares itself.

An RFID tag would never be as inexpensive as ink lines printed on a label. Still, a tag was simple electronics. The couple of cents an RFID tag cost were insignificant compared to the faster, foolproof checkout it enabled.

"You're *so* good at spotting new products before they become hot," Dad began saying. I understood his surprise. Did you know just one in ten new food products survives even a year? After a few demonstrations (I called both Yebeg Wot, an Ethiopian lamb-in-red-pepper-sauce dish, and organic mushroom burgers before either was featured in *Grocers Weekly*), he began stocking pre-trendy and high-margin, ready-to-go meals on just my "intuition."

I knew better than to try an explanation. The RFID scanner in my pocket, its sensitivity boosted by a few tricks I'd mastered in college, invisibly polled the carts of every shopper exiting whatever big-box retailer I chose to loiter by. Dump the data into a PC, sort, and *voilà*: market research. But catching fads was only postponing the inevitable, unless—fat chance—Mom and Dad could match big-box volume and buying power.

At this point I was actually starting to feel a bit like Charles Boyer, whom I had finally gotten around to scoping out on **imdb**. Boyer had done a ton of movies and TV I'd never heard of, and a few I had. In a world of 500-channel digital cable, "The Rogues" was always on some network. Damned if he wasn't suave, and who *doesn't* like to see scoundrels get their comeuppance?

So, in a way, Plan B was Dad's fault.

RFID applications are not limited to checkout. The newest thing in groceries is smart shelves. Picture a smart store that with a few microwave pulses identifies every jar of pickles and can of cranberry sauce in stock, including those orphaned items abandoned aisles away from where they belong. It's now possible to signal a merchandise management system—even before the shopper meanders to the front of the store—that it is time to reorder something.

Plan B required a newer gadget, one that took me inside the stores instead of staking them out. Wouldn't it be interesting, I had decided, if merchandise management systems were to believe that phantom jars of sauerkraut were selling like hotcakes? That quarts of eggnog were being abandoned in freezer cases? It didn't take much to make my little gadget pulse random UPC, batch, and package numbers as I roamed the aisles. My inventory gremlins were ephemeral—but, I guessed, troubling enough to reintroduce into the ordering loop safely fallible and inefficient humans. Judging from the recent occurrences of stock boys and girls wandering the aisles with clipboards, my first several ventures had been successful.

On foray number eight, the feds nabbed me.

After 9/11, everyone said everything had changed. After the 2/4 dirty-bomb attack on the Super Bowl, everything finally did. The new **Homeland Security Bureau** was the most visible proof. The newest domestic intelligence agency was not known for its candor. It appeared in media reports as Homeland BS far more often than innocent typos could explain.

I was driven by two taciturn feds to the headquarters of the country's newest intel agency. Growing up in outer metro DC, I had endured too many school field trips downtown to expect aesthetics from modern government buildings—but this recent construction was just stunningly ugly. My impression, as our nondescript sedan swept past armed guards and a security gate into the underground garage, was of a concrete castle rendered by MC Escher.

I didn't see how what I had been up to could be illegal . . . but oblivious and impervious as I was then to current events, I also knew the government had taken to making rather expansive assertions under the **Patriot Act**. It did not help that my perceptions of the FBI, a big chunk of which had become a core component of the HSB, had been formed by "The X-Files."

By the time they laid it out to me in a spartan, windowless room, I was numb with shock. Big Bob's had no intention of sharing their sales data, so a case could be made for theft. The exceptional sensitivity of my Plan A RFID receiver notwithstanding, I had had to stand on Big Bob's property—the parking lot—to get useful signals. That added a possible case for trespass. And, they mused, how confident was I a jury wouldn't find hacking the most credible explanation for the indoor signals my Plan B transmitter had been emitting?

Trespass? I had bought something on every trip, which made me, in technical terms, a *customer*. Theft? Rival retailers had sent secret shoppers into competing stores since forever. More than once Dad, having spotted a furtive note taker, had offered another store's spy a cup of coffee and a chair. Polling RFIDs just made the data collection more efficient.

But possibly I had started down a slippery slope by injecting gremlins into Big Bob's inventory statistics. How many, in a jury of my supposed peers, would be people whose VCRs endlessly flashed 12:00 (any jurors who still owned VCRs would be worrisome enough) and whose children dutifully reset their digital clocks twice a year? Could those peers be convinced my simulated RFID responses were *not* a hack attack? How much was I willing to bet on that?

As my peril began to sink in, the special agent in charge hinted obliquely at the real deal. What the bureau truly wanted was my evident smarts on RFID transceivers. Mine had better range than the gear they were buying.

The best I could hope for in this situation was massive legal bills I would be years in paying off. Worst case would be legal bills plus who knew how much jail time?

What would you have done?

It was only much later that I realized the one thing the feds wanted above all else: to *avoid* a trial.

Despite a life-long fascination with the space program, there was never any realistic chance I would become a rocket scientist. As kids, sparklers were the only Fourth of July fireworks my brothers and I were ever allowed—and the way Mom winced on those rare occasions Dad brought sparklers home sucked all the fun out of the experience. Then **Sojourner** rolled its first few yards onto the Martian surface. Problem solved.

NASA, it turned out, was not the only group that developed robots. By the time I graduated from college, DARPA—that's the **Defense Advanced Research Projects Agency** was putting more funds into robots than was NASA. I'd never had any interest in defense contracting, but lots of DARPA-supported research was and is just way cool, cutting-edge stuff. That's how I wound up working for a Beltway Bandit on a DARPA contract. My bosses no doubt thought about one kind of dual-use for the new technology while I was imagining another . . . and while I nursed my dreams, if and when NASA ever again had money, of someday building robots at JPL.

It did not, amid the never-ending and ever-expanding war on terror, take much to outspend NASA on robots. My piece of the DARPA project was, not surprisingly, on the electronics side, and the budget scarcely covered salaries. To keep costs down, I did my proof-of-concept work using what the govvies call COTS. That's "commercial off the shelf", an acronym which, despite the plain semantics of its phrase, had been nounified. I needed a radio link between a lander and its rover—or, at customer briefings, between a war fighter's handheld controller and the tiny, semi-autonomous scout vehicle it controlled. The cheapest, most accessible COTS used unlicensed radio spectrum. You know: the frequencies used by low-powered gadgets like **WiFi** wireless LANs and cordless (not cellular) phones.

It was the damnedest thing. My rover would work just fine for days and then, for no apparent reason, it would glitch. Long story short, there was intermittent interference on the command link. My colleagues razzed me about my ill-advised choice of frequency (I didn't mention the dearth of cordless phones on Mars), and, rather than rebuild, we moved the project into a shielded lab. It didn't help.

Okay, NOW, long story short. Much time and expensive test equipment later, the problem was traced to several items of new clothing.

Would you care to guess what inexpensive labeling mechanism also uses low-power RF at unregulated frequencies?

⚜

There's no reason to drag my erstwhile employers into this, not that much detective work would be necessary to identify them. For purposes of this history, "the corporation" will do just fine. Given the dual-use nature of my work, and who was funding it, I had been asked to apply for a Top Secret clearance. I had reluctantly gone along, comforted by the two-plus year backlog in clearance investigations. I was new enough to the real world to still be thinking in college student time: Nothing matters if it can be postponed past the end of a semester.

My bosses at the corporation were beyond ecstatic when I mentioned a friend-of-a-friend introduction to an HSB project manager interested in synergies between my current work and Bureau needs. The HSB got a fast-tracked research project, the corporation got a sole-sourced contract, and I got a bonus and an impressive sounding title. HSB tracked down my long-dormant clearance application.

After my clearance came through, miraculously processed within a few weeks, I finally began to understand the Bureau's interest in me.

You can be excused if you believe an RFID can only be read from inches to a few feet away. The reason, when you approach the subway turnstile, you must hold your smart card right next to the sensor is *not* that the embedded RFID tag can't be sensed from much greater distances. Precisely because cards can easily be read from several feet away, the same pulse that wakes up and momentarily powers your smart card is activating the cards of everyone near you. Your card must be within inches of the sensor to make its reply sufficiently and unambiguously stronger than all others. The transit folks want to know whose account to decrement for the fare.

After uninvited RFIDs made my robots malf enough times, I concluded it was easier to teach 'bots to filter out unexpected return pulses than to strip-search everyone entering the lab. Filtering: It sounds deceptively simple. It's not. Think about coping in real time with arbitrary numbers of RFID tags. Each tag might emit any possible product code or serial number. Each signal as detected by the robot varies unpredictably in strength and direction as I or my co-workers pace. The same filtering technology, repurposed in my homemade scanner, is what made my parking-lot forays productive. The trick was to capture, not reject, the streams of RFID reports.

The HSB wanted my signal-processing logic—and they wanted me to keep enhancing it.

<hr>

Bureau folks never refer to their headquarters as headquarters, only (in hushed tones) as the John Ashcroft Building. That's generally abbreviated JAB, and the same wags that dubbed the organization Homeland BS speak as disparagingly of the Junior Achievers Building.

Hushed tones or irreverence? That choice nicely encapsulates my months of ambivalence. No matter how often I returned, the boxy, mostly windowless JAB never lost its hunkered-down, fortress-like aspect. But once I went through the curbside row of massive concrete obstacles unsuccessfully masquerading as planters, passed three tiers of badge readers and armed guards checking photo

IDs, penetrated the maze-like corridors into the heart of the structure, an eerie surrealism always manifested itself.

Flyers that advertised carpools and retirement parties were taped beside doors secured by cipher locks and ominous warning signs. Armed agents in well-tailored suits were outnumbered by casually dressed electricians, programmers, janitors, and clerks. Stacks of still-boxed computers on pallets lined the halls, but it took weeks—and then, only if you knew whom to sweet-talk—before the Security and Infrastructure folks would hook one up. Parts of the interior were under construction at all times, providing isolated workspace for some investigation or other, and altering pedestrian traffic flow from month to month. Yet somehow, despite all the security, random artisans were allowed into JAB to sell ugly handicrafts at tables in the cafeteria. And somehow, even in the very bowels of JAB, gear would regularly go missing from labs.

My new career had me conflicted from the start. It was hard *not* to feel good about helping stop the bad guys. I didn't know, nor did I think I needed to, who was caught and how. It was sufficient to hear vaguely that terrorist plots were being disrupted. Evidently I also had no need to know exactly how my ever-longer-range receivers were being applied; in my mind's over-imaginative eye, I envisioned agents tracking unsuspecting bad guys at a discreet distance. At some level, I recall feeling Rogue-ish—but more like the crazy-coot uncle than a main character. Than like the dapper Marcel St. Clair played by Charles Boyer. And at yet another level, I have to admit, I was a kid set free in a toy store. Where homeland security is concerned, money was never an issue. It is hardly coincidental that the Beltway Bandit pronunciation of HS Bureau became Hasbro.

On the other hand, this simply wasn't a line of work I had ever thought to get into, nor was I getting a single robot an inch closer to Mars or Titan. Nor was I helping Mom and Dad. My new, very humorless, customers had made it *abundantly* clear that my RFID trolling expeditions were over.

In short, I was confused.

Then **Mechanicsville** happened.

CNN played softly 24/7 on a dozen TVs mounted high up on pillars throughout the JAB cafeteria. I was on an early lunch break, escaping the computer-room chill of my lab, when murmuring broke out. On-screen, flames engulfed a red barn, surrounded at a safe distance by flasher-equipped unmarked cars, ambulances, and two fire trucks. A trim HSB helicopter had landed to one side of the frame, its rotor still spinning lazily. The screen crawler gave the then-unfamiliar town name in Iowa.

All around me, "Waco" was getting mentioned a lot.

The **Branch Davidian** references were prescient. That is, although I don't think the HSB agents all around me knew it at first, children were dying in the conflagration: a high-school science club.

Many network exposés and blogs later, you know what none of us knew then: It was only a gung-ho young teacher trying during spring break to excite kids about physics through model rocketry. That—and some bitter irony here—regulatory overkill.

Respect for a parental phobia has kept my knowledge theoretical, but I understand model rockets. The fuel of choice is ammonium perchlorate composite propellant. If **APCP** happens to sound familiar, it's probably because APCP fuels the solid rocket boosters of the space shuttle. APCP is a rubbery mixture of salts, powdered metals, and resins that ignites at about 500 degrees Fahrenheit.

The thing is, APCP falls within the purview of the post-9/11 **Safe Explosives Act**, which means permits, finger-printing, and background checks before anyone is allowed to buy the stuff. The funny thing is, APCP doesn't explode;

it merely burns like the dickens. If you do buy it, the feds are allowed onto your property at any time and without notice to check for its proper storage.

The Cedar Rapids Rocketeers, like similar clubs, cooked up their APCP from unregulated precursor chemicals, just as farmers mix explosives to blow up tree stumps or "dig" irrigation ditches. It's all perfectly legal, under a **personal use exemption**. You might ask: How does one prove personal use? Is it not better, in our dangerous world, to err on the side of caution?

The final count was twenty-six dead: eighteen kids, the teacher, and seven parents.

Based on "a tip," HSB had begun what spokespeople called an "unscheduled inspection." Most people who see HSB's own video of swooping helicopter and onrushing cars think: raid. "Tragically," the final report concluded, "the unexpected arrivals appear to have caused the unintended indoor ignition of one or more model rockets. A rapidly spreading fire resulted. This only reinforces the tragedy of citizens working with such dangerous, generally illegal materials."

⋯⋯

Like most small businesspeople I know, Dad has little respect for economists. "If you took all the economists in the world and laid them end to end," he likes to say, "they wouldn't reach a conclusion." And, "Economists correctly predicted nine of the past five recessions." That last one, it turns out, is attributable to an economist.

My ambivalence about HSB ended with the cold shower that was Mechanicsville. There were real human consequences when domestic intelligence foiled nine of the past five terrorist plots.

Mechanicsville and the subsequent investigations raised plenty of questions. One of the most obvious, still officially unanswered, was, "Who tipped off HSB?" That is, who somehow confused a science club with terrorists? HSB did not reveal its sources, of course. I heard just enough hallway chatter to know that the question worried the hell out of people and enough to disbelieve the media speculation that Homeland BS was covering for some naïve or competitive or vindictive classmate of the victims, lest others hesitate in the future to inform.

⟨═╼╾═⟩

Two kinds of people work in JAB: those who carry guns and those who don't. The latter (which includes contractors like me) tend not to get much respect. Too many of the former know squat about computers. In 2003, the **FBI was training agents how to use a mouse**.

And yet, the modern approach to security is all about information.

Unless you've been on Titan, you must know passenger screening became serious business after 9/11. The last time I checked (**Airline Disclosures of Passenger Information**), six airlines and two big reservation systems admit to having shared at least samples of their passenger data with the Transportation Security Administration. No one asked the passengers if they cared to be part of the experiment.

After 9/11, everyone demanded to know why the FBI hadn't known ahead of time. No matter how many hostile operations were prevented in the intervening, fairly peaceful years, the question came back, big time, after 2/4. One result was establishment of the HSB. Not coincidentally, the biggest technology project the HSB now has going is its Consolidated Data Warehouse, the mother lode of information about *anything*. I had no need to know what was in it, nor did I, but it was clear that the approach being taken to better connecting dots in the future was: collect lots more dots.

Dots like: Several of the Cedar Rapids students had recently purchased "extremist Islamicist literature." That literature, as NBC News broke soon after this HSB explanation, was extra-credit reading in the curriculum of a World Civ class.

For a time I had a privileged user account on CDW. Designing gadgets did not require any access, let alone privileged access, but my testing collected scads of RFID transaction data, which I had kept, in my HSB lab, within a database management system. When a dayshift database administrator on CDW announced her vacation plans, I got volunteered to backfill.

My new, unwanted DBA task required occasional poking about the database, just to make certain everything was operating okay. The cardinal rule is: never look up yourself. It's apparently bad form to check whether you're under investigation (evidently, double agent **Robert Hanssen** monitored his own records at the FBI for years for signs of suspicion). One thing I looked up instead, as a sample query, involved press reports of the Mechanicsville situation. A security admin spotted my query in an audit log, and my wrist got slapped. I wasn't on the approved list of people to be accessing such a sensitive matter.

Too late: I had already clicked through to long lists of annotated RFID transactions associated with the investigation. I had glanced at a few, and one I couldn't get out of my mind: the tires of a parent's SUV, recorded by a Wave-N-Go pump at a Mechanicsville gas station. There was no record of a purchase, as though the stop had been for directions or a bio-break.

Clearly, the gas-station chain was providing company data to the feds. Was such surveillance illegal? Unethical? Creepy? Was this different from flight records, which, since 9/11, few expected to remain private?

I was still wrestling with those questions when I noticed one of the chains providing RFID data to the HSB was Big Bob's.

I was more facing my TV than watching it when the last puzzle piece fell into place. Had I been paying attention, I would have simply zapped the commercial. The ad did not even penetrate my consciousness until well into the next segment of the sitcom. If my TiVo thought it strange that I backed up to re-screen a commercial, it did not comment.

The ad was for a high-end washing machine. Accompanying a close-up of a red sock atop a mound of pink underwear, the voiceover declared, "Make such tragic accidents a thing of the past." I froze the frame. It would indeed be great if my red socks and my tidy whities declared themselves to my washer. What was decidedly *not* great was the sudden epiphany that my socks and undies were likely announcing my presence to every RFID scanner I passed. As in, every big store I entered; every subway turnstile I passed, even if I'd bought my fare card with cash; every Wave-N-Go gas pump . . .

Feeling stupid—why had I compartmentalized the RFID-in-clothing problem as purely an in-the-lab issue?—I unearthed my homebrew scanner from its place of exile at the bottom of a desk drawer.

The newer half my wardrobe had RFID tags. My wallet was filled with them.

<hr/>

If you have not yet joined a **currency exchange**, you should.

In much simpler times, people worried that newfangled credit cards were an invasion of privacy. There would be centralized records, somewhere, of what you bought when. People who worried about such records—some of them, obviously, Doing Bad Things—would use only cash.

Surely you've heard about the supposed nutcases who wear tinfoil-lined hats to hide their thoughts from the aliens. Well, my *wallet* is now foil-lined. New Euro notes carried embedded RFID tags as long ago as 2005; for

several years now, new US currency shared that "honor"—
to prevent counterfeiting. Here's what they don't tell you:
You can be traced by the money in your pocket. Each bill in
your wallet was associated with you when you received it at
the bank lobby or ATM or in change at a store. It stays
associated with you until a bank or store cash register logs
its receipt. Tagged bills mean that even buying things with
cash is no longer anonymous.

Are you still wondering about currency exchanges?
That's a bunch of folks who meet for the sole purpose of
swapping their cash. You can do it out in the countryside
somewhere, far from any possible RFID poller, although
there are obvious risks to carrying large sums of cash to an
isolated rendezvous. A better solution is a shielded room (in
technical terms, a Faraday cage). Copper window screening
works nicely, as long as you remember to cover the floor,
ceiling, and door, too. RFID interrogation signals can no
more get in than microwaves can get out past the similar
mesh embedded in the glass of microwave oven doors.

Click here for **plans to build your own currency
exchange.**

⟨⟨⟨ ⟩⟩⟩

RFID chips are tiny. RFID tags generally are not,
because the antennae must capture enough power to oper-
ate the silicon chip. The typical antenna occupies a couple
square inches. That means you can find—and disable—the
tags. After I calmed down from my red-sock epiphany,
that's just what I did. If my story has made any impression
on you, you will, too. I used a scanner to look for them; if
you lack access to a scanner, pay close attention to big
labels, overlapping fabric, and wide hems. If a garment
crinkles, check there between cloth layers.

Shoes are harder. Taking them apart to find the tags
that are almost certainly there will probably destroy your
footwear. I zapped mine with a focused microwave beam

until their chips fried. A bit of shoe polish covered the resulting scorch marks. (You *might* be able to microwave your shoes, but I don't recommend it—especially if they have steel shanks.)

You may be asking: Why? Why did I disable the RFID tags in my clothes?

No one had cause to be tracking me. Maybe *that* was my reason. That the tags helped retailers manage their inventory was no reason for me to be marked like a prospectively wayward cat. I was offended, damn it. Sitting in my newly RFID-free apartment, stewing in high principle, paranoia, and self-righteousness, my thoughts turned to the tires that had led HSB to Mechanicsville. Outside I went.

My car, it turned out, was filled with RFIDs, and not only in its tires and the E-Zpass transponder clipped to the sun visor. Even if I could take the car apart, some pieces were likely unzappable.

Which left what?

I could replace my car with a clunker too old to contain RFIDs. I could, in theory, keep a clunker running with old parts from junkyards. My suspicions were by then in full bloom. I found myself wondering why the NHTSA had suddenly decided a few years earlier that tires had an aging mechanism (**Tire Expiration Dates**) distinct from tread wear. Was age-related rubber deterioration real, or was it disinformation to get RFID-tagged tires onto every car in the country? Frying an RFID embedded in a tire would soften the surrounding rubber. That couldn't be good.

You're overreacting, I had lectured myself. Three hundred million Americans and almost as many vehicles, ever more tags on each, every day passing within range of, well, I had no idea *how* many RFID-sensing tollbooths and point-of-sale terminals. How could HSB possibly keep up with that data geyser? They would have to concentrate on small subsets already known for some reason, by some conventional investigative means, to merit scrutiny.

Wouldn't they?

Perhaps you are enrolled in one or more **merchant loyalty programs**. Knowing what you buy, and when, and
where, has value. That's why so many stores (but *not* mom
& pop) discontinued coupons in their newspaper ads, but
happily provide discounts once you disclose your customer
ID. You regularly buy canned soup, so it seems harmless
when they tempt you at the checkout with a deal on crack-
ers. The results can be both humorous and off-putting when
your favorite bookseller makes recommendations for you
extrapolated not only from what *you* read, but also from the
gifts you've purchased for your quirkiest friends and relatives. It gets downright creepy when your pharmacist spec-
ulates from your prescriptions that, for example, you have a
likelihood of erectile dysfunction, and mails you a Viagra
coupon and the advice you discuss it with your doctor.

Those are trivial examples of **data mining**. Remember
Dad and his disdain for economists? Economists predicted
recessions by mining data long before that term came into
vogue. Their models, of ever-growing sophistication and
ever more voracious appetites for data, hunted for correla-
tions, trends, and clustering. But correlation is different
than causation, which is how they predicted nine of the
past five recessions. These flawed readings of the economic
entrails and commercial tea leaves—they're almost funny
until misinformed government policy ensues.

Data mining is a big deal now in homeland security, and
rightly so. Way back in the Cold War, West German federal
police broke the infamous Baader Meinhof gang by hunting
for prime suspects: single men without cars registered to
their names, who paid their apartment rent and utility bills
in cash. Estimates vary, but the federal police may have sur-
veilled, by emergent techniques not yet called data mining,
up to five percent of the adult West German population.

Data mining can be powerful and productive. It's a good
thing when phone-call patterns give warning of an immi-

nent terrorist strike. But when HSB—and I speak now of former colleagues who are honest and honorable people, who in my mind, notwithstanding my current fugitive status, I consider my friends—detects nine of the *next* five terrorist attacks?

That's how you get a Mechanicsville.

*

The red-sock incident happened on a Saturday. The following Monday I had a DBA shift, filling in for my still-vacationing colleague. Feeling a bit like Marcel St. Clair, I did a few "Is it still running?" checks of CDW.

Sturgeon's Law posits that ninety percent of everything is crap. Either Sturgeon was a cockeyed optimist, or he knew nothing about software. The data warehouse required constant babying, reconfiguring, tuning, restarting . . . pick your euphemism for "fixing." Driving the process was a mix of recurrent and ad hoc queries, by which to gauge how well the temperamental software was behaving that day. In the ad hoc category, I queried with a few presumably innocent product RFIDs I'd recently captured with my scanner: tires on a friend's car, a second cousin's new penny loafers, a case of beer in the storeroom of the bistro where I had eaten dinner the previous night. I thought nothing of the gaggle of feds clustered across the lab at one of the security administration workstations. Secadmins are a breed onto themselves; it is their nature, like birds, to flock.

I was staring at the screen in frozen disbelief, at a column of time-tagged hits that tracked my buddy's car around town yesterday, when an HSB guy—the gun-toting, agent type—sauntered over and tapped my shoulder. "A word to the wise, Zach. Checking out your friends and neighbors is not allowed either."

I went outside for lunch that day, and never came back.

*

Which brings us to the end of my cautionary tale. If I am not simply deluding myself, if this blog has a readership beyond seething HSB agents, we may even be, to borrow a phrase from Winston Churchill, at the end of the beginning.

That is all very metaphorical, of course. I am going to be very vague about where, physically, I am. While I am being metaphorical, I will go so far as to admit a return to my roots. I am toiling once again at a mom & pop store. It's someplace that pays me in cash, and that—like *my* Mom's and Dad's place—still uses those quaint, low-tech devices which, although called cash registers, register no information about the currency therein.

To anyone from HSB viewing this: Maybe it's a grocery. Of course, it could as easily be a dry cleaner, a hotdog stand, or a used-book store. Perhaps it's none of those.

In short, my hypothetical Dear Reader, I've gone underground. The Ten Most Wanted Fugitives list calls me a cyber-terrorist.

HSB now claims I've hacked into the transactional databases of American companies. Not so. At worst, I've grazed the database of *one* company, Big Bob's. In my opinion, that hardly rises to most-wanted status.

HSB would also have you believe I brazenly engaged in a nefarious spying operation from within the bowels of JAB itself. Once again: not so. I'll admit—I have admitted—to a few peeks. I'll assert every DBA and sysadmin there does the same. Vigilance in the search for bugs in crappy, over-priced software is no vice.

Why, then, is HSB after me?

It all keeps coming around to Big Bob's. You've already read my after-the-fact reasoning (rationalizing, if you prefer) about the field trips to Big Bob's that brought me to HSB's attention. But the friend's tires that surfaced in the CDW, just before I went to lunch and never returned, were bought at Big Bob's. By inference, Big Bob's provided the data to HSB. Who else could tie those specific tires to that friend? Not that Big Bob's alone could possibly have had enough RFID readers, widely enough dispersed, to have captured the peripatetic course around town of those tires.

The quicker I am taken into custody, the sooner this narrative, in its many reincarnations and mirror sites on offshore servers, stops. HSB does not want to reveal its plans—devised, I will postulate, with only the best of intentions—to track everyone, everywhere, at any time. They want at all costs to keep secret the clandestine co-opting of Big Bob's, and countless other retailers, into Big Brother.

I keep remembering that agent's "friendly" advice. CDW had associated me with my second cousin from across town and the college buddy with whom, at the last minute, I had gone to dinner. My query had been enough to trigger a real-time alert at a secadmin workstation.

Many of you are thinking: HSB has no reason to watch *me*. *I've* done nothing wrong.

I'm relating this story to make you consider one central fact: *I* did nothing wrong, either.

⸙

What you do now is your choice. My free advice is join a currency exchange. Trade shopping lists with your friends. Pay with cash, and patronize stores with old registers. Carry your purchases in a foil-lined shopping bag. Remove those RFID tags that are safely removable.

But if you want to do more. . . .

I have a new calling, and the spare time to indulge it: very specialized circuit design. I've concentrated on gadgets for all things RFID: **detecting**, **spoofing**, **jamming**, and **frying**. The frequencies used by RFIDs are unlicensed, making my hobby (except perhaps when zapping others' chips) entirely legal.

What these devices have in common is the long-term effect of their deployment. Widely used, they will degrade databases reliant on RFID-based tracking. If you believe that following your every move and viewing your every purchase should be more difficult than typing a simple query into a government database—if you place any value on your privacy—such degradation is a good thing.

Perhaps you have the skills and equipment to make these devices. Any savvy teen with access to a modern high-school electronics shop can build them. And they offer a productive new use for that old, wireless PDA that hasn't seen the light of day in months ;-)

Check back often for updated designs.

I've put on indefinite hold my dream that a robot of my design will roll onto Mars or Titan. My robotic aspirations have been repurposed toward a different world: the RFIDsphere. Imagine armies of tiny RFID spoofers and jammers set loose to roam, to mimic codes they encounter, and to inject RFID gremlins throughout their random travels.

How polluted must the data sources for repositories like CDW become before we're all freed from incessant surveillance?

Herewith two parting comments for my friends at the Homeland Security Bureau, and especially to those of you on the hunt for me. First, you have not heard the last of The Rogue. Second . . .

Tag. You're it.

INTRODUCTION TO TIGERS IN THE CAPITOL
Ernest Lilley

One of the most notable features of the Capitol is the steady flow of tourists wandering around the monuments. They come from all over the world, and as Jane Lindskold points out, they may yet come from further than that. I think this is part of the city's charm, Americans stopping by to check up on their taxes at work and aliens dropping in to see what a place of power is like, and maybe hope a little will rob off. It looks bigger on TV.

Jane Lindskold's tour guide is the man who saw his vision of a planned city unravel according to the expediencies of the moment. Who better? And of course, the more things change, the more they stay the same.

TIGERS IN THE CAPITOL

JANE LINDSKOLD

The mistake was when they let that dragon bite get taken out of it back in 1846. Or was that 1847? I don't suppose a year matters, not after all the time that's passed since.

Not that giving up the land was the first mistake they made. That was just the big mistake. The first mistake they made was taking me off the job, figuring a bunch of Masonic morons could pull off the trick. Hah! There's more to creating a fortunate city than slapping on a lot of charms after the buildings are up.

Charms. Sigils. Emblems. Mirrors. Those're the kind of fix you throw in when a city grows from the ground up, grows from nothing. You know how most cities are made. Maybe there's a place where a couple of roads cross, then someone has the good sense to set up an inn, and someone else sets up a livery stable, and maybe a shop, and next thing you know there's a village, maybe a town. Or maybe there's something geographical about why people settle in a place and stay, a mountain pass, say, maybe a harbor or river crossing.

That's how Oxford got started, so they say. Ox-ford. Get it? These days, though, these days when people hear 'Oxford' they don't even hear what the word means. It's like the meaning of the word's all vanished, come to mean highbrow and intellectual and lots of colleges and chapels. Well, let me tell you, there were some fixes thrown in there. Otherwise, the place would have lost its identity long ago.

Come with me. I'll show you what I mean. Don't worry. I know the city is dangerous, but I know it like the back of my hand. Stupid saying. Do you know what the back of your hand looks like? What I mean is that I know Washington, D.C. like the inside of my heart.

Where we are now, this used to be the Mall. My idea that, not that they followed my design. I would have had more trees for one thing, more formal gardens. I think I had Versailles in mind as a model. Versailles impressed me, even if the people who lived there didn't. The designers had a good idea with Versailles, lots of open space, big avenues; problem is those avenues went nowhere. Mine, now, mine wouldn't have suffered from that mistake. I'd have tied them in to existing roads, built a grid around them. Logic and beauty in one package, but did anyone listen?

Those avenues . . . Those got me into trouble let me tell you. Know why? I'll tell you. Okay, General Washington— he'll always be General to me, not President, because that's how I came to know him—picked out this area as the new site for the capital city. Not the greatest location in the world, to be honest. Swampy land. Bad drainage . . . And the summer heat! Nothing like as hot as it gets these days, of course, but these days you can get away from the heat. Then you couldn't.

But the General needed a location where the federal government could afford to buy enough land for an entire city. He certainly wasn't going to find real estate bargains in some settled area.

You're right. There was a town already here. George-town, they called it, for one of the other Georges not for the General. That's confused generations of school kids, let me tell you. I mean, Washington for the city, George for the town. Makes sense, if you look at it as a kid would. But Georgetown as a separate entity is gone now, officially merged with the larger city in 1871. Its vanishing was a foreshadowing, I think, of what would come.

Where was I? Right. Avenues. Now, my plan called for a

number of large avenues connecting various key sites and incorporating the existing roads at the same time. It was a good plan. I still hold to it. Let me tell you, I bet that the drivers in the twentieth and twenty-first centuries—that's back when every family seemed to have two or three personal vehicles—I bet they would have liked my broader avenues. But the idiots who arranged to purchase the land for the Federal City . . .

What? You didn't know? Oh, yes, what you've read in the history books is true. Yes, the good states of Maryland and Virginia donated the land for the Federal City, but in a sense they just dedicated air. What Maryland and Virginia did was donate their claim to tax and make law in those designated square miles. Pretty easy way to be generous when you think about it. Neither Georgetown nor Alexandria were great commercial centers, and including them made the donation seem all the grander.

Maryland and Virginia's donations created a nice, tidy diamond of land with the corners pointing in the four cardinal directions. Auspicious placement, until Virginia got pissy over something or other and took back their chunk of land, including Alexandria. I'm pretty sure that happened in 1846.

That messed up the dynamics of the site. The city lost its perfect balance, became weak in the south. It's no great surprise that when the trouble came that nearly split the nation, it came from that weakened southern portion.

Anyhow, although Virginia and Maryland donated the land for the Federal City, the individual landholders were not dispossessed of their claims. I firmly believe they should have been. A blank canvas was what was needed to make a truly ideal city. The owners could have been compensated with lands from elsewhere. . . .

But this is water down Tiber Creek, and Tiber Creek is long, long gone, turned into a canal, then buried under asphalt. I suppose it survives as a sewer. Nasty end for what was a bright little waterway.

Now, to explain the fate of my magnificent avenues, Congress or whoever made such decisions, had decreed that while owners would be paid for land to be used for public buildings, the owners would not be paid for land intended for roads. The argument was that the proximity to these roads would be reward enough.

Believe me, many of those greedy landowners knew they would soon be rich, but still they did not see why the avenues needed to be so wide. These fools had no vision for the future, and they lacked my special knowledge of what would guarantee a fine and prosperous city.

So my avenues, my beautiful, broad avenues, were sacrificed. Soon thereafter, so was I. After I lost my official standing no one would listen to me, not even when I tried to tell them what a terrible thing they had done.

No. I am not speaking merely of narrow roads contributing to traffic congestion! Roads carry more than people and commerce. Roads carry energy as well. I see you understand. I'm surprised. Oh, yes, well, I have heard of feng shui. Who hasn't these days? However, the Chinese and those many nations who have adopted their customs and philosophies do not have a monopoly on geomantic wisdom. Are you surprised to find that I knew similar lore way back in the 1790's?

When my beautiful roads were cut off or narrowed, the flow of energy through the city was similarly disrupted. Those roads that remained were left unpaved for a long time and one of the first attempts to pave Pennsylvania Avenue involved using wooden blocks. Wooden blocks in a swamp. I know. I know. It's hard to imagine, but true.

Later, I managed to convince a man they called Boss Shepherd that good roads—and sewers to keep them clean, along with sidewalks for the foot traffic—were key to the city thriving. Boss Shepherd maybe went a little crazy with his projects, and he couldn't restore my beautiful avenues, but he did some good. No more would we have major avenues paved in wood. Good asphalt finally sealed down the mud. At last my Grand Avenue was there, and the fine buildings to line it came in time.

What is it? Why do you look so strange? Why are you looking at your little hand computer? You say Boss Shepherd performed his works in the 1870's? What of it? Of course, I was there. I tell you, this city is my heart. Now, listen.

However, destruction of my beautiful roads was nothing to what happened to the Mall. I had oriented the Mall so that the Capitol (we called it the Congress House then) would be at one end on a hill overlooking the surrounding city. The President's House—it wasn't officially called The White House until much later, Theodore Roosevelt's administration, I believe—was built on a flat area off the Mall. This was a significant choice, because if the two buildings had been placed on the same alignment, the two branches of the government would have been in continuous opposition.

Yes. You're right. Such conflicts happened nonetheless, but give and take resolved even the most ferocious disagreements. This would not have happened if I had not planned so magnificently, I assure you.

But I was telling you about the Mall. I had intended the Mall to be a place of open spaces, filled with gardens and fountains. Since you are a student of feng shui, you know that both gardens and fountains serve to recirculate energy. Instead of these dynamic energy conducting constructions, the Mall was left as blank open space amid which the tremendous energies of this ruling city surged, eventually ebbing to no positive end.

However, although unseen, these energies were felt. Before they drained away, their unseen permutations served to confuse and delay those who must travel between the Congress House and the President's House, or to other points in the city. Chaos rather than productive order ruled. Even I who loved the embryonic city as a father loves a promising child, even I could hardly blame those who wished to abandon Washington City after the British invaders burned the President's House and several other building in 1814.

After all, what was there to keep? What was there to tend? A dream. A promise. Ah, my friend. Even with your gaze so high above mine, I can see your eyes narrow as you contemplate the irony of this statement. Yes. Let us walk, I will tell you how I redeemed my beloved city, at least for a time.

The Mall was the key to that redemption, but it was a key with no teeth. The city was founded in the 1790's. A few essential landmarks were created in the intervening years. The best of these was the monument to General Washington that was begun in 1848, but even that was not finished for another twenty-some years. The Washington Monument has always been a construct plagued with problems. Despite the fact that their popular name would make you think they know something of stonework, those Masons have no idea how to build solidly, yet they had the effrontery to aggrandize themselves with more than twenty inscribed tablets lining the obelisk's interior walls!

But I am distracted from my point. You have a question? You ask how the condition of the Mall could be the key to the city's revitalization? Yes. I agree with what you say. There were other essential turning points in Washington City's history. Certainly, the revision of its governmental system in 1871 helped. Certainly, the efforts of many men to make it a functioning city rather than merely a symbolic location helped. However, these efforts merely made Washington a capital city. From the very first plans I presented to General Washington, I wished to create a fortunate city, a dynamic place where creative energies would flow for the benefit of all.

John Adams was the first president to reside in the President's House. When he moved into the yet unfinished structure, Adams made a pious prayer that all who dwelled within those walls would be good men who would rule justly. He focused narrowly on the inhabitants of one house. My wish was grander, for I wished my creation to invigorate and inspire all who would participate in the grand democratic experiment. The Mall, with its ability to channel and recirculate energy, was key to my goals.

As I said, the city was founded in the 1790's. A mere fifty years later, many people had no idea that the Mall even existed. The open spaces had been overlaid with shabby temporary structures. A railroad ran through it, stopping at the steps of the Capitol. My gardens and fountains either had not been built or had been poorly placed. There were periods when the Congress nearly auctioned off the land. During the Civil War cattle were penned around the base of the incomplete Washington Monument. Only President Lincoln's insistence assured that construction on the Capitol dome continued. He had the wisdom to understand that buildings have power beyond their physical forms, even beyond their ability to serve as symbols.

The years of the Mall's decline were a bad time—for the city and for the nation—but the coming of the hundredth anniversary of the city's founding awoke shame in impor- tant people. At last they realized how the loss of the grand dreams for the capital city had hurt the image of the nation as a whole. They set out to repair the damage, and I did my part to steer them into remembering my plans.

Don't look at me that way. You, looking like you do, standing there and daring to define what is possible. Let me tell you, my skinny friend, when I was born you would have been considered a lot more impossible than I am.

That's all right. I understand. I forgive your momentary incredulity. People raised as you are know so much, but you've forgotten a great deal in order to learn what you know. Of course, I don't mind finishing my tale. Let's walk a little.

See that mud flat? That's where the Tidal Basin used to be. The Jefferson Memorial is that green lump behind it. The area once looked very elegant, but I could have warned them they were making a mistake when they built the Tidal Basin. Standing water is dangerous, and not just because it breeds disease. Running water brings things, and, yes, it can carry things away, too, but the Potomac curved enough to leave more good than it took away. The Tidal Basin though . . . Well, it did a bit of rising and falling, but when the tides were low; there was too much standing water, too much stagnant decay.

Another problem from the consideration of design is the opposition of the Jefferson Memorial to the President's House. Remember what I told you earlier? That's the very situation I was trying to avoid when I placed the Capitol and the White House. The orientation opposed the past and the present, set them against each other. That's never a good thing, and was especially bad with Jefferson being one of the framers of the Declaration.

I heard that when Ronald Reagan was president he said he liked to stand in the White House and look at Jefferson and have Jefferson look back. Past and present, present and past staring at each other. I don't fancy that Jefferson would have thought much of an actor being elected president either. I can't imagine that Tom's looking back would have been very friendly.

I'm not going to bore you with what was done in the renovation from the 1890's and after. You've seen pictures of the end results: the open, tree-lined Mall, the museums, the marble facings on the grand buildings. That's the Washington, D.C. that everyone remembers, the city they think has been in place forever and ever.

The commissioners in charge of the renovations did a good job. Too much time had gone by for my plans to be followed precisely, but even so I'm not lying when I say that they served as direct inspiration. Why, some of the commissioners even went and toured Versailles. That's where the idea for the Reflecting Pool came from.

I know. I know. More standing water, and that's a problem, of course, but the Reflecting Pool is different from the

Tidal Basin. It gave back sun and sky, and that's energy circulation of a kind. The pool also provided a reflection of a monument built to honor one of the greatest idealists ever to sit in the White House—and I don't mean Woodrow Wilson either. Abe Lincoln was a much more practical man. I liked him.

But I wander from the point. My point is that at last the Mall had become what it was supposed to be from the start, an open space, one that circulated energy, replenished inspiration, and created opportunities for greatness. The museums that came to line it reminded people of what humanity was capable of achieving in arts and sciences. The monuments and memorials, scattered and tastefully placed, reminded people of the best of human aspirations. Even that Masonic Temple to General Washington finally looked right in its new setting amid the broad, green expanses. It encouraged one to look up, to remember the heavens above.

If you think it's a coincidence that the greatest era of United States influence came after the Mall became the entity I had envisioned from the start, well, you're wrong. It was no coincidence. Your history books will give you many theories, many flat out explanations, but the truth is that finally the nation had a heart and soul, a place where the multitudes could gather—quite often literally—and remind those in charge that they were representatives of a democratic government, not despots.

I suppose you could call the decline that began in the late twentieth century some sort of congestive heart disease. The Mall gradually became too cluttered. Everyone wanted to be represented in some way, shape or form.

The trend started simply enough. Disagreement over the Vietnam War had torn the nation apart. Some people felt Vietnam had torn at the nation worse even than the Civil War had done, but I was there for that earlier conflict, and I think they're wrong. Anyhow a memorial recognizing the veterans of the conflict in Vietnam was looked upon as a good thing, a healing act.

I didn't disagree, but if I had known what was coming, I would have started screaming before the first shiny stone was in place. I didn't, and by the time I realized what was happening, I could no more stop it than I could add width to my avenues or make Virginia spit back the part it had bitten out of the land it had granted to the Federal City.

The manner in which the Vietnam Veteran's Memorial was altered from its original design was a foreshadowing of what would happen to the Mall as a whole. There was the wall with all those inscribed names, but that didn't satisfy some folks, so they had to put in another statue with heroic soldiers to make them happy. Then they had to add the memorial to the nurses.

Don't get me wrong. They're touching pieces in their ways. The problem was that inclusiveness, that attitude that everyone is right if only you see things their way, had come to dominate. Even the Masons were closer to right with their big Father of our County pointing up at the sky. That at least gave us all one father, no matter where we were born. Yes. There were tablets commemorating different groups and states, but they were inside. Unity. Oneness was proclaimed outside where everyone would see it. This new approach glorified fragmentation rather than unity, and that was dangerous.

And more monuments followed the one to the Vietnam Veterans: FDR, Albert Einstein, Korean War, World Wars I and II, Signers of the Declaration of Independence, Signers of the Constitution, every President who had a backing or a trust fund, even the purchasers of goods for the United States Armed Forces. They all had to have their place on the Mall. Nowhere else would do. Nowhere else would provide equality.

Monument after monument, the crowding continued. There's only so much space on the Mall. Within a century of the dedication of the Vietnam Veteran's Memorial, you couldn't walk a foot without some plaque or hologram shouting out to remind you that someone else had done something special. Statues lined every path. There was no room for public gatherings because the memorials had taken all the open space.

Do your history books contain the incident when some jokers managed to project an image on the side of the Washington Monument that read "THIS IS A MEMORIAL TO THE FORGOTTEN"? I'm not surprised. It was a shameful time.

But there was another effect to this clutter, one much more serious. Without the free circulation of energy, thoughts once again became cluttered. Focus narrowed to minutiae. The big picture was lost. Special interest groups on all levels blocked anything that would stop what was important to their one little group.

By then, largely because of events that took hold when the United States was at the peak of her power, the world was no longer a series of isolated nations. Economies were interlocked. More seriously, ecosystems were becoming interconnected in a fashion that would have taken thousands of years before. The early indications of this were evident even in the twentieth century. They were widely recognized by the middle of the twenty-first, but no one did anything.

Why? Because it was someone else's special interest, not theirs, and nothing remained to remind people we were all in this together. So biologists warned about invasive species. Climatologists fussed about global warming. Anthropologists worried about loss of the past. Educational specialists focused on managing the present. No one had much concern for the future. On and on and on . . . I don't need to go into further detail, do I? You can see the results.

Everyone worried about one or two little things. No one wanted to face that it's all interconnected. With the Mall reduced to a memorial to special interests, there was nothing left to remind us we were one nation. No longer were we indivisible. Instead we were infinitely divisible.

Plague finally forced people to make the connections

that they had been denying, and by then it was too late to save the situation. There'd been warnings in the twentieth century that more and more diseases were becoming resistant to treatment. In the twenty-first century, tuberculosis resurfaced as a serious concern. Diseases flew on jumbo jets. West Nile Virus. Dengue Fever. Asian Bird Flu. Tiber Malaria. Mississippi Flu.

A medical system that had been shouting—as a special interest—that it could not cope with an aging population and a decreasing pool of medical professionals gave up trying to save everyone. Those without comprehensive medical coverage died in droves. As these were often the laborers, other elements got out of hand.

For the first time in centuries, the United States faced famine. Moreover, invasive species of other types got ahead of efforts to clear them away. Waterways were jammed with zebra mussels. Leafy spurge took over areas used for grazing cattle. Kudzu and honeysuckle swallowed buildings in the south, then crept ever further north. Tamarisk drank dry rivers that carried water throughout the thirsty west.

Global warming proved a real contributor to all these problems. Warmer weather let thrive mosquitos and other insects that carry infection. Warmer weather means that freezing temperatures don't kill back invasive plants. Warmer weather means rot, decay, and contamination. Pretty soon, no place wasn't warm enough for various nasty things to survive and invasive species have incentive to mutate.

Washington, D.C. was situated far enough south to be hard hit early on. For a while people tried living in their sealed and air conditioned buildings, but eventually an exodus began. The city deteriorated further. The museums were closed. The animals in the National Zoo broke loose and joined the host of invasive species.

The people who fled D.C. carried the problems with them, problems of attitude as well as of illness. They spread. You've seen what happened. You probably have a better perspective on those events than I do.

D.C. had been intended to be the nation's capital. If I had been given my way, it would have been the nation's heart as well, but no one was listening. I stayed. I did my best. Maybe someday someone will come and clear the kudzu off the monuments, scrape the mussels and algae off the pipes. Maybe someone will clear the tigers from the Capitol and the constrictors from where they coil in Lincoln's lap.

If they do, I'll be here. I'll try and tell them what they need to do to make the city live again. I certainly hope they're as good listeners as you have been.

You're from Mars you say. Tell me. What's it like? Is there anything to those canals I've heard about? I've always thought they must have been put there for a reason.

INTRODUCTION TO AGENDA
Ernest Lilley

Travis Taylor is exactly the sort of polymath superman that I'd managed to convince myself existed only in Golden Age SF novels, which consoled me after a childhood reading classic SF where the hero is brilliant, athletic, socialized and well connected. He's sort of an updated Richard Ballinger Seaton (Doc Smith's Hero from The Skylark of Space series), working on advanced propulsion systems for NASA, while bringing a collection of Buckaroo Banzai like skills, including rock star and martial arts expert, along for fun. And did I mention that he's not just a rocket scientist but a redneck rocket scientist? Score another point for the Space Program's legacy, not only the industrialization of the South, but the creation of new types of thinkers, or maybe the resurrection of the American inventor.

In "Agenda," we get a story that will hopefully raise hackles on everybody's necks at one point or another, whether from the enlargement of "America" or the persistence of political perversity. It's definitely SF, but the future envisioned is one that rolls forward from here, instead of looking backwards from some arbitrary state, and it's one that leaves me with a slightly unsettled feeling. Who could ask for anything more?

AGENDA

TRAVIS S. TAYLOR

"Yes, Howard-son, but out of nearly two billion people we only have eight senators and only twenty-two representatives. How is that fair representation, Howard-son?" Congressman Zhi muttered and shrugged his shoulders as he took his seat next to the esteemed gentlelady from Nebraska and fellow independent Congresswoman Sharon Howard.

"Mark, Mark, that is a century's worth of water under the bridge just like your faked up Chinese accent. And after all, your ancestors started the war, not mine." Sharon grinned and elbowed her colleague from the great state of Henan. "Shhh. I think it's starting."

"My accent is authentic, mind you. War? Humph, it only lasted three days."

"Yes but how many millions died in those three days, huh? Now shush. I want to hear this." Sharon leaned back in her chair and thought to her *staffer* a few instructions.

Johnny, translate this immediately and run it in American real-time for me.

Sure thing, Congresswoman.

And as soon as it is over I want immediate wide sample polling data all the way out to Mars. I need to know how I should vote after all.

Yes, ma'am.

"The Chair recognizes the honorable gentlelady from the great state of Nigeria. Mrs. Amaka Chi you have the

124

podium." The Speaker of the House of Representatives of the United States of America banged the gavel and sat down.

Amaka Chi was approaching eighty-nine years old and could remember before Nigeria had been *joined* to the United States, but the last thirty years or so of her life had led her to truly believe that the Great Capitalists could accomplish anything. In fact, in her lifetime she had seen the eradication of famines and diseases and tribal war that had forced her beautiful homeland to be a third world slum for ages. But that was no more. As soon as Amaka realized that the Americans would change her country and elevate its economic stature in the world she had put down her freedom fighter's banner and rifle and picked up a copy of the Great Constitution. Her people from the state of Nigeria would long remember what she had done for them—what she would do for them.

Amaka flipped her long dark hair over her shoulders and leaned her long slender two-meter tall frame against the podium. She smiled first to the Speaker and the Vice President and then turned to the floor facing both houses of the great governing body at once—along with the entire seven billion voters in the solar system.

Okoro, play me the speech in native tongue and translate on all channels in all tongues.

Yes, your highness.

"Mr. Speaker, Mr. Vice President, Colleagues of both great houses and from all seven hundred and thirty states and territories of our great nation, I thank you for having me speak with you tonight." Amaka smiled and nodded then cleared her throat lightly and smiled again.

"I rise tonight to talk to you about what I think is certainly one of the gravest issues to face this Nation in the twenty-three years that I have had the honor of serving in this body."

"In this great Congress, Mr. Speaker, I have taken much pride in working with Members of the other parties on national security issues, and I have been one of the first and few to acknowledge that many of the struggles that we have won in this body were unfortunately against the White House. Issues that the current administration thinks will go unnoticed or that it feels unworthy of attention involving national security were brought to light by due diligence and were won only because we had the support of strong leadership on the Democratic side, the Independent side, and the Republican side as well. I give those comments today, Mr. Speaker, because I want to focus on what is happening with the debate surrounding the investigation we performed via the Tau Ceti Commission, of which I was a member, and the resultant information that has been put forward to the American people about a matter that needs to be thoroughly investigated."

"As you well know, Mr. Speaker, after the unfortunate events and breakdown of diplomacy with the Separatists at the Tau Ceti Accords we have been forced to maintain a tight grip on new technologies that could be used for destructive purposes. An example of this is our new quantum membrane transportation system that will allow us to transport supplies and people the vast distances between stars in mere minutes. The details of this technology have been kept out of the public information simply because we fear that if the Tau Ceti Separatists controlled such technology that they may use it for a preemptive strike against American targets. The Separatists could have an army on our doorstep in no time catching us off-guard and decimating our system's defenses."

"Now would the folks in the Tau Ceti system make such a move against us? You bet they would. It has been part of the Separatist Faith that all others outside their religion are subhuman and are a pestilence to their way of life. In other words, there is no room in the universe for any faith other than theirs."

"I bring this up, Mr. Speaker, because the Tau Ceti Commission report was completed almost nine months ago by forty-three of us from both houses of Congress and from all three parties. We took great pride in the fact that we worked in a nonpartisan manner with the sole driving philosophy of understanding the Tau Ceti problem and shoring up America's national security to prevent attacks like the one we had last week against Luna City. If the quantum membrane transportation technology details were kept Top Secret, how, I ask you Mr. Speaker, did a ship loaded with Gluonium appear in Lunarspace and then detonate dead center of the great Luna City? We are fortunate our Earth defense shield grid frequencies were not compromised as well or it could have been Earth that was attacked! Again, how Mr. Speaker were the fanatic followers of the Separatist leader Elle Ahmi able to kill millions of American citizens on the Moon before our defense net even knew there was a ship coming?"

"The reason is quite simple, Mr. Speaker. Somehow the Separatists were given the designs of the transportation technology! Mr. Speaker, I want to call attention to my colleagues here tonight and to the American people listening and watching throughout our great system to this article found in the July 1st, 2125 issue of U.S. News and System Report entitled *Destruction from Outside the Universe* documenting the annihilation and destruction that would be caused by a terrorist attack from M-space. In this article, Mr. Speaker, is an artist's conception and illustration of the prototype QMT-4 transportation system. Mr. Speaker, in 2125, this was classified and is still today. So how did the detailed design information of a Top Secret program appear in a magazine article three years ago?"

"Mr. Speaker there is only one explanation. The White House, in 2125, leaked this document to U.S. News and System Report, giving the entire populace of the solar system including the Separatists' ambassadors and businesses, through this article, access to the design of the QMT-4 transportation technology. The White House has time and time again looked the other way when it has come to national security and why? How could the Executive Officer and Commander in Chief of our Great Republic be so care-free in protecting our security?"

"But how deep does the problem go, Mr. Speaker? When this article first appeared, the Department of Defense, the Senate Select Committee on Intelligence, The Defense Appropriations Committee, and the FBI all began internal investigations as to who would have leaked this design of the QMT-4 to this particular magazine. Mr. Speaker, on several occasions I have been approached by members of these investigations that were told to stop the investigation because they knew where it was going to lead!"

"In this hand I hold a document that will indeed tell us where the investigation was going to lead. This is a manifest of campaign funds for the Democratic National Convention for the previous two elections. On page two hundred and thirty-one of the document we see that there is an allotment of funds that add up to be on the order of a billion dollars to the DNC from more than thirteen different Separatist organizations. At the time of the elections this information would have been little more than information to be spun against the DNC candidate as sympathizing or having a soft spot for the Separatists. But in light of the events on the Moon I say we can no longer follow that line of reasoning."

"Mr. Speaker, I call tonight to the American people for an official authority to impeach the President of the United States of America on the grounds of treason for leaking information to the press that in turn has lead to the deaths of millions of American citizens!"

"HEAR HEAR!" erupted from both sides of the house. They all had a finger they could point and now somewhere to point it besides themselves. The White House was the perfect patsy. Amaka finished her speech and stood tall and stern at the podium looking up at the Speaker for a motion and welling with pride at the response her speech was getting.

"Harrumph!" Congresswoman Howard rose applauding and shouting.

"Order! Order!" the Speaker of the House banged the gavel a few times. "Do I have acknowledgement for the motion on the floor? Mr. Talbot of New Zealand, you are recognized!"

"The great state of New Zealand seconds the motion to vote for impeachment proceedings, Mr. Speaker!" the Republican politician pumped his fist in the air and then clapped his hands.

"We have a second of the motion. We will all now vote yea or nay to proceed with an impeachment process of the President of the United States." The Speaker banged the gavel once again. "Open voting will be allowed for three minutes."

***

"I tell ya Thomas, I just don't believe it. I've been the man's bodyguard for six years and have yet to see him do anything that I thought was untoward. I mean, you've seen how he reveres his wife and daughter, right? He's just not that kind of man." Clay Jackson adjusted his personal shield system and then straightened out his tie. Clay holstered his two mini M-blasters behind his back on his belt clips and then slid his sports coat on checking the hidden pockets throughout it to make certain the knives, daggers, throwing stars, stunners, and miniature explosives were all still accounted for.

"Well, that Nigerian Congresswoman seems to have him dead to rights, Clay. The hearings don't seem to be going in his favor either. I know what you mean though. I'd have never thought it." Thomas closed his locker and adjusted his tie. The two men had been partnered for more than ten years and assigned to the White House for most of that. "I guess you just can't trust politicians can you."

"I just can't believe it. Oh well. Personal thoughts off,

professional thoughts on." Clay nodded to his partner that it was time to go to work.

You read me, Thomas?

Loud and clear, buddy.

Good. I'll check us in. Clay nodded with the slightest gesture to his partner as he slid his sunglasses on and activated the sensors on them. The display panels in the lenses activated and began downloading situational awareness data.

HQ one six zero zero Pennsylvania, over. He thought on the wide area net link.

HQ one six zero zero, here.

Clay Jackson, on.

Thomas Washington, on.

Roger that, Clay Jackson and Thomas Washington. I read you on site, lower security locker room. Shift transition is go.

Roger that, HQ.

"Well you have to believe that the Independents and the Republicans are just loving this. The impeachment hearings are not going in favor of the Democrat President and the most unbelievable thing here is how *little* the President has come out and said in his defense. Is it a sign that he's given up?" Walt Mortimer of the Washington Post summed up his talking points and waited for more crossfire debate from the roundtable.

"Walt, I disagree with you, as usual." Alice St. John of the Review was quick to add comment. "The President shouldn't come out and start blasting back at these allegations while there are legal proceedings taking place. I think he is doing the right thing by keeping a low profile and honorably accepting whatever consequences may come."

"Then you believe he's guilty then?" Britt Howard the show's host asked.

"Well, that is for the impeachment process to show, but from all the evidence the public has been shown so far I would say he has to be," Alice replied.

"That raises the question to all of us here around the table. Guilty or not guilty?" Britt nodded as he named his guests. "Walt?"

"Guilty."

"George?"

"Guilty."

"We know Alice's vote is guilty. And I guess I vote the same. So the four of us here all believe the President is guilty. What do you think? We'd like to see your response. So, please go to www.roundtable-news.com/todayspoll and let us know what you think.

⚜

President Moore sat quietly looking out the window of the oval office. The view had pretty much been kept the same for centuries. There were actually laws in place that kept architecture to heights below the peak of the Washington Monument and there were other regulations that maintained the Capital City's aging charm intact. *It's a Great city*, he thought.

But his mind was elsewhere. What was happening to him? He had come this far and had done great things, but to go down this way he could not allow. He was being set up, but by whom? Sure there had been donations from the Separatists' PACs and corporations and it was likely that all three candidates had received similar donations. That was nonsensical and circumstantial evidence that would go nowhere. But to tie that in with the leaked classified documents was enough to impeach him. But President Moore knew that he had not leaked those documents or ordered them leaked. It just did not make sense to him. He thought to himself that if he were going to do something like hand over the System to Elle Ahmi and her fanatical Separatists there seemed to be better ways than just leaking documents to the press. No, he was being set up—framed. *Who had the most to gain?*

Congresswoman Amaka Chi sure was getting a lot of face-time with the public. She had gained the most as far as he could surmise. *Could it be that simple*, the President thought. *Is this just a bunch of smoke and mirrors to create a windfall of publicity for a practically unknown congress-woman?* The President considered the possibility as he stared out the window at the south lawn.

He would get to the bottom of the situation. After all he was still the President of the United States of America and he had called in some favors. An investigation into the complete membership of the Tau Ceti Commission was being conducted—an investigation that nobody in the public knew about—and soon he would have some answers.

⬥

"Mr. President, sir, I am not certain we should be here without backup and prescreening the area," Clay Jackson cautioned as his eyes and sensors continually scanned the dark alleyway that led up to the dock and pier at the end of King Street.

"Relax, Clay. Nobody knows we are here and besides, this is Old Town Alexandria, we'll be fine," President Moore assured his bodyguard as he tossed breadcrumbs off the pier to the ducks swimming in the Potomac.

"Sir, somebody is coming," Thomas Washington nodded his head up river.

"Relax boys," the President said calmly and tossed the last bit of crumbs into the water and then dusted off his hands by rubbing them together.

A man dressed in a rather average looking suit and tie approached them cautiously. The lighting on the pier was a bit low for the two Secret Service agents to capture clear images even with the infrared and ultraviolet sensors. Somehow he was jamming them.

"Mr. Jackson and Mr. Washington don't bother trying to scan me. It will be futile. Mr. President, I believe this is what you are looking for." The man held out a memory patch. "And I assume when I check my funds, that I'll have what I'm looking for?"

"Yes, yes, of course," President Moore replied. "Now let's have it." He held out his hand and met the elusive figure's grip in a handshake. *Abigail, download and store all information on this patch.*

Yes, Mr. President.

"I see," President Moore grinned. "Ah yes, it was worth every penny meeting you Mr. Smith."

"Likewise, Mr. President. Have a good evening." The man said as he slipped back into the alleyway shadows.

⋘⋙

"In surprise to everyone from Sol to the Oort Cloud today, the impeachment hearings of President Moore were brought to an abrupt halt. The Attorney General today released evidence that indeed the blueprints for the QMT-4 transportation technology were leaked to the press but not by the White House. It turns out that the blueprints were altered and then leaked to the press by the FBI as part of a sting operation to uncover a double agent in the Department of Energy laboratories at Los Alamos. Since the sting operation was ongoing and classified in a compartment that the Tau Ceti Commission was not privy to, they reached the conclusion that real information had been leaked. Apparently none had. The interesting question that was left lingering was if the leaked information was false, how did the Separatists develop the M-space transportation technology? The Attorney General replied that just because the Separatists are fanatics does not mean that they don't have smart scientist working for *them* also . . ."

"Indeed," President Moore switched off the television and chuckled lightly to himself. "Congresswoman Chi will just have to wait at least two more years before getting me out of office. And then she will still be beholding to me." Moore swiveled his chair around to relax, gloat, and stare out the window of the Oval Office for a second or two but his moment of relaxation was interrupted by a faint crackling *hiss* sounding behind him that was followed by a short burst of white light. Without turning to see the cause President Moore smiled again—*an M-space transportation directly to the Oval Office and through the security shields could only mean one thing.*

"You shouldn't be *here* Elle, someone could be watching." He scanned around the office nervously.

"Relax, Alexander, I've got the dampening field on. Nobody will see or hear a thing. If they do, I'll take care of it."

"Right."

"I see you managed to escape a disaster," the Separatist leader said and plopped down into the President's lap kissing him deeply.

"Yes, I did. It was just an overzealous Congresswoman from Nigeria trying to make a name for herself. We all have skeletons you know and the lovely Mrs. Amaka Chi did not want hers to go public." He laughed and kissed her back and then held her at arm's length. "But, hey, with no help from you, I might add. What is with this attack on Luna City? You're not supposed to be ready for any attacks for at least another year. And why Luna City?"

"That wasn't my doing. It was yours." Elle Ahmi poked her finger at the President's chest playfully.

"Not mine."

"Well, yes and no. One of your damned CIA agents infiltrated us and discovered our plans." Elle explained between kisses. "She was good, real good. She killed most of the crew on board that ship and liberated it away through M-space back to the Sol system. She was about to blow the whole thing. But fortunately, one of my special operations teams, ahem, *volunteered* to M-space onboard the ship and detonate it at the last minute. They cut it close and barely were able to detonate the cargo before she could send out a distress call." Elle gave him one last kiss and stepped a few meters from him.

"So, our plans have not been compromised?" President Moore grinned.

"No darling." Elle winked and activated the M-space generator and vanished with a crackling *hiss* and a flash of light.

"Excellent!"

Introduction to *A Well-Dressed Fear*
Ernest Lilley

Since I wanted as much a futurist collection as an SF one, Barbara Chepaitis' story, full of political intrigue among ESPers, stepped a little outside my comfort zone, though for me to rule out psi powers as possible future tech is a bit on the conservative side of science. What I really think is technology may well provide ESP like powers, but if it does it will be to the many, not the few. That's ok. I don't need to be comfortable all the time, and I did say I wanted different points of view. Her main character is a therapist and sometime covert operative in B.A.'s version of a PSI Corp, who doesn't need any convincing that absolute *power* corrupts absolutely, or that you can't tell a book by its cover.

A Well-Dressed Fear

B.A. Chepaitis

Crystal glasses held by pretty people gleamed under the cut glass light of chandeliers. Conversation, soft laughter and demure music wafted around the room where an intimate group of two hundred or so people gathered at the cocktail party of Senator Jarret Daimler, candidate for President of the United States. Jaguar Addams, her tall, slim form swathed in gold silk that fit her like a second skin, lifted an impeccably broiled scallop from a tray and brought it to her mouth.

She sensed Alex looking at her from where he stood on the broad curved staircase. She didn't turn. They weren't supposed to acknowledge each other. He was here not as Alex Dzarny, Planetoid supervisor, but as Jonathan Bass, Post press, some hair dye, glasses and a little facial plastique altering his visage enough that if she didn't know him, she wouldn't know him. But she found his thoughts easily and spoke to him subvocally.

What? she asked.

Alex subdued a smile. *Nothing, Jaguar. Enjoying the food?*

My tax dollars at work. And the best thing about this damn assignment so far.

Alex agreed, but didn't get a chance to reply because at that moment Senator Jarret made his entrance, to applause and cheers.

He was a handsome devil, Jaguar thought, with his dark hair, chiseled face, deep eyes that seemed to see everything.

He made a brief speech of welcome and gratitude that said little but said it well, and started working the crowd. Not for the first time, she wondered why she'd said yes to this.

She was a teacher on Prison Planetoid 3, where she worked with criminals; rehabbing them by making them face their fears. Daimler was not a criminal, unless you felt that way about politicians. Of course, she generally did. But that wasn't why she came. The Senator had invited 100 people from ordinary walks of life for this campaign trail party. He wanted to honor those he called Ordinary Heroes. And he specifically requested Jaguar Addams.

She would have declined, but their Board governor suggested she go because the Senator was on the Appropriations committee in charge of their budget. She grumbled, but bought a new dress. Then, the night before she was to get on the shuttle for the home planet, she'd entered her apartment to find General Durk sitting on her couch.

She took one look at him and held her door open. "Get out."

"No," he said. "Not yet. Close the door."

"Get out, rat fuck," she amended, continuing to hold the door open. He gave a quick nod and an officer appeared, entered the apartment and closed the door for her. She put her hands on her hips and tapped a foot hard. He remained relentlessly seated. "The last time we met, you almost got me and Alex killed," she said. "I doubt you have anything to say I'd care to hear."

"You're wrong. You're going to Senator Daimler's party," he remarked, a statement rather than a question. "And he was one of ours."

"One of your what?"

"Special Ops. He worked with us on psi capacity projects. He's a practiced empath."

At this, she went quiet. A practiced empath was running for President.

"I don't know what he's up to," the General continued. "I want you to find out."

"He's up to about 45 percent in the polls. What else can I tell you about him?"

"I don't need you to tell *me* anything. I just want *you* to find out about him. What he is."

"What for?"

"Because if you don't like it either, you're the only person I know who might stop him."

"Maybe I want an empath in the Oval Office. It'd serve my interests better than your outfit."

"Maybe," he said. "But if I'm right, then you take care of it. I'll send you flowers."

With that, he rose, nodded to her courteously, and walked to the door. The officer opened it for him, saluted, and they both made an exit, leaving Jaguar to stand and gape.

Soon after Alex called, saying the General had also been to see him, but hadn't said much more than he did to her. Only gave him a press pass and ID to go with her and keep an eye on things. He'd cleared it with their Board governor already. Everything else remained a mystery.

"It's just the General's prejudice showing," Jaguar said. "He doesn't want an empath as his Commander in Chief."

"Maybe so," Alex said. But he didn't seem convinced.

Now Jaguar licked at her fingers and watched the Senator go from one person to another, speaking briefly, shaking hands, putting a hand on a shoulder and gripping it then releasing it, always looking directly into the eyes of the person he spoke with, his face seeming to say that who they were and what they wanted was the most important thing in the world. He had the iconic male authority conservative Americans loved, and the open charm liberals flocked to.

When he reached her, his practiced glance took her in quickly, showing an appreciation that couldn't possibly offend. "Dr. Addams," he said, "I'm so glad you could make it. I've been watching your work for some time, and I wanted to make sure you got some recognition for it."

He offered his hand, took hers and held it in both of his briefly, looking directly into her face. As she'd planned if she was given the opportunity, she made herself open to more than just the social gesture, touching him empathically, letting him know she was doing so.

The touch he returned was as intense as anything she'd ever felt. There was no hesitation. Just a sudden and total flooding of her consciousness with his presence, and a total awareness of what that presence held. It was brief, but in the seconds it occurred she swam in deep waters, in an oceanic pulse of power. Then he released her hand. She worked to keep her face neutral.

"Would you mind walking with me?" he asked courteously, as if he hadn't just swarmed her. "I have a few questions about the Planetoid I'd like to ask you, since I have you here."

⟨≈≋≋⟩

As Alex watched from his place on the staircase, he was surprised to see the Senator taking the room with Jaguar in this cosy way. He wasn't wasting time. But then again, neither was she. From what he'd seen she'd made empathic contact and was following up. He didn't dare listen in, though. They couldn't risk it if the Senator was what the General said he was.

But then, a shift in the room's energy, drastic and unpretty, stopped him cold.

He blinked, looked to the entrance, to the rear of the room.

Six men, blue suits and white shirts, nothing special, but they were converging, and they had . . . something.

Jaguar. At two o'clock. Three, armed.

She whipped her head up at the contact and saw what he saw.

Got 'em. Are there more?

Three. Mine. Go.

They both moved.

She went through the crowd so quickly nobody had time to wonder, and then she kicked at the hand of one man, a weapon flew end over end. The other made a move for her, but she ducked and he went over, and that was all Alex saw because he was busy with his own, had one on the ground and was looking into his eyes, which told him things he wasn't ready to hear. He stood caught in new knowledge and a precognitive swirling of information beyond it until someone threw something incendiary and the air was filled with screaming, fire and smoke.

Before the room disappeared, Alex turned and saw the Senator, still calm, gathering people, herding them to the exit. In the smoke he caught a whiff of something nasty. Something that shouldn't go into the lungs. Through the noise, he sought Jaguar's thoughts.

Jaguar. Something in the smoke. Suspend activity. You know how.

Alex, he's . . .

But the rest was garbled, and then the room went very dark.

<hr />

Waking was a slow process, like walking uphill out of fog into a clearing. Unconsciousness receded from her. She opened her eyes, and blinked around.

The fog was gone, but it was still deep night, she supposed, because it was very dark. She lifted a hand and hit hard steel two inches from her face. She looked down at her body, covered in a sheet. A quick pat up and down revealed no bandages. She was not broken or punctured.

Above her she saw only dull metal. It was cold, thickly dark. Bracing her legs against the back portion of her prison, she kicked hard, and slid suddenly into a room dimly lit with fluorescents. She rolled over onto her feet and stood, looking around.

"The Morgue," she muttered. "Damn." She looked behind her and saw that she'd just emerged from a drawer labeled with the name Jane Doe.

Alex had instructed her to suspend her physical state. Little breath, heart slowed enough to seem stopped. This was a technique most practiced empaths knew. Because of it, they'd taken her for dead and brought her here. She wondered who else had joined her for the post-party morgue bash. She wondered how long she'd been here. She wondered where Alex was.

She checked other drawers and saw more Jane and John Doe labels. She opened a few and saw faces badly burned, caught in grimaces of pain and terror, faces blue with suffocation. Then, more methodically, she opened the John Does, counting one, two, three, four, holding her breath with each one. Then, the last one. She closed her eyes, offered a brief prayer to her most powerful gods, and pulled it open.

Empty. No one at all. She felt her legs go shaky. Alex wasn't here.

Then the door to the room opened, and a young man strolled in, pushing a cart, whistling. She turned to him, her sheet dangling loosely in her hand.

Where's my clothes?" she demanded. The intern blanched, backed up, and ran away.

In very little time the room was crowded with people, including the ME, all of whom wanted to know how she felt, who she was, and pushing unwanted medical attention on her.

"I don't need a hospital," she insisted. "I need some clothes and a cab."

She was desperate to ask about Alex, but knew she couldn't. If they let her go she could check at admitting to see if he was in the hospital. As it was, she could learn nothing except that Senator Daimler's party left ten killed, many injured. Senator Daimler himself was the hero of the day, subduing the terrorists and dragging people out of the fire.

"They say Daimler took them down?" she said.

"It's all over the news," the ME affirmed. "Him and some woman from the Planetoid. He's going crazy trying to find her, said she saved everybody's life."

"Huh," she said, not really surprised that nobody noticed Alex. He was good at being invisible when he wanted to be. And the media would pick the best story and stick with it, regardless. She hoped her face wasn't visible in any of their footage.

"You must be admitted for tests," a doctor insisted. "There may be residual damage."

"Did they use biobombs?" she asked.

"No, thank God. If there was, we wouldn't be here like this, without gear."

"Then get me some clothes," she said. "Get me a telecom so I can contact my people on the Planetoid. And get me out of here."

When they scurried off she simply wrapped her sheet tightly around herself, and walked out.

⚜

By the time she was out of the building she was dressed decently in scrubs she'd picked up along the way, and nobody seemed to notice that she was barefoot. Not even the front desk, where she learned that Jonathan Bass had not been admitted. She regretted the loss of the dress—it was a nice dress—but even more she wished she had something to put on her feet. With no cab money she had to walk, and the streets in this part of town weren't that clean.

She hadn't gotten more than a few blocks when she also wished she was on a crowded, well lit street, as she became aware of a large dark car trailing her, going slowly as if they were looking for something or someone. She walked faster, and the car caught up, pulled over.

A man emerged from the back seat. She kept walking until he was right at her back and then she swung an arm around, clipping him hard at the throat. Before he could react she heel-kicked his knee, brought a knee to his important parts, and smashed a fist upward at his nose.

He went down nicely, but someone else got out of the car. "Don't move," a voice said quietly. "Not even a little bit."

She stood very still, eyeing the laser fire weapon he pointed at her. With his free hand he opened the back door of the car, and Senator Daimler rose up out of it, grinning at her.

"If you ever need a job as bodyguard," he said. "I'll hire you."

❦

"Tequila if you have it," Jaguar said. "Anything else if you don't."

"Tequila it is," Senator Daimler said, and from the bar at the far wall of his living room, he poured her one, brought it to her.

"I'm sorry about your agent," Jaguar said as she took it. "But I don't think I hurt him badly."

"Just his pride," the Senator said. He raised his scotch and took a sip. He'd brought her back to his home, saying she could regroup there before the official investigators found her. He'd gone to the hospital to be there for those who lost loved ones, and to try and find her. He heard first that she was dead, then that she'd walked out, for all any-one knew, naked.

"The naked part was wrong," she noted, looking down at her scrubs. "Senator, do you have any idea who did this, or why?"

"It's HATE–Hate America to the End–claiming credit. They've promised to disrupt other campaigns, too. We're not sure where they come from, but we'll find out," he said, looking grimly determined. "Is there anything you noticed that would be helpful?"

"No more than anyone else there," she replied.

"That's not true," he said. He put his glass down on the buffet, moved closer to her. "How do you want to do this, Dr. Addams?"

"Do what?"

"Talk to each other. You already made empathic contact, so you know about me, and I certainly know about you. Do we dance around it, or should we be direct with each other?"

She raised cool sea-green eyes to his face. "I'm here to learn about you, so direct is good."

At this he raised an eyebrow. "Learn about me? Why?"

"Because I heard some things. I want to see if they're true, so I'll know who to vote for."

The corner of his mouth lifted in a grin. "Are you sure?" he asked and in his question she heard both threat and dare.

In answer, she lifted her hand to his forehead and brought herself in to his thoughts, felt the moment of empathic contact folding over them, his deeply blue eyes assuming the proportions of sky in her mind.

⚜

They stood in a blank space, in an absence of time. She was here. Wherever here was.

Where? she asked.

Here, he answered. *Everywhere. Where I am.*

Events swirled around her. Time was a strange attractor, spinning complex patterns. She knew this. She'd been with Alex when he occupied Adept space and knew the whirling of time, its circular motion.

But then . . .

Then his eyes, seeing all of it, his hands moving,

spinning events this way that way, taking what it saw and shaping

Shaping futures seeing everything because he was more than Adept

What was this? What was he?

Hands that would change the world utterly.

His hands would remove a terrible danger from the world. He would rise with joy to begin a new age of peace and prosperity, stopping even death. Even death. He knew how.

And he wanted her there.

She pulled back. It was too big. What he knew. The raw power he had to make use of it. He was not simply an Adept. Adepts saw possibilities. He created them. He had knowledge from the beginning of time through the future, and with political power he'd use that to remake the world. A tingle ran up her spine, as if she was in the presence of every deity she'd ever spoken to in the dark nights of her own soul.

"What are you?" she gasped, speaking aloud.

She felt his laughter ringing inside her. *You know. I was there at the beginning and I see the end. In power, I'll stop time and death. Be with me.*

She knew the energy of power in its most elemental forms, loved the taste of it on her tongue, the feel of it in her skin. What he offered would be more than bliss. He read this in her and drew her closer.

More than bliss. More than bliss. All her past, all present worries, all hopes for the future, all was subsumed in the curling energy of a man who could truly rule the world. She could give herself totally to this, relinquishing anything she'd ever had or been to it because who wouldn't do so? It was like death, inevitable, like life, inexorable. It was everything.

Then, with piercing clarity, she knew something else.

It was not hers.

It simply was not hers.

With supreme effort, she stepped back, held a hand out

to keep him away. "No," she said, voice tight and thin. "No more."

He stayed still. "Am I going too fast?" he asked gently, quietly.

She regained composure, shrugged. "Maybe dinner and a movie would be a better start."

He smiled at her. "If you need time, I understand. The investigators will want you to stay in Washington for a while, so there's no rush."

"None at all," she agreed.

* * *

She was still shaky when she got to her hotel, mind racing over what he'd shown her, what it meant. She forgot to stop at the desk to ask for a key. She realized that when she stood in front of the door to her room and saw she didn't need one. The door was already open.

Just a crack. Just enough to tell her someone was there, or had been. Why, she wondered, did they leave the door ajar? Unless whoever it was wanted her to know.

She entered the room and once inside, closed the door, heard the lock click into place. She stood with her back pressed against it, breathing quietly. Shadows in the dark made themselves known as objects. Lamp. Bed. Desk.

She took a step forward. Another. One more.

The move, when it came, was quicker than thought. A hand wrapped her wrist, pulled her around. She was pressed against warm flesh. Her mouth was pressed against another mouth and she was being kissed, held close. It was Alex. He was alive.

When the kiss broke, she reached up and touched his face. "You have an interesting definition of no contact," she noted.

"I like it," he said.

"So do I. Did you follow me out of the hospital?" she asked.

"I did. I saw Diamler's car. Tell me what happened next."

"Easier this way," she said, and called him into empathic contact, where she took him to the place Daimler had shown her, let him see what Daimler was. When she finished, he was quiet.

"The General was right," Jaguar said. "Daimler's got it in spades. Adept, hypnopath, empath, you name it. And he'll use it. Create a *Pax Americana* like none we've ever seen."

Alex heard the excitement in her voice, but also the reservation. "But?" he asked.

She shook her head. "I don't know. Alex, you're an Adept. Maybe you understand it. Is it inevitable that someone with so much power throws as much dark as light?"

"Not inevitable," he said, "But with Daimler–both are there."

"And what he showed me–the disaster and the triumph –is it true? Can you tell?"

Alex considered. Adepts generally saw possible futures, but occasionally they'd see one clear line that ran straight to only one result. Those times rang like crystal flicked hard. As Daimler's vision had.

"It's true," Alex said. "Very true. And very big. He'll change the world."

"For the better?" she asked.

"Yes. He's placed at a cusp of events. He'd turn the world back to sanity at a moment of great insanity. He reads the past, the future as far as it goes, and he has the intelligence to work with it. He has the attributes of a god, Jaguar. Except . . ." Alex ran a hand through his hair.

"Except," she agreed. "Alex, he wasn't afraid. When the gunmen hit the room."

"He wasn't afraid because he knew they were coming," he said.

"Because he's an Adept?"

"No," he said. "Because he hired them."

He saw her swallow hard. She'd suspected this. "Are you sure?" she asked.

"One of the gunmen was an empath," Alex explained. "When I got him down, I did a quick read. They were his people. That's how he knew they were coming."

Jaguar went still. "Why?" she whispered.

"For a sure win. This clinches it for him. Now he's a high profile hero, fighting the bad guys, saving the people. It's a paradox, Jaguar. He's compelled to do the good he foresees, and he'll use any means to make sure he can do it."

She frowned. "Ten people are dead. Not including the gunmen."

"It was a willing sacrifice for the gunmen. They did this for him."

Jaguar closed her eyes and let that sink in. Of course. When he showed her who he was, she felt the same. She would do anything; give up everything. But she'd been called back by the truth. Knowing that a simple truth, once discerned, was more precious than any power.

Two small lines of tension knit themselves into her forehead. "What if he doesn't make it to the Presidency, or he dies? This disaster he'll avert—will it happen?"

"That's unknown. But all the other good he'll do won't happen. Only he can do that."

"Then what do *we* do, Alex?"

"I don't know," he said.

"We can do nothing," she said hesitantly. "Walk away. Let him win."

They could. And they'd have perhaps the greatest ruler in history. But they'd have a ruler, not a President, because all that would end, too. "Is that what you want?" he asked, knowing her answer meant a great deal personally as well as in the world. He could walk away, but he doubted Daimler would let her do so. If she didn't see that, she was already under his spell.

She said nothing. He put a hand to her face and called her thoughts to his.

Is it what you want? All his light, his gifts, bought with the coin of the soul? He'll take nothing less, Jaguar. Do you want him?

He felt her tug against him and he released her. It was easy enough for him to choose. He hadn't tasted Daimler's power, the future he offered, as directly as she did. Small price the ephemeral soul must seem for guaranteed safety in a world made new. He waited as she closed her eyes, wrestling with what she'd experienced. A biblical moment, he thought. She wrestled with angels. With demons. She wrestled with a god.

How can I choose for the world, Alex?

Choose for yourself, Jaguar. See who you are. Be what you see.

Another moment of grappling. Then, as if she was herself dispelling demons she swept a hand out. "He lied," she said. "And his lies got people killed. He should be my prisoner, not my President. Certainly not my god."

Alex breathed in deeply, which told him he'd been holding his breath.

"We'll have to go public," she continued. "Tell what we know."

"We have no evidence," Alex said. "and who'll believe us against him? He's the media's happy ending, a man with everything he wants–except you."

She startled, her head jerking up, and then tried to cover it with coolness. "You knew that?"

He lifted a shoulder, let it fall. Of course, the gesture said.

"Still," she insisted, "we have to do something."

"How?" he asked.

"In Christian terms, he's both god and antichrist in one. Let's put him to the test and see who wins." She raised her hand in the sign of the empath. "See who you are. Be what you see."

Alex's face grew tight. Empathic reflection? Face his fear? "He'll swallow you whole, Jaguar. Besides, there's nothing in him to work with. That kind of power doesn't know fear."

"Sometimes," she said, "that kind of power fears itself."

"He knows you. He knows what you'll do and he'll be prepared to meet it."

A corner of her mouth turned up in a smile. "He doesn't know me, Alex. Nobody does, except, maybe in your better moments, you."

He saw the clarity of her integrity, the profound nature of it. He couldn't stop her. She'd take the risk. But she wouldn't take it alone.

"Okay, Dr. Addams," he said crisply. "Tell me what you have in mind."

⋘⋙

"I have no desire to rule," she said to Senator Daimler. "I'm not built that way. But you seem certain."

"Of course I am," he said. "How can you doubt it? Haven't I shown you enough to know?"

They were back in his house, after a day of press conferences where she was at his side, demurely telling reporters that she was only doing her job at the party, and like the Senator, she hoped the group that staged this horrendous act would be apprehended. Already Daimler took her arm as if it belonged to him. Already he was grooming her for her role as his partner.

Now he came and stood in front of her, lifted a hand and ran it softly down her cheek. "Is it Alex?" he asked. "Is that what's bothering you?"

She raised her eyes to his, and said nothing.

"I know he was there," Daimler continued. "I couldn't let him live. You understand that."

"That's what it's like, being a god," she said quietly. "You get to make those choices."

"Yes, Jaguar. You will."

"Show me," she said. "Show me all of it. Then I'll know."

He pressed a hand against her face, drew her close, pulling her into the raging complexity that he was. She felt it taking her, lifting her, carrying her. Tornadoes. Great tearing motion she was helpless against, so she didn't fight it, but let herself be carried by this, no human, no humanity only a god a demon a god great energies pouring their being into the . . .

It is mine.

A moment of panic. Alex was right. Nothing to work with here. He was a god and his capacity for good seduced her, he was a demon who held her and the power that fueled both was bliss to swallow her whole. And she would be his foil, his mirror in which he'd view his triumph. She reached for it, tasted it, fell into the center of it where she saw

All he was, made of all that and it was . . .

Nothing.

Nothing.

The world, made of words, unmade by lies. The essence of nothing no being an unspinning of time and space and matter and . . .

It's mine. I give it to you. To the world.

The emptiness seared her, made her want to turn her face and weep. Yet, the good was there, cupping the hollow space and which would win? She would have to find out.

She blinked. Moved closer. She would be his mirror. He would see all, except her.

She raised a hand, palm forward, her flesh a mirror, reflecting back to him all that he was, amplifying it. His face a mask of triumph, he moved to it, power drawing him, engulfing him.

See who you are. Be what you see.

Heat pulsed from within him, then through him to her and back to him, heat joining heat and power growing, energy massing in.

He moved to it. He reached for it. It was all he was, and it engulfed him.

The flash fire that exploded in the room was not something she expected, but then, she didn't know what to expect, never having taken down a god before. In the moment it splashed into flame she curled herself into a ball and rolled, away. Away.

Then, hands reached for her, pulled her through smoke and fire, and somehow she was on her feet, running, being dragged away, away.

When the world came back into focus, the first thing she saw was the branches of a tree. She was lying under it, staring up. Closer than the branches was Alex's face, looking down at her. Behind her was Senator Daimler's house, in flames.

She took it all in.

"He's gone, isn't he?"

"Yes," Alex said. "And all he might have been or done."

"Alex," she whispered, "Did we just save the world, or end it?"

"I don't know," he replied. "I don't know."

Introduction to Civil Disobedience
Ernest Lilley

I considered getting a story from Joe a major coup, because works like the *Forever War* have had tremendous impact on the intersection of politics and science fiction, and because he's always been a favorite author of mine. His vision here is prescient, plausible, and darn twisty. Jump in.

CIVIL DISOBEDIENCE

JOE HALDEMAN

I'm old enough to remember when the Beltway was a highway, not a dike. Even then, there were miles that had to be elevated over low places that periodically flooded.

We lived in suburban Maryland when I was a child. I remember seeing on television the pictures of downtown Washington after Hurricane Hilda, with the Washington Monument and the Capitol and the Lincoln Memorial all isolated islands. My brother and I helped our parents stack sandbags around our Bethesda house, but the water rose over them. Good thing the house had two stories.

That was when they built the George W. Bush Dam to regulate the flow of the Potomac, after Hilda. (My grandfather kept mumbling, "Bush Dam . . . Damn Bush.) That really was the beginning of the end for the UniParty, a symbol for all that went wrong afterwards.

The politicos claimed they didn't cause the water to rise — it was supposed to be a slow process, hundreds or even thousands of years before a greenhouse crisis. I guess they built the dam just in case they were wrong.

Then there were three hurricanes in four weeks, and they all made it this far north, so the dam closed up tight and people in flooded Maryland and Virginia could look over the Beltway dike and see low-and-dry Washington, and sort of resent what their tax dollars had bought. Maybe what happened was inevitable.

Over the next decade, the dikes also went up around New York, Boston, Philadelphia, Miami, The Hamptons, and Cape Cod. Temporary at first, but soon enough, as the water rose, bricked into permanence. While suburbs and less wealthy coastal towns from Maine to Florida simply drowned.

By the time the water got to rooftop level, of course all those towns were deserted, their inhabitants relocated inland, into Rehab camps if they couldn't afford anything else. We spent a couple of years in the Rockville one, until Dad had saved enough to get into an apartment in Frederick. It was about as big as a matchbox, but by then we two boys had gone off to college and trade school.

I was an autodidact without too much respect for authority, so I said the hell with college and became a SCUBA instructor, a job with a future. That was after I'd been in the Navy for one year, and the Navy brig for one week. Long enough in the service to learn some underwater demolition, and that's on my website, which brought me to the attention of Homeland Security, about a day and a half after the Bush Dam blew.

Actually, I'm surprised it took them that long. Most of my income for several years had been from Soggy Suburbs, diving tours of the drowned suburbs of Washington. People mostly come back to see what's become of the family manse, now that fish have moved in, and it does not generate good will toward the government. They've tried to shut me down a couple of times, but I have lawyers from both the ACLU and the Better Business Bureau on my side.

I returned to my dock with a boatload of tourists, only four, in the bitter January cold, and found a couple of suits and a couple of cops waiting, along with a Homeland Security helicopter. They had a federal warrant to bring me in for questioning.

It was an interesting ride. I'm used to seeing the 'burbs underwater, of course, but it was strange to fly over what had become an inland sea, inside the Beltway dike. The dam demolition had been a pretty thorough job, and in less than a day, it became as deep inside the Beltway as outside. They can fill up the collapsed part and pump the water out, but it will take a long time.

The guy who did it called it "civil disobedience" rather than terrorism, which I thought was a stretch. But he did time the charges so that the flooding was gradual, and no one drowned.

Since I was a suspected terrorist, I lost the protection of the courts, not to mention the ACLU and the Better Business Bureau. They didn't haul out the cattle prods, but they did lock me in a small room for 24 hours, saying, "We'll get to you."

It could have been worse. It was a hotel room, not a jail, but there was nothing to read or eat, no TV or phone. They took my shoulder bag with the book I was reading and my computer and cell.

I guess they thought that would scare me. It just made me angry, and then resigned. I hadn't really done anything, but since when did that matter, with the Uniparty. And not doing anything was not the same as not knowing anything.

The smell of mildew was pervasive and the carpet was squishy. When we landed on the roof, it looked like about four stories were above the waterline. I couldn't see anything from the room; the window was painted over with white paint from the outside.

Exactly 24 hours after they had brought me in, one of the suits entered through the hotel room door, leaving a guard outside.

"What do you need a cop for?"

He gave me a look. "Full employment." He sat down on the couch. "First of all, where were you . . ."

"I get food, you get answers."

"You have that backward." He looked at the back of his hand. "Answers, then food. Can you prove where you were when the dam was sabotaged?"

"No, and neither can you."

"What do you mean by that?"

"Food."

Yet another look. He stood up without a word and knocked twice on the door. The guard opened it and he left.

A few minutes later I tried knocking, myself. No result. But the man did come back eventually, bearing a ham sandwich on a Best Western plate.

I peeled back the white bread and looked at it. "What if I don't eat ham?"

"You left a package of sliced ham in your refrigerator on K Street. You ordered a ham sandwich at Denny's for lunch on the 28th of November. I checked while they were making the sandwich."

Now *that* was scary, considering where my refrigerator was now. I tore into the sandwich even though it was probably full of truth serum. "If you know so much about me," I said between bites, "then you must know where I was at any given time."

"You said that neither you nor I could say where we were when the dam blew."

"No . . . you asked where I was when it was *sabotaged.* That could have been a week or a year before the actual explosions. The saboteurs were probably back in Albania or Alabama or wherever by then."

"So where were you when it blew?"

"At my girlfriend's place. It rattled the dishes and a picture fell off the wall."

"That's the tree house she's squatting in, out in Wheaton?"

"Home sweet home, yeah. Her original apartment is kind of damp. She paid a premium for ground floor. Wrong side of the Beltway."

"So we only have her word for where you were."

"And mine, yes. What, you don't have surveillance cameras out in Treetown yet?"

"None that show her place."

I guess it was my turn to respond, or react. I finished the sandwich instead, slowly, while he watched. He took the plate, I suppose so I couldn't frisbee it at his head, take his keys and gun, subdue the guard, steal the helicopter, and go blow up the New York dike. Instead I posited: "If the saboteurs could have been anyplace in the world when it blew, what difference does it make where I was?"

"You weren't in town. It looks like you knew something was going to happen."

"Really."

"Yes, *really*. We got a warrant, and a Navy SEAL forensic team searched your apartment."

"Are my goldfish all right? Water's kind of cold."

"It's interesting what's missing. Not just toiletries and clothes, but boxes of books and pictures from the walls. Your computer system, not portable. All the paper having to do with your business. Your pistol and its registration. You moved them with four cab rides between your apartment and the Sligo dock, all two days before the Flood."

"So I moved in with my girlfriend. It happens."

"Not so conveniently."

I tried to look confused. "That's why you're on my case. I'm one of the dozens, hundreds, of people who moved out of D.C. that day or the next?"

"You're the only one with underwater demolition training. On that alone, we could haul you down to Cuba and throw away the key."

"Come on. . . ."

"And you were already on a watch list for your attitude. The things you've said to customers."

"The apartment was too expensive, so I got back my deposit and moved out. My girlfriend . . ."

"A week before the first of the month."

"Sure. It was . . ."

"In a blizzard."

"Yeah, it was snowing. No problem. Or the cabbie's problem, not mine. We wanted to have Christmas together."

"For Christmas, you just sort of boated through twelve miles of blizzard. By compass, for the fun of it."

"Oh, bullshit. I just kept the Beltway to my left for ten-some miles and turned right at the half-submerged Chevron sign. Then about a hundred yards to a flagpole, bear left, and so forth. I've done it a hundred times. You try it with a compass. I want to watch."

He nodded without changing expression. "One of the things we lost when the dam blew was a really delicate sniffing machine. It can tell whether you've been anywhere near high explosives recently. The closest one's in our New York office."

"Let's go. I haven't touched anything like that since the Navy. Four or five years ago." I'd been in the same house with some, but I hadn't touched it.

He stood up very smoothly, one flex, not touching the arm of the couch. I wouldn't want to get into anything physical with him. "Get your coat."

I got it from the musty closet and shook it out, shedding molecules of mold and plastic explosive. How sensitive was that machine, really?

He knocked twice and the cop took us to an open elevator. The buttons under 4 were covered with duct tape. The cop used a cylindrical fire department key to start it. "Roof?"

"Right."

"Where's my stuff?" I said. "I don't want to leave it here."

"We're not going anywhere." He buttoned up his coat and I zipped mine up. We got out of the elevator into a glassed-in waiting area and went out onto the roof. There was no helicopter on the pad. Not too cold, high twenties with no wind, and the air smelled really good, almost like the ocean.

I followed him over to the edge. There was water all the way to where the horizon was lost in bright afternoon haze, the tops of a few buildings rising like artificial islands in a science fiction world. Behind us, the Beltway with almost no traffic.

"It's quiet," I said. Faint rustle of ice slurry below us. I peered over the rusty guardrail and saw it rolling along the building wall.

"They said 'Power to the People.' This isn't power to anybody. It's like the country's been beheaded."

I didn't say that if you're ugly enough, extreme cosmetic surgery could help. I might be in enough trouble already.

"Whoever did this didn't think it through. It's not just the government, the bureaucracy. It's the country's history. Our connection to the past; our identity as America."

That was something Hugh was always on about. The way they wrap themselves in the flag and pretend to be the inheritors of a grand democratic tradition. While they're really alchemists, turning the public trust into gold.

"Hugh Oliver," he said, startling me.

"What about Hugh?"

"He disappeared the same time you did."

"What, like I disappeared? I left a forwarding address."

"Your parents' address."

"They knew where I was."

"So did we. But we've lost Mr. Oliver. Perhaps you know where to find him?"

"Huh uh. We're not that close."

"Funny." He took a pair of small binoculars out of his coat pocket and switched them on. The stabilizers hummed as he scanned along the horizon. Still looking at nothing, he said, "A surveillance camera saw you go into a coffeehouse in Georgetown with him last Wednesday. The Lean Bean."

Oh shit. "Yeah, I remember that. So?"

"The camera didn't show either of you coming out. You're not still there, so you must have left through the service entrance."

"He was parked in the alley out back."

"Not in his own car. It had a tracer."

"So I'm not my brother's car's keeper. It must have been somebody else's. What did he . . ."

"Or a rental?"

That much, I could give up. "Not a rental. It was clapped-out and full of junk."

"You didn't recognize it?"

I shook my head. Actually, I'd assumed it was Hugh's. "Why did you have a tracer on his car?"

"What did you talk about?"

"Business. How bad it is." Hugh's a diver; not much winter work. Idle hands do the devil's work, I guess. "We just had a cup of coffee and he drove me home."

"And what did you do when you got home?"

"What? I don't know. Made dinner."

He put the binoculars down on the railing and pulled out a little sound recorder. "This is what you did."

It was a recording of me phoning my landlord, saying I'd found a cheaper place and would be moving out before Christmas.

"That was at six twenty-five," he said. "When you got home from the coffeehouse, you must have gone straight to the phone."

I had, of course. "No. But I guess it was the same day. That Wednesday."

He picked up the binoculars again and scanned the middle distance. "It's okay, Johnson."

The big man slammed me against the guardrail, hard, then tipped me over and grabbed my ankles. I was gasping, coughing, trying not to vomit, dangling fifty feet over the icy water.

"Johnson is strong, but he can't hold on to you forever. I think it's time for you to talk."

"You can't . . . you can't do this!"

"I guess you have about a minute," he said, looking at his watch. "Can you hold on a minute?" I could see Johnson nod, his upside-down smile.

"Let me put it to you this way. If you can tell us where Hugh Oliver went, you live. If you can't, you have this little accident. It doesn't matter whether it's because you don't know, or because you refuse to tell. You'll just fall."

My throat had snapped shut, paralyzed. "I . . ."

"You'll either drown or freeze. Neither one is particularly painful. That bothers me a little. But I can't tell you how little guilt I will feel."

Not the truth! "Mexico. Drove to Mexico."

"No, we have cameras at every crossing, with face recognition."

"He knew that!"

"Can you let go of one ankle?" He nodded and did, and I dropped a sickening foot. "Mexico returns terrorists to us. He must have known that, too."

"He was going to Europe from there. Speaks French." *Quebec.*

He shrugged and made a motion with his head. The big man grabbed the other ankle and hauled me back. My chin snapped against the railing and my shoulder and forehead hit hard on the gravel.

"Yeah, Europe. You're lying, but I think you do know where he is. I can send you to a place where they get answers." He rubbed his hands together and blew on them. "Maybe I'll go along with you. It's warm down there."

Cuba. Point of no return.

My stomach fell. Even if I knew nothing about Hugh, I knew too much about them.

They couldn't let me live now. They'll pull out their answers and bury me in Guantanamo.

Johnson picked me up roughly. I kicked him in the shin, tore loose, ran three steps and tried to vault over the edge. My hurt shoulder collapsed and I cartwheeled clumsily into space.

Civil disobedience. What would the water feel like?

Scalding. Then nothing.

INTRODUCTION TO THE LONE AND LEVEL SANDS
Ernest Lilley

Looking for a range of viewpoints, it only seemed right that I ask a Libertarian for a story for this collection. I discovered L. Neil Smith with his first novel, *Probability Broach*, followed by *The American Zone*, in which our universe is connected to a series of parallel continuums, and the action takes place in an alternate southwest where an armed society really is a polite society and Admiral Heinlein is fondly remembered. Smith calls himself one of Heinlein's children, and that's surely true, but he's also an offspring of Raymond Chandler, whom I'm just as much a fan of. Personally, I think that the Libertarian notion that you can get along with hardly any government is pretty wishful thinking, but certainly no more so than a belief that politics . . . or science . . . or religion holds the answers to creating a perfect world.

Writing about the near future is a dangerous business, it should be noted. When we received the story, it had a bit about the uncovering of Watergate's "Deep Throat" that the real uncovering of made necessary to revise. I like a little mystery in my world, so I was a bit saddened by the event. If anyone decides they'd like to drain Loch Ness to settle that debate, you can expect me to picket.

Fortunately the story didn't hinge on the point, and stands quite well on its other merits.

The Lone And Level Sands

L. Neil Smith

I met a traveler from an antique land
Who said: Two vast and trunkless legs of stone
Stand in the desert. Near them, on the sand,
Half sunk, a shattered visage lies, whose frown,
And wrinkled lip, and sneer of cold command,
Tell that its sculptor well those passions read
Which yet survive, stamped on these lifeless things,
The hand that mocked them and the heart that fed;

And on the pedestal these words appear:
"My name is Ozymandius, king of kings:
Look on my works, ye Mighty, and despair!"
Nothing beside remains. Round the decay
Of that colossal wreck, boundless and bare
The lone and level sands stretch far away.

—Percy Bysshe Shelley, "Ozymandius"

The guard said, "Pardon me, Miss Ngu, may I please have your autograph?"

Llyra stood on the slowly moving slidewalk with her husband Morgan and their three children, taking in the amazing sight of the famous Leaning Monument of Washington. The guard, who was no more than a ticket-taker in point of fact, had apparently run all the way from his glass booth at the entrance of the Mall to catch up with them. Now the man bent over, hands on his knees, trying to catch his breath, as well.

By special arrangement with the Seaboard Weather Control Company, a holosign over the entrance had informed them, the onetime capital city of the Old United States and East America was kept authentically hot and humid all year round. As a result, all of them including the guard, it appeared, felt authentically sticky and uncomfortable.

"Sure," Llyra told him cheerfully over the somewhat alarming sound of the man's wheezing. "Are you all right? Do you have something for me to write on?"

He levered himself upright again, looking flushed. Except for a fringe of reddish hair above his ears, he was completely bald, and bright pink from his chin almost to the back of his neck. He needn't have been bald, of course practically nobody in the rest of the Solar System was these days, old-fashioned laws forbidding genetic therapy had long since been repealed, or were simply ignored, but the East American people largely remained prejudiced against "fooling Mother Nature."

He fished around in his antique gold-buttoned blazer, a patch on the breast pocket displayed a System-famous company logo surrounded by the legend, "Ejtofz Entertainment Enterprises", producing a scrap of paper.

"I'm okay, thanks, Miss Ngu," he told her, looking to her husband, as well. "I'm originally from Flagstaff, see? Old Arizona? Eighteen years I've lived and worked in the District and I'm still not used to the damn artificial climate." He glanced down at the children. "Pardon my French."

Morgan laughed. "That's okay, Fred." He'd looked down at the man's nametag. "We speak a lot of French, ourselves." In his way, Morgan was just as illustrious a personality as his wife, but she was the one who got asked for her autograph and he'd long since grown accustomed to it.

Llyra spoke up. "I'm sorry, Fred. Where are my manners? This is my husband, Morgan Trask, my son Emerson, my daughter Julia, and our baby daughter Ardie in the pram." As she spoke, she signed the scrap of paper, dating it July 2, 2145. A sudden wave of nausea and foreboding swept through her, as it did sometimes. She'd had another of her bad dreams last night and awakened shaken and sweaty but she ignored it.

"It's very nice to meet you all." said the guard, shaking hands with the couple's eight-year-old son and five-year-old daughter. "Thank you, Miss Ngu. You know, we see quite a few celebrities here, but . . ." he held up the autograph. "Well, my wife will be so pleased." He departed at a considerably more leisurely pace than he'd arrived.

They all looked up at the monument again, sitting about a hundred yards away. The only thing holding the tower up seemed to be a pair of structural carbon cables, stretching from the pyramidal top, against the direction it was leaning, and anchored in the ground. They were smaller, but similar, Llyra realized, to the big cable, over 22,500 miles long, that they'd ridden down on from synchronous orbit this morning.

It was hard to believe that, in times past, thousands of groups, military veterans, racial minorities, trade organizations, labor unions, animal rights advocates, and environmentalists like the Sierra Club, All Worlds Are Earth, and the Mass Movement, had rallied here, sometimes by the millions, to state their case and make their demands. Now it was just a huge empty space Llyra and her family had almost to themselves.

"Ejtofz Entertainment Enterprises must be too cheap to spring for antigravs," Morgan observed.

He'd pronounced the name "Eye-tovs." Llyra thought it must be Hungarian or Lithuanian or Serbo-Croatian or something. The company had just bought the entire city, everything inside the legendary Beltway and was intending to make a theme park of it.

"They're still relatively expensive," Llyra replied. "And they're power hogs."

"Yeah, but if nothing is done to prevent it, someday this

monument will collapse, leaving a long, broken line of rubble, the Washington Memorial Wall."

Between them and the monument, a life-sized hologram in quaint early 19th century clothing appeared and politely introduced itself as Parson Mason Weems. It spoke of General Washington, about the monument itself, and apologized for an apparently famous untruth it had once told about a hatchet and a cherry tree in its biography of the first American president.

"Just think." Llyra said. "One little fib, not quite three and a half centuries ago, and now he'll be apologizing for it until the sun burns out."

Morgan laughed.

"When Washington retired after two terms," the hologram continued, "He . . ."

"Be quiet, now." Llyra's husband told the hologram. "And please go away."

The hologram promptly vanished.

Morgan Trask was tall by nearly anybody's standard, six feet nine inches. Although he was heavily muscled and in excellent condition, strangers usually thought of him as skinny, owing to the proportions involved. He had strong Nordic features, although most of his ancestors were Irish, and long blond hair presently pulled back in a ponytail. He wore what served as casual street clothes in the Moon's largest city, Armstrong; to the natives of Earth they looked like pajamas, or surgical scrubs and a small plasma pistol high on his right hip.

Born and raised in what might as well have been an interplanetary colony, a village built under an atmospheric dome east of L'Anse Aux Meadows on the northernmost tip of the Great Northern Peninsula of the Unanimous Consent Confederation of Newfoundland, Morgan had been the Solar System's Olympic gold medalist in men's figure skating.

Now he turned to his wife, catching the eye of his two older children, as well. The third, Ardie, was in her stroller, more or less oblivious to anything except her toes. "Somebody told me that when Washington was a general, Congress put him on an expense account, rather than a salary, and he used it to buy livestock for the farm he shared with Martha."

The baby began to fuss a little. Increasing the flow of the air curtain that protected her child from the climate, Llyra raised her eyebrows. "Is that true?"

He shook his head. "Don't know. It's just what somebody told me. When he got elected President, he wanted the same deal but they turned him down."

"Gosh, I wonder why."

Twenty-eight year old Llyra Ngu Trask was nearly as tall as her husband, six feet seven inches, and similarly muscled, although with all of the curves appropriate to her sex. She, too, had been an Olympic gold medalist, in women's figure skating, at the age of sixteen. Blond and fair, with just the faintest hint of her Asian forbears in her hazel eyes, her height was nothing extraordinary where she came from. She'd been born and brought up on the terraformed asteroid Pallas, at one twentieth of a standard Earth gravity. It had taken her years to work up to skating on Earth, but in the end, she'd been the first female to perform a quintuple Salchow in a one-gee field.

For the past ten years, she and her husband had been coaching young Olympic hopefuls, as well as future show skaters, at the Robert and Virginia Heinlein Memorial Ice Skating Arena—"the Heinlein"—in Armstrong City in the Moon. The waiting list for their services, famous from Mercury to Pluto, was long and those on it would now be disappointed.

They had returned to Earth with their three small children for what could possibly be the last time, to see a few sights they thought were important. After Washington, their plan was to visit a handful of other North American cities and pay a visit to Morgan's parents in U.C.C. Newfoundland, before heading for Egypt. Next month they would board the *C.C.V. Prometheus*, bound for an ancient alien interstellar jump device recently discovered at the edge of the Solar System. It would take them to another star system and the beautiful Earthlike planet, Paradise.

Those who wished to retain a sense of perspective had named the planet's single extraordinarily dark and smooth-surfaced moon "Parking Lot."

One sight they wanted their children to see was the former capital of the former United States of America, the last government of any consequence on Earth. Ejtofz Entertainment Enterprises had begun its renovation of the mostly abandoned city by restarting the famous moving walkways that took visitors from one point of interest to another.

As they'd seen, holograms of important biographers acted as guides to the various monuments and memorials. Cameras, computers, and other electronics were allowed inside the park in a city that had once required a police permit for a camera tripod but only at their owners' risk. Uncountable trillions of electronics-eating anti-surveillance nanites were still active from about a century ago, when people finally grew tired of being watched and listened to all the time.

"Mommy, what's that?" Emerson asked suddenly.

"Don't point, dear, it's not polite. Anyway, your eyes are better than mine. I can't quite . . . why, I think it looks like somebody in a hoverchair."

The instant the whole family turned to look, the figure took a right angle and vanished behind a statue of Hillary Rodham Clinton that, in the style of her times, had been made from crushed aluminum cans.

"Maybe somebody from your neck of the woods, Honey," Morgan suggested. "Somebody who can't tolerate the new treatments for gravity." All five of them had suffered numerous injections, tests, physical therapy, and other indignities to be here, including the baby.

"Maybe," Llyra answered. There was something unsettling about that figure, but she couldn't put her finger on what it was. "Let's go have some lunch, shall we? I saw a little cafe over by the Schwarzenegger Pavilion."

⚜

"Do you think there's bugs in there?" Llyra's five-year-old daughter Julia asked as they approached the next memorial on their itinerary, a site mostly known, these days, for its appearance on antique coins and currency. Not all such collectibles were rare. Toward the end, the East American government had cast this particular president's likeness into a thermoplastic five million dollar coin, circulating enough of them, it was said, to fill one of the smaller Great Lakes.

Emerson gave his sister a nasty snicker.

"This is a pretty good climate," said Morgan, "for all kinds of nasty bugs."

They'd seen some of the city proper, before coming to the Mall. So far they'd visited the apartment building where Wesley Snipes had supposedly lived in the twentieth century movie *Murder at 1600*, the basement parking garage where "Deep Throat" had met with reporters Woodward and Bernstein, and a Catholic girls' school where a barricaded twenty-first century President Horton Willoughby had finally been persuaded to surrender and resign from office over the Martian scandal.

There was still a military tank long since rusted and inert standing at every important intersection of the city, left over from the turbulent final days of the Homeland Security era. It was difficult for Morgan and Llyra to keep their eight-year-old son and five-year old daughter from climbing on them; it looked like fun to the adults, as well.

Later this afternoon they planned to visit the Hall of Fictional Presidents, with its host of robotic and holographic representations from Raymond Massey to Harrison Ford, Gene Hackman, Ronny Cox, and Martin Sheen.

"And snakes!" Emerson added. "I wanna see some snakes!"

One of the few drawbacks to living in the Moon was that the children could only see wild animals by going to the zoo. The boy devoured everything he could read and watch on the subject. That had been one reason they'd decided to head for the stars, and a new planet. There he could run through the woods and see new life that very few human children or adults, for that matter had ever seen. There was a danger in that, of course, but pioneers like Arctic colonists and Pallatians welcomed it, for the freedom and opportunity that came with it.

The monument before them was a gigantic rectangular building entirely surrounded by columns. Inside, one of the presidents sat on what was unmistakably a throne, looking down at the visitors who came to see him. The monument, however, was overgrown with semitropical weeds and vines, beneath which two centuries of graffiti had left not a square inch of stone unmarked. One of the columns at the entrance was broken, leaving a gap like a missing tooth in the face of a street tramp.

Before they came within fifty yards of the memorial, another holofigure appeared before them, both of its arms extended, palms outward.

"I'm sorry," said the hologram. "The public may not enter this structure, as it's overrun with dangerous insects, snakes, rats, and bats."

"Bats!" exclaimed both older children at the same time, Emerson with excitement, Julia in horror. Llyra felt some nameless dread wash through her again. It had been like this for half her life, ever since her ill-fated trip to Mars. She shook it off, as she always did, and concentrated on the hologram.

"I was Thomas DiLorenzo," the figure wore a jacket and tie from the early twenty-first century, "one of Abraham Lincoln's last biographers. Over the past century or so, the man's image and place in history have become somewhat tarnished, as it has become clearer what he did and why. Fundamentally, he allowed six hundred twenty thousand individual human beings to die violently and many more to be wounded, raped, and impoverished in order to preserve a mere political construct."

"But he freed . . ." Llyra began. Earth history wasn't her strong suit.

"A claim," the hologram went on, "was often made that Lincoln ended slavery, but not only did his Emancipation Proclamation free nobody, all throughout the war, Washington's capitol dome was being renovated by slaves. And Lincoln stated frankly that if he could have preserved the Union by keeping slavery in place, he would have done so. What the man did, instead, was to spread it everywhere across America, by introducing military conscription and income taxation, the two most pernicious forms of slavery that continued for another hundred and . . ."

The hologram's voice was overpowered by a roaring noise overhead. They all looked up to see one of the new antigrav shuttles its underbelly polished like a great curved mirror clawing its way into the midday sky, headed for the Moon, or possibly one of the Lagrange positions.

Some people still preferred spaceships to the orbital elevator the Trask family had ridden down on. Those like the vessel overhead were faster and more direct, but a great deal more expensive. The Trasks had taken a small space hopper from Armstrong City in the Moon to the pinnacle of the nearest space elevator, there were now six of these altogether, all of them built by Llyra's father, who had also terraformed Ceres, and ridden it to Fernandina in the Galapagos Islands on the equator. From there, a hypersonic atmospheric cruiser had flown them to Baltimore in East America. After visiting the H.L. Mencken Shrine, they'd taken an almost empty hoverbus to the former national capital.

Antigrav technology, a leftover, archaeologically, from some ancient civilization gone for a billion years, had come back from the stars with Mankind's first interstellar exploratory vessel, the *Fifth Force*. The shuttle overhead was lifted by antigrav, but driven by fusion engines that human beings had invented all by themselves. The lower portion of the vessel's hull was reflective because, for a great many years, the dying East American government had taken to using tactical lasers to shoot down aircraft it believed had violated its airspace.

Eventually one of them, a freighter full of frozen buffalo meat from Nebraska bound for L5, had crashed, wiping out the town of Bricktown, New Jersey. Several armed parties of West Americans had infiltrated the laser installations and destroyed them. Now the lower hulls of spaceships were polished, partly as decoration, but partly as a reminder and a warning.

The hologram continued through the noise of the climbing vessel, but it was movement in the corner of her eye that captured Llyra's attention. "Don't look now," she told her family quietly, "but the person in the hoverchair is back."

The apparition was closer now, less than a hundred yards away. The chair was big and bulky, technology at least a century out of date. Despite the temperature and humidity, the figure in it was swathed in a heavy blanket, with a scarf over its head and a muffler around its neck.

Once again, as Morgan and the children turned, the chair lurched abruptly to one side and vanished behind a commemorative stele dedicated to Helen MacClellen Willoughby, sometimes known as the "Fist Lady."

Llyra discreetly checked the weapon she carried under her short jacket, a hypervelocity .11-caliber electric pistol. She'd been one of several hundred victims aboard a hijacked spaceliner when she was younger, half a lifetime later, she was still having nightmares about it, and had solemnly sworn that she would never let herself be disarmed again.

Although she and Morgan strove to live as normal a life as they could, especially for the sake of their children, they were both as famous as any figure skating champions had

ever been, and they were accustomed, and tried to stay prepared for, odd behavior from the public. Llyra had experienced trouble before with innocent but overly enthusiastic
fans, and even genuine stalkers, although learning that she
could handily defend herself and her family usually discouraged them.

"Next on your itinerary," said the hologram, "is the
monument to one of the last Chief Executives of the United
States—although by then, most people called it East
America, President-for-Life Maxwell Promise."

⚓

The Trasks had not lingered long at the Maxwell
Promise Memorial. It was a huge, windowless cube, one
hundred old-time meters on a side, constructed of welded
and riveted metal at least six inches thick. Nobody seemed
to remember anymore what was on the inside. One small
door required a special electronic ID card to open it, and
such cards had not existed for decades. In the open, there
were surveillance cameras every couple of yards around the
perimeter, gutted long ago by tech-devouring nanobots, and
doubtless many hidden cameras and microphones, equally
non-functional.

The sides of the grim, imposing building were scorched
and scored by firebombs and grenades, pocked-marked by
bullets. The holographic guide to Promise's life and time, an
exiled historian who had lived in the Moon, had taken
delight in describing the way the man's lifeless body had
been dragged through the streets by his own bodyguards,
to demonstrate to the public beyond question that he had
finally been deposed.

Gratefully, the family skipped ahead to the monument
dedicated to the best remembered of the American presidents, Thomas Jefferson, whose ideas and ideals had finally
triumphed after nearly three bleak centuries of shrinking
human freedom.

"It could never have happened," opined Jefferson's holographic biographer, one Albert Jay Nock, a man dressed in early twentieth century clothing, "without the other settled worlds to preserve his memory, practice what he preached, and bring it back home to Earth. Jefferson had his predecessors, his friend Thomas Paine certainly influenced him strongly, as did Trenchard and Gordon's *Cato's Letters*, and his successors, but he was the first to tell a king where to get off."

Perhaps she was biased, Llyra thought, but it was a beautiful building, sparkling white, circular in floor plan, with a graceful domed roof supported by columns, and a classic stoa or covered porch. Three short flights of gentle steps led to the entrance. Inside the center of the monument, a bronze statue of the third president stood, there would be no throne in this place, under his own words, inscribed high on the wall above him: "I have sworn upon the altar of god, eternal hostility against every form of tyranny over the mind of men."

A small group of individuals was busy sweeping the floor, cleaning the walls and columns, and gently polishing the coppery brown statue of the author of the Declaration of Independence. "Any of the workers you see around you," explained the holographic biographer, Nock, which had followed them inside, "represent Thomas Jefferson clubs from all over North America, the planet Earth, and even the Solar System, who, since the collapse of the East American government and Park Service, have taken it upon themselves to clean the monument and maintain it in good repair."

"That's kind of nice," said Morgan.

"Unfortunately," added the hologram, "those groups, at least here in North America, seem to be dwindling in number and enthusiasm, and it's feared this monument may eventually begin to decay like all the others here."

A cool breeze blew in from the front of the monument, off a body of water called the Jefferson Basin. Turning to look out over the water, Llyra saw one of the strangest things she'd ever seen. It was the hoverchair person again, and the chair was somehow climbing on mechanical legs, awkwardly and haltingly, up the lowest tier of steps leading toward the monument.

She'd known such a thing was possible, but had never actually seen it before. Among the other Settled Worlds, those seriously injured or ill depended on medical technologies that had often been outlawed on Earth, relying on gravity that was only a fraction of the Earth's to help them recover. On Pallas, sick and healthy people alike commonly used flying belts.

"I'm going to see what this is all about right now," she told her husband, sweeping away the feeling of dread and panic that had arisen within her. He put out a hand and brushed her arm, but didn't try to stop her. Instead, as she descended the top two flights of stairs, he watched her back.

The person in the chair had seen her coming. As soon as the chair reached the landing between the first and second flights, it pivoted around and headed back down toward the basin again. Before Llyra could catch up, a thin scattering of other tourists on the steps looked at her oddly, it had reached the slidewalk and sped away on a cushion of compressed air.

Morgan and the children joined her on the landing.

"I don't know," she told her husband, sitting down on the steps. "Maybe it's just me. But this business is giving me the oddest, unsettled feeling." Something about it kept reminding her of her girlhood ordeal.

"It isn't just you, kiddo. Somebody is definitely following us with what my old psychology professor at Memorial called an approach-avoidance problem. You know we could skip the rest of this, and go back to Baltimore. I'm having a hankering for a big seafood dinner stuffed red snapper, maybe, or broiled lobster. What do you say?"

She shook her head. "It goes against my grain, is what

I say. If we do that, I'll always wonder what it was all about. Wouldn't you, too?"

Sitting down beside her, he laughed. "Other people can have all the psychological problems their little hearts desire, my love. They're absolutely free, and the supply is endless. All I give a damn about is you and these street urchins we seem to have picked up somewhere." He tousled the hair of his son, who looked up at him with trusting eyes, then hugged his older daughter. "I'll be happy just to get them and you, too, away from this pathologically civilized planet."

"Spoken like a true Newfoundlander," Llyra said. He laughed again and began whistling "The Star of Logy Bay", his favorite Newfoundland song.

The truth was that, coming from the tiny town of Curringer on Pallas, she shared his feelings on the subject completely. She'd grown up flying hundreds of miles by herself, over untamed wilderness haunted by dangerous animal predators, just to skate on a frozen pond, and she longed for her children to be able to thrive in an environment like that.

"So what do you say," Morgan asked, "shall we shuffle back to Baltimore?"

"That's 'shuffle off to Buffalo' and not on your life. There's a mystery here of some kind that has to be solved, Morgan, or I'll never feel right about it." She put a hand on his arm. "But I need you to back my play, all right?"

"Uh-oh," Emerson stage-whispered to his sister. "He's sunk." Julia nodded and giggled.

Morgan straightened his back, attempting to regain some dignity. "Unaccustomed as I am to thinking of myself as anybody's sidekick, even yours, darling girl, when have I ever failed to back your play?"

"Very well, let's go on with the tour and see what happens."

Morgan was the first to notice and comment on the fact that the automated slidewalks seemed to be taking them from monument to monument in a pattern that made no sense. Washington's tipsy obelisk was at the opposite end of the Mall from the weed-grown Lincoln Memorial. Promise's scorched metal cube was on the opposite side of Jefferson's gleaming memorial, which was all the way back and around the Basin.

"I'll bet I know why, too," Llyra suggested. "Millions of people used to come here. Some centralized computer system somewhere is running a program originally designed to prevent too many tourists at a time from visiting any one of the memorial sites. Each time we stop somewhere and start again, it takes us to the least-crowded site we haven't seen yet."

Morgan grinned and nodded. "All that, and she's good-looking, too."

"But there's hardly anybody at all here today, Mommy," Emerson protested.

"Yes, dear," she told the eight year old. "But the system isn't quite smart enough to realize that, so it keeps shifting us all over the place as if it were a hundred years ago and there were still thousands of people on the Mall." She looked to her husband. "It's sort of a parable about government in general, isn't it? Govern, and if there's no real governing to do, govern anyway. I'm glad we Pallatians gave it up."

"You gave it up before you had it," he agreed. "And we Newfies headed north to get away from it. Though not before the Canadian federal government raped the outports." It was an old story and a bitter one that began with the seal fishery being outlawed at the behest of a handful of Hollywood stars throwing thousands out of work and nearly ended with a formerly proud, hardworking, outdoor people being jammed into the fetid capital city of St. John's and put on welfare.

Until the northern colony movement began in protest.

Now the family came to the Ronald Reagan Memorial, probably the most photographed object in North America, a hundred-foot titanium statue of a western-style rider on horseback, with the traditional high-heeled, pointed-toed boots and spurs, broad-brimmed hat, bib-front shirt, calf-skin vest, and fringed leather chaps over his jeans.

About the former president's waist in an elaborately tooled belt, he wore a pair of giant single action Colt .44/40 revolvers. There was a colossal Model 1892 Winchester, presumably chambered for the same caliber cartridge, in his saddle scabbard. The alloy used had turned purple over the years or had been that color to begin with; but in a triumph of art and science, both of the horse's front feet were high in the air.

Unfortunately, the monument was covered with bird lime, and there were nests in the cowboy hat, the saddle-bow, and the lariat coiled on the saddle horn. There were the inevitable graffiti, and everything on the statue below eye level looked as if it had been pounded on and dented with sledgehammers.

Llyra wasn't certain what the monument was supposed to signify, and Morgan, who grasped it intuitively, was at a loss to explain it to her verbally. Emerson shouted "It's a *cowboy!*" which seemed enough explanation to him. He loved western movies and was looking forward to having his own horse or some alien equivalent when they reached Paradise.

Julia, with her grandfather's eye for engineering, wanted to know why the horsie didn't fall down.

"Cantilevers," her brother told her smugly.

"Why can't it lever?" she asked.

Emerson peered at her suspiciously. She returned an innocent look, but was not too young, not in this family, anyway, to make atrocious puns.

"What do you know about this guy Reagan?" Llyra asked. Morgan was from what had once been Canada, and might not be expected to know about this man, but all she knew about Earth history herself was that her ancestors had left the planet to avoid seeing any more of it being made.

Morgan said, "I know my granddad used to go on and on about him. He gave people an illusion of liberty, an illusion of progress, an illusion he was getting government off their backs, while all the time it grew larger and freedom shrank. He was proof, to Granddad, that politicians are all evil, no matter what they mean to be. That's why civilizations fall and this place is a ghost town. It reminds me of Palenque, somehow, a deserted Mayan capital I visited when I was a teenager."

"That's pretty harsh, don't you think?" She winked at him.

"Reagan made possible every atrocity that happened afterward. He shifted their war on drugs into high gear and destroyed the Bill of Rights. That's what's harsh, not telling the truth about him. This monument is a joke."

Llyra shook her head. It took a lot to make her husband lose his sense of humor. Then again, his grandfather had been close to him and still was. He had taught Morgan to fish and hunt and survive in the Arctic.

They were about to leave for the next stop, when the figure in the hoverchair appeared from around one end of the Reagan monument, where an outsized hoof had concealed it. This time it bore straight for them. Morgan put all three children behind him and laid a hand on his plasma weapon, while Llyra stood to one side, preparing to set up a crossfire.

The figure raised both its hands; crossing them and waving them, as if to say, "Don't shoot!" Then it reversed itself and disappeared around the horse once more. By the time the Trasks had followed it, it was gone.

Again.

⚓

The Franklin Delano Roosevelt Memorial lay on the opposite side of the Basin inlet from the Jefferson Memorial.

However, instead of a single great structure, it was composed of a series of low outdoor "rooms" full of bronze sculpture and relief carvings, each of which commemorated a distinct phase in Roosevelt's presidency, from the Great Depression through the Second World War, and formed a sort of half-maze along the shore. At one time it was said to have been the most popular of the attractions along the Mall, but it was empty and neglected now.

Weeds grew up between the paving blocks.

Dry waterfalls and fountains gathered leaves that had obviously been there for years, rotting and turning into black soil. Again, graffiti defaced the monument, blotting out the former president's famous sayings that had been inscribed there late in the twentieth century.

"Look, Mommy and Daddy, a doggie!" It was Julia who was excited this time, rushing to the oversized bronze replica of Roosevelt's famous scottie Fala, not noticing the dramatically cloaked president sitting to its left. Llyra thought it didn't look quite as cute once the scale was established. The expression on its face seemed rather menacing.

Roosevelt struck her in much the same way. Whoever had created this memorial had imagined the man as benevolent, but Llyra knew because Morgan had told her that, imitating several of his predecessors, his policies had actually prolonged the economic crisis for twelve years. In the end, to bail his failed administration out, the man had done all he could to precipitate an unnecessary war that had killed sixty million people, worldwide, and left Europe and Japan in ruins.

That was what Morgan said, anyway.

The sculpture here was fascinating, though, she thought. Llyra's mother, a scientist specializing in finding new uses for asteroidal materials, had taken to sculpture recently, using the iron, nickel, cobalt, and other metals so abundant in the Asteroid Belt. The sculptures in this place were of traditional material, but the long line of hungry men waiting to be fed, for example, was beautifully done, and the voluminously caped president looked like a fictional arch-villain.

"*Mommy!*" Julia screamed, pointing back the way they'd come. The five of them were suddenly trapped, hemmed in by the walls of the monument. Julia hid behind the out-sized bronze dog. Emerson wedged himself in behind the president, and Morgan pushed Ardie's pram in with him.

The hoverchair was here again, headed directly for them.

Llyra drew her pistol, noticing that Morgan had drawn his own. The person in the chair seemed to bear an eerie resemblance to the figure of Roosevelt behind her. The chair drew up, almost to Llyra's feet and stopped, without its occupant making anything resembling a threatening gesture.

There was a long silence, then, "Please don't hurt me. I mean you no harm." It was a woman's voice, a weak and quavery one at that. "All I want to do is thank you, and to ask you to forgive me, if you'll be kind enough."

"Forgive you?" Llyra tucked her weapon away, counting on Morgan to protect her if she'd made a mistake. "I don't even know who you are."

The woman reached up slowly and unwrapped the muffler from around her neck. She then uncovered her head and face. "I'm sorry, I just get so cold these days."

Llyra blinked. Somehow the woman looked familiar, but the younger woman couldn't place the older woman's face. "Are you all right?" she asked.

"No, dear, I'm not all right. I'm very old and I'm very ill. But that's actually the reason I wanted to thank you. You'll have to excuse my earlier shyness; this isn't an easy thing to do. But I read that you and your family are going to leave the Solar System, and I called in every favor I had left to track you down here before you go."

"But why?"

"You may not recognize me. We never met. But twelve years ago, when you were just a girl, I was the international director of the Mass Movement."

"Anna Wertham Savage," Morgan supplied. He holstered his weapon and stood beside his wife, putting his arm around her. "You people claimed that importing raw materials, agricultural products, and manufactured goods from the Moon and the asteroids would change the mass, and therefore the motion of the Earth's crust, relative to the core, causing slippage and buckling that would destroy civilization and maybe all life on the planet."

Llyra remembered hearing about this woman. It had been a violent splinter of the Mass Movement, Null Delta Emm, that had hijacked the liner. Several people had died on both sides. And now she wanted to apologize?

"I didn't approve what was done to you, Miss Ngu—Mrs. Trask; they went ahead and did it without my approval. They're all dead now, and there is no more Mass Movement. I saw to that. Later, I acquired the disease I suffer from, a very old-fashioned one that can be cured in a few hours most places in the System. But not in the former Commonwealth of Massachusetts, and not in the city of Amherst, where I have lived most of my life. I was just supposed to be quiet and die, slowly and painfully because some people and I used to be one of them; loathe technology and loathe themselves, and all human life, even more."

"What does all this have to do with me?"

"You showed me the way, don't you see? You went from one twentieth of the Earth's gravity to become a champion here. You survived a crime that nobody was supposed to live through, and helped turn the tables on the criminals. Now you and your family are going to the stars. If you can do that, I can go to the Moon where even as sick as I am, I can walk again, and where they will cure what's wrong with me and give me a new life."

Llyra stepped forward and knelt beside the woman's chair. "And you went to all this trouble . . ."

"Because I had to. Because I wouldn't feel right until I did. They say that everybody has at least one great leap in them. This is mine. I may never do anything adventurous or daring again, but at least I will have done this."

Llyra shook her head. "I don't know what to say."

"I do," Julia chirped. "Say, 'You're welcome.'"

INTRODUCTION TO THE EMPIRE OF THE WILLING
Ernest Lilley

Australian author Sean McMullen fulfilled my desire to go to the far ends of the earth for perspectives, and even a bit beyond, as the story he came up with was the second alien story that I let in. But Australians are aliens too, right? So why should I be so picky about what planet a character is from? I've been a fan of Sean's since first reading his *The Centurion's Empire,* and that admiration was increased when he produced the remarkable post-apocalypse series that begins with *Eyes of the Calculor.*

I think there are some interesting ideas in here, echoed again later in James Alan Gardner's story "Shopping at the Mall" and I'm really glad I looked for extra-American viewpoints. Oddly enough, they're less cranky than the homegrown variety. Maybe they're just being good guests.

THE EMPIRE OF THE WILLING

SEAN MCMULLEN

I was focussed into the mind of an Australian businessman as he landed in Washington. We had determined that there was something strangely invisible about being an Australian traveller in America. Australians have never done anything to unduly antagonize the Americans, and being foreign they get away with being unfamiliar with Washington. Why did I not notice the signs of danger? Quite simply, there were none. No other space faring power had taken over Earth, and there were no signs that anyone had ever tried—although the Terrans had alien conspiracy theories that were so ludicrous as to be funny.

Washington is the capital of the United States, the greatest power ever to dominate the planet Earth, so naturally it was scheduled to be conquered first. I booked into a five star hotel, but dressed in casual clothes before I set out to begin my survey. I had to look like a tourist because, incredibly, the city which is the seat of government of this nation is heavily dependent on tourism. People actually enjoy looking at the buildings from which they are governed. Even more strangely, they are encouraged to do so by their rulers. This was seen as a fundamental vulnerability in the Terran species. Notice that I say was, rather than is, but I am getting ahead of myself. The hotel staff booked me into a tour without so much as asking for authorization from even a minor official. It was to cover the White House and the Capitol, the twin centers of American government.

From media broadcasts we knew that the White House is the headquarters of the government for the nation, and it is where the president governs. Congress also governs the nation. When I first learned that the nation had two governments, I thought it was a bizarre joke. The Congress meets in the Capitol Building, but its members do not live there—unlike the president, who lives in the White House. Sometimes. As far as I can tell, the function of Congress is to antagonize the president. Congress is composed of two groups, the Senate and the House of Representatives. The Senate is less representative than the House of Representatives. This appears to be because the Senate is composed of two members from each state, and the states are not uniform in population. The members of both bodies pass laws and spend the money of the people who vote for them.

I still cannot distinguish between the two factions that dominate Washington, the Republicans and the Democrats. The Democrats believe in republics, and the Republicans believe in democracy. More or less. They are called parties. The president can be from either of the parties. Generally. Either party can dominate Congress, but even when the same party dominates Congress as the president comes from, it does not always support him. Somehow this unstable and convoluted arrangement works. Mostly.

Trying to understand Washington is a somewhat thankless and depressing task. I must admit that I gave up my own attempts after two days, and ordered that our mindfarers should be sent in as soon as I had prepared the way for them. The mindfarers would embed in the minds of all members of the government, learning their secrets and procedures, and sending data back to our computers so that a governance model could be built. The Washington system is so complex that no one person can understand it without the aid of a hyper-associative computer. The Terrans, of course, do not have hyper-associative computers, so no Terran can understand how Washington functions. Members of any other species would be very nervous about such a state of affairs, but American Terrans do not seem to mind.

There are seventeen minor parties in Washington. The smallest party is the Happy Birthday Party, which has one member. When scanned, his mind was preoccupied with introducing a bill legislating for free beer for the Happy Birthday Party. He did not believe that there was any chance that the legislation would be passed, but introduced it every few months in order to justify his allowance as a member of Congress. The largest minor party is the Liberal Family Party, which favours repressive laws to protect traditional family values. I have not been able to determine the nature of traditional family values even using mind scans. A scan of five party members revealed that two of them were embezzling party funds, two were having extra-marital affairs, and the fifth wanted to have an extra-marital affair if only he could find someone interested in him who was unlikely to reveal the story to investigative journalists. Affairs are recreational reproductive activities between Terrans that they prefer other Terrans do not find out about.

On the positive side, within a week I had obtained the mind signatures of two hundred and ten of the members of Congress, and I knew that getting the signatures of those remaining would be easy. The president met a delegation of congressmen on my ninth night in Washington, so I acquired his mind signature easily. By the end of my second month I was able to report that our mindfarers had established themselves in key minds throughout the whole of Washington's administration. There they waited, trying to learn enough about Washington to take control.

❦

Why did we not just take over? After all, we had the president, the vice-president, his cabinet, and the whole of Congress. All I can say is that I was nervous about not understanding the system. We had to learn more about the dynamics and workings of the government before assuming control of it, so the mindfarers remained passive while let-ting their hosts go about their business. Their observations poured into our operations center, gradually building a computer model through which we could assume control of the US, because although the Americans could run Washington without computer assistance, *we* certainly could not. The sheer volume of matters involving decisions, patronage, factions, public perceptions, and private reali-ties made me wonder how this primitive world's leaders were able to cope at all.

We were staggered to discover that five thousand four hundred and forty variables were required to run the Washington computer model. Why, we all asked, were there so many? After all, the figure was two orders of magnitude above the governance standard on other civilized worlds. Much of this complexity seemed to come from the phenom-enon of lobbies. Once elected, one would expect that a politician would be left alone to govern, but not in Washington. The Terrans have developed an art form out of exerting influence without having real power or authority. Many of the decisions about laws and spending are deter-mined by people who have not been elected, or by a minor-ity party holding a balance of power.

Other lobbyists use protest marches. These are gener-ally groups of twenty or thirty individuals that are repre-sented as groups of two or three thousand by sympathetic media networks, or as two or three by networks that are less so. Media managers vary considerably in their political orientation, which is partly influenced by those who own their media company, those who pay bribes, those in a position to accept bribes, those who know which Terrans in the company are engaged in secretive recreational repro-ductive activities (often with members of lobby groups), whether the sponsors of the media company support the lobby group, and whether the news item will affect the number of people watching the media broadcasts—the last-named factor known as "the ratings."

There are also email campaigns, where people organize groups of like-minded people to send messages via computer networks to specific congressmen and women in order to influence their decisions. Some of these people are not like-minded, however, they just lobby in return for a commission. These lobbyists are controlled by lobbyist businesses. Senators and House members are lobbied by voters, by groups of voters, by organizations representing groups of voters, by organizations pretending to represent groups of voters, by organizations supposedly with the best interests of voters at heart but with no links to the voters, by organizations representing shareholders—some of which are sometimes voters and by organizations interested in making money by persuading the politician to do something illegal in return for a bribe. The politicians, in turn, spend their time trying to persuade all of the foregoing people and organizations that they are doing what they are being lobbied to do, while they actually follow the party's hidden agenda which is determined by a few individuals, who are in turn lobbied by all the foregoing individuals and organizations.

The president and congressmen—and women—also lobby organizations to let them appear on media shows in order to lobby the very people who are lobbying them in the first place. You can see why I dared not let the mindfarers try to take over. Who is running the place? This was not merely my question, but the question in many Terran minds that I scanned—most of whom were meant to be running the country. Some think it is the president, others think it is all elected officials, some suspect it is bureaucrats, some think it is alien spies (as if!), while a few even think it is the people by means of their elected representatives. Actually, nobody has much of a clue about how Washington governs, but everyone has a vague concept of it, although none of those vague concepts even comes close to reality.

Elections in general and voting in particular were no less confusing as we struggled to understand what we were to take over. Candidates do not try to convince voters that they have their concerns and interests at heart, they instead tell them what they *should* be concerned about. Worse, because most of any major party's voter base is unswervingly loyal, the candidates spend most of their time courting undecided voters, having already told their loyal supporters what they ought to be concerned about as loyal party members. This all means that party policy is determined by small groups of voters whose opinions are not those of the major parties. I must confess that at the end of my second month in Washington I was close to concluding that the system was beyond comprehension and totally out of control. Although people called "the founding fathers" were supposed to have designed the system, the system does not appear to have been designed by anyone. It more or less evolved from the original model without any discernable plan or agenda.

⁂

I was on a bench, eating my lunch on the broad strip of parkland downhill from the Capitol Building when I noticed that a man was watching me. He was badly groomed, scruffily dressed, and drinking spirits from a bottle concealed in a paper bag. I reached out and gave his mind a minor push, to make him lose interest in me. To my astonishment, he snared my influence, drew his own control tendrils along it, and locked me into a state of catatonia. He was a combatant, not a diplomat. He could have killed me then and there.

"You are Labarrvien-18-I of the Administral," he said aloud, smiling. "It's a pleasure to meet you."

Whoever he was, he knew! There was another force abroad on this world.

"I'm from the Oligarron," he continued. "Been here nine years. Got a garbage skip behind the Smithsonian. People avoid the thing because I maintain a neural push. Being a mindlord I can do that. Come over some time, we can talk over beans and EU vodka."

He got up and sauntered off into the lunchtime crowds. My release was abrupt and traumatic when it came, and I flopped back on the bench, gasping with relief and shock. Those around me stared, then tried to seem uninvolved. For some minutes I remained on the bench, thinking through what had happened, and what I had been told. A mindlord of the Oligarron, here! The thought was alarming in the extreme. True, he had caught me off-guard, yet even had I been ready I could never have resisted his grip. Nine years, he had said. The Oligarron had more than twice the number of client worlds than the Administral, in fact it was seen as a great coup when we had focussed out mindfarers into Earth. The world was deep within the Oligarron's fiefs, and the area was heavily shielded. We had assumed that there was some world of great significance in the region, and that it was Earth. A mindlord living in a garbage skip. The very thought had me reeling. No mindlord that I had ever met had lived on an estate smaller than Washington itself. They were powerful beyond comprehension, and so wealthy as to defy belief.

I was still living in a five star hotel. The staff knew me, and I was known to be seen with senators and members of the House. People actually lobbied me, and I was earning a modest income by influencing the politicians. The hotel staff were paid by spotters to check which guests were picked up by which limos, and from a limo database they determined who was being entertained by who. This information was then sold to lobbyists who stayed in the hotel, who then lobbied people like me. These people then rated us according to our effectiveness, which was in my case, very high. This information was in turn sold to lobby brokers, who set up meetings between people like me and people with both money and a need for influence.

The whole lobbyist exercise had been very profitable for me on several levels, and foremost was the training in the workings of Washington's decision making processes. Now there was a mindlord on the scene. He had probably been monitoring me from the day I arrived. Certainly he could have broken my mind with very little trouble, and nobody would ever have known, yet all he had done was invite me to his garbage skip behind the Smithsonian.

⚜

I spent three very distracted days, completely at a loss about what to do. Within a mile or so of my hotel room was a mindlord living in a garbage skip. The thought was beyond all credibility, and at first I could not really accept it. Resolving that our first encounter was somehow a trick, I threw out a mind-cast, compelling several dozen police to converge on the Smithsonian's loading bays to check a suspicious character living in a garbage skip. Members of the National Guard met the police and quite an impressive shootout ensued. Both sides were convinced that the others were terrorists wearing stolen uniforms. In the aftermath, everyone seemed inclined to overlook the man living in an overturned garbage skip. After this, I needed no more convincing. He was indeed a mindlord.

The matter of what to do came next. I spent several days trying to think of how to eliminate the threat. My conclusion was always that the mindlord could not be beaten. Finally a lateral alternative came to me. Any mindlord who meant me harm could have had me dead by now. Thus the fact that I was still alive obviously meant something.

I set off for the Smithsonian. Finding the skip was no easy task. The mindlord had pushed it out of people's minds, so I had to secure two guards to escort me as I did a manual search of secure areas. The skip was lying on its front, the lid tied up to a nearby wall with discarded cables and baling wire. Beneath this awning was the mindlord's throne, which was a packing case upholstered with polystyrene form-fit packing. He was cooking something in a pot. Two mangy cats lounged nearby.

"Labarrvien-18-I!" he called cheerily as I approached. "I was wondering when you would call by. Send your guards away and pull up a box."

"They were only with me to keep humans from asking questions," I explained as the guards walked off, now blind to us.

"Quite so, I don't like humans either. Cats, on the other hand, are much better. These two are Dido and Anaes, they adopted me."

"Er, I don't follow."

"I was reading Virgil when they arrived, so I called them Dido and . . ."

"No, er, I mean . . . I'm not sure."

"You mean why did they adopt me. Cats can see into your soul. These two strays accepted me for what I am. Nobody has ever done that. I am only wanted for my influence, or power, or wealth, or connections, or even recommendations. Dido brought me a mouse this morning. When I looked into her mind, I saw that she was merely concerned for me because I was looking thin. Such a selfless act, I was moved to tears. I'm cooking it up with a can of beans."

"You're going to eat it?"

"Why yes. You can hurt a cat's feelings if you waste a good mouse."

I resisted the urge to vomit. This was a member of the Oligarron's inner advisarium, a noble who determined the destiny of a thousand or more worlds.

"So, ah, may I ask why you are here?" I continued tentatively.

"Oh, Dido and Anaes need looking after."

"You live in a garbage skip in Washington to look after two cats?"

"Well, that may be an exaggeration. They are my friends, I just like to be with them."

"Look, about my mindfarers . . ."

"Silly people, cats are much better company."

"There were no other mindfarers active on this world when I did my survey."

"True."

"But you were here first."

"Also true."

"But you have been here nine years. This world could have been proclaimed as your Oligarron's fiefdom."

"Very silly idea."

"My lord, I do not understand."

"You will, eventually."

"I suppose you want us out of the minds of the Terran politicians."

"Personally, I would not be seen dead in a Terran politician's mind, but there's no accounting for taste."

"So you do not mind if we gather in this world?"

"No, oh, would you like a kitten? His name is Petronius."

I was handed a small, rather greasy ball of greyish fur. One does not decline a present from a mindlord, so I accepted the little animal and put it in my coat pocket.

⚜

Back in my hotel suite I scanned the kitten's mind for spy-riders, then took it to a veterinarian's clinic where it was treated for worms, fleas, tics, mange, and various dietary deficiencies before being given a bath and having its teeth cleaned. I returned to the hotel, where a minor suggestion within the kitten's mind taught it to urinate over the shower's drain hole. Leaving him with a bowl of water and a saucer of Kitty Delights, I cast my mind out to the Administral's nearest fiefdom for status reports.

All was quite tranquil beyond Earth. Nobody else had been aware of the mindlord. I checked with the Administral's secure link. There were no problems at all with the Oligarron's forces. I learned that the local govenance directant had organized several peers to lobby the Allocator

General for twice as many mindfarers, which—he said—would make the conquest of Earth even faster. I failed to see how two mindfarers per politician could help matters, but nobody took my advice on that matter. I returned to my host's mind, made sure that Petronius was safely asleep on the spare pillow, then fell asleep myself.

The following morning I attended to a number of lobbying commissions, then met with some senators. The mindfarers riding each of them reported odd behaviour among their longer serving colleagues. Some mindfarers were actually considering resigning. Three or four had already done so. No mindfarer had *ever* resigned during a campaign. I returned to the hotel too distraught to think, then spent an hour watching America's Funniest Bungled Holdups while drinking beer. It had a strangely tranquillizing effect on my mind.

Within three days, another nine mindfarers had resigned, abandoning Washington and its politicians. By now I suspected that I knew the cause. Taking Petronius in my pocket, I returned to the mindlord.

"How do they do it?" I asked as we sat watching my kitten showing off his newly clean fur to Dido and Anaes.

"Who and what?" asked the mindfarer, who had closed down his higher senses for reasons best known to himself.

"How do the Terrans force us to leave their politicians and return home? That's what happened to your people, was it not? You came, you conquered, then your mindfarers started to drift away."

"Yes. Sort of."

"But what do the Terrans do to us? I checked with those mindfarers who returned home. None were damaged or traumatized. Most had even more drive than ever before."

"Just as happened with us."

"So what did you do?"

"I found this skip, then I furnished it. The cats moved in later."

"But why did you stay here?"

"Because there was nowhere to go. Have you noticed that a packing case upholstered with polystyrene is remarkably comfortable as a chair? Even the best of hotels do not have chairs that treat you as kindly as mine do."

⁂

It was no surprise that mindfarer resignations continued over the following days, but there were always new mindfarers to take over. Leaving my host asleep, I returned to a reference databank and did some extensive research. This sector of space had once been the preserve of the Beauricians, but fifteen years ago the Oligarron's people had began to assert dominance here. The Beauricians fell back, and for a time it seemed likely that they would become a client protectorate of the Oligarron, but then the Oligarron seemed to loose direction. That had been eight years ago. The dispute had exhausted both sides, however, so that our Administral was now able to encroach on the disputed zones.

Earth had been claimed by both the Beauricians and the Oligarrons, yet had not been conquered. There was something about Earth . . . and then I had it! At least I had a fairly firm theory, anyway. I composed a formal formulation, had my staff draw up a computer model, ran it with the test data, then sent the results to the Administral with just an executive summary. I had learned that technique from Washington lobbyists. Nobody ever reads a full report, so the less you submit, the more liable people are to read it. Within an hour I was rewarded by contact with the Administral himself.

"You are saying that this Earth government, this Washington, is a system that repels invasion by its very nature?"

"The model indicates that, your lordship," I replied.

"But this is very significant. Why, a system such as this could proof all of my worlds against invasion with no need for costly battle fleets and border patrols. Why did the Beauricians and Oligarrons miss it?"

"I cannot say."

"I notice that both systems went into decline within a year after attempting to invade Earth. Explain this."

"I believe that they were so traumatized at not being able to take over a small, insignificant world like Earth, that it caused internal instability. It is like the bite of a poisonous insect. The initial bite's pain makes you withdraw, but the poison causes you distress long after the actual bite."

"Really? So what is your recommendation to counter this?"

The Administral had actually asked for my recommendation! This meant that I was being considered an advisor! I had, of course, anticipated this, and had thought out a course that was both inspired and feasible.

"My feeling is that they *persisted* with trying to invade Earth. What they *should* have done was change their approach to passive observation."

"But that is what we are doing now, yet our mindfarers are still being repelled."

"True, but with every mindfarer who spends time in Washington, we gain more data for our models. Even better, we get no sense of defeat, because we *know* that we are reverse engineering one of the most powerful yet simple defensive weapons ever devised."

There was a pause while the Administral considered my proposal. When he came back, his tone was strange, almost conspiratorial.

"Your logic cannot be faulted," he announced. "The study of Washington will be intensified, and there will be no attempt at takeover for now. With yourself, as a member of my inner chamber of advisors, an estate and palace will be allocated to you on the world of Marvielle."

"Administral, your generosity both overwhelms me and does me honour. However, I do have a request to make of you."

"A request?" he exclaimed, the beginnings of affront already in his tone. "Speak."

"Of all those to spend time in Washington, only I have shown no tendency to want to leave. I believe this might be worthy of study."

"Ah, true, yes!" he responded, all at once friendly again. "But why?"

"I alone do not ride in the mind of a politician."

"Ah yes. Yes! Return, then, study this clue as much as you will."

My host opened his eyes in the hotel suite. I reached out and picked up Petronius.

"I went to sleep a mere minion, and I have awoken as one of the most powerful advisors in the galaxy," I announced to the kitten. "What about celebrating with breakfast?"

Petronius sat on the table eating bacon pieces from a bowel while I had coffee and cereal. Casting my mind out to the registers, I noted that new mindfarers were already pouring into the minds of Washington's politicians and officials to fill the vacancies. I had deduced Washington's secret. All that I had to do now was work out that secret's mechanism. With Petronius in my pocket, I set out for the Smithsonian yet again.

"Where is he?" I asked as the mindlord waved languidly to me from the shelter of his skip's lid.

"She, actually. Come along."

A seven minute walk brought us to Valentina's Original Hamburgers, a rather scruffy place with laminex tabletops and uncomfortable metal chairs. It was jammed solid with customers, and a queue extended half a block down the street outside. I was not surprised when the mindlord was given preferential treatment by Valentina, who left her rather harassed staff of seven to attend the other customers.

"Labarrvien-18-I, I've been watching you, you're a good

boy," she declared before I could open my mouth. "Burger with the lot, cheeseburger, and mince for Petronius, Lyndy. Two black coffees, one cappuccino, and a saucer of milk."

"How did you know . . ." I began.

"Come *on*, mister, we're all professionals here. Emel, is he really as good as you say?"

"He got closer than we did, Val."

"Hey, but he had our examples to work from. Come *on*, Labar, just kidding. Through here, into my office."

Two hamburgers and three coffees, probably ordered by customers in the queue, arrived before I had even managed to sit down. War Mistress Vale N'10 of the Beauricians made sure that Petronius was settled on her desk with his saucers of full milk and hamburger meat before turning her attention back to me.

"Nice cat," she said, sitting back in her chair. "You know, I always say that you can tell nearly everything about a person from their cat."

"But if they don't have a cat?" I asked.

"Then they're not people. How is the burger?"

"Better than the meals in my hotel," I said without exaggeration.

"All organic, you know? What goes in has no steroids, hormones, antibiotics, GM, insecticides, nothing. No hydroponics, either, and the eggs are free range."

"The taste says it all," said the mindlord, his mouth full.

"So, you made the Administral's Governance Chamber, congratulations!" said Valentina, reaching out and slapping my shoulder.

This time I did not even bother to show shock that she knew what should have been one of the most closely guarded secrets across a hundred thousand worlds.

"Thank you," I muttered.

"Got any plans?"

"Plans?" I echoed suspiciously.

"You know, where to settle. Emel has his garbage skip, I've got the burger bar, so what's it to be for you?"

"Well, I thought I might keep up being a lobbyist."

"Not bad, but I think you'll get bored with that before long. Tell you what, here's my card. Next time you find yourself short on comedy after eleven some night, give me a call and we'll do the bars."

<hr />

And that was all the information I obtained from War Mistress Vale N'10 of the Beauricians. I spent five weeks of futile liaison and surveillance as the Administral's mindfarers came and went, before deciding to accept Valentina's offer one Saturday night. Three hours and five very peculiar bars later, I found myself stark naked and flat on my back in her apartment above the burger bar while she introduced me to recreational reproductive activities, Terran-style.

I awoke at seven, with Valentina sprawled half over me. Petronius was asleep on a pile of her discarded clothing.

"You awake?" the Beaurician asked.

"Er, yes."

"That was fun, we've got to do it again."

"Um, why not?"

"That Emel, he's too laid back to be fun. Just likes to sit on his butt and watch life cruise past."

"I'd noticed."

"And you, Labar, have you worked it out yet?"

I thought for a moment, then concluded that there was no point in pretending to be evasive or stupid.

"Er, no."

"I'll give you a clue. What happens to your mindfarers when they leave Washington?"

"Nothing. I did think of that. All have successfully returned to our system, and are very productive and loyal servants of the Administral. Those that I questioned said that it was not so much that they wanted to leave Washington, so much as a need to return and use new ideas they had learned."

"Precisely. When I realised that *my* people were doing that, I actually ordered the Beaurician battle fleet to come straight here and slag this planet down to the mantle. Then I remembered that Lilith was here, and that I had to get her to safety first."

"Lilith?"

"My tabby cat."

"Of course, how silly of me."

"Anyway, I'd had a chance to cool down by then, and I realised that it was too late for we Beauricians. On the other hand, were the Oligarrons to discover this world, they would go straight to the capital of the greatest power."

"Washington."

"Guess what would happen there?"

"I am trying to do just that."

"The same as happened to us."

"Which is?"

"The same as is happening to you."

———

In return for a promise to call around after eleven on the following Saturday, I got a shower, a coffee, and a hamburger with the lot and a saucer of milk for Petronius. With the young cat asleep in my coat pocket, I wandered the streets, deep in thought but short on conclusions. Something about Washington had caused two superpowers to . . . change. On the other hand, they were both still functional. I checked what records were available through official channels. There was nothing but the usual propaganda.

On a whim, I phoned Valentina.

"I don't suppose you could give me a couple of powerful Beaurician names and a scandal that they'd rather people did not find out about?" I asked.

"I can, but it will cost you."

"And what will the cost be?"

Half an hour later I was in Valentina's office. In return for providing her with a size 14 black g-string edged with red lace and with "I DID IT UNDERCOVER IN WASHING-TON" embroidered on the crotch in small letters, I was told three Beaurician names and the details of a rather nasty scandal involving the supply of Oligarronese warp drive engines for the Beaurician battle fleet with 'FABRICATED BY BEAURICIAN AUTOMATA' stamped on them.

Armed thus, I gained access to the Beaurician information system and spent a week exploring the enemy's data vaults. I then compared the information to what I had access to in the Administral's domain. When I finally finished, I contacted the Administral and delivered a report flagged with the highest priority that I was authorized to issue. The Administral got back to me promptly enough, but I was merely thanked for my diligence and told not to worry.

This caused me to give up completely!

I purchased a bottle of EU vodka, sat on the edge of a gutter, and drank about half of the contents. I then went over to Valentina's burger bar, where she helped me drink the rest of the bottle. We proceeded to the mindlord's garbage skip, picking up another bottle of vodka on the way.

"Well now, judging from your condition, you worked it out," said the mindlord genially, removing Dido and Anaes from his spare chairs. Valentina and I sat down.

"I told the Administral, and he actually said it was a good thing!" I exclaimed as Valentina handed the new bottle to the mindlord.

"You sound surprised," he replied.

"He said that Washington's style of government was a perfect way to pacify client worlds. They spend so much time floundering about with lobbying through the convoluted established channels that nobody ever manages to get a proper conspiracy going."

"Where have I heard that before?" laughed Valentina.

"He also said that it was a great way to give factions within his own government an illusion of power while tying them in knots."

"And it will," said the mindlord.

"He thinks he can control it," I sighed.

"They all think that," said Valentina.

"And here was I thinking that Washington was somehow repelling mindfarers. All the while they were falling over themselves to get back into our own worlds to apply the Terrans' political convolutions to enhance their own careers and fortunes. Government by incomprehensibility and self-interest is spreading across the galaxy."

"In some other Terran nations they do it even better than the Americans," said Emel.

"It's the end of civilization as we know it!" I moaned. "The Administral's entire government has been screwed by a nation whose GDP is less than his entertainment budget."

"Speaking of being screwed, are you coming back to my place?" asked Valentina.

"You dirty little boy," laughed the mindlord.

Over the following week I moved out of the five star hotel and into the apartment above Valentina's burger bar. So many important and influential people patronized the place that my lobbying business actually flourished.

It was a year later that the mindlord, Valentina, and myself were sitting on that park bench downhill from the Capitol Building. The spring weather was unseasonably warm, and there were more tourists about than usual. The mindlord had his EU vodka, Valentina had a takeaway coffee, and I was finishing a hamburger with the lot.

"The Rim Stars' Communedium managed to focus a pathfinder into Washington last night," the mindlord announced.

"Was it a mindfarer?" asked Valentina.

"Empathian," replied the mindlord.

"Should be good for a laugh," I said, settling back with my head on Valentina's lap as yet another galactic super-power began to slide into the empire that Washington did not know that it owned.

INTRODUCTION TO HAIL TO THE CHIEF
Ernest Lilley

Allen's done some terrific work envisioning the future, or the present from the past, in novels like *Tranquility Alternative* and his current *Coyote* series. He badly bent one of the constraints I had set up for the anthology . . . no blowing up the city. The story does a terrific job of expressing how technocratic/SF types really feel about being governed by politicians, with the wry and deadly humor that marks much of Steele's short work.

HAIL TO THE CHIEF

ALLEN M. STEELE

It's a spring morning sometime in the 26th century–no one can know the date for certain; the last calendar has long since dissolved into the muck left behind when the glaciers finally receded–and the President of the United States wakes up in what's left of the Oval Office.

Sunlight streams in through battered windows that lost their glass many years ago, causing him to snort and scratch at the fleas that crawled upon him from the pile of animal skins he uses as a bed. Rolling over, he opens his eyes to cast a bleary gaze at the sun. He's tempted to go back to sleep, but his stomach is growling, and besides, there's affairs of state which must attended.

So he staggers to his feet and lurches out on the balcony. Beyond the swamp that overruns what used to be the South Lawn, a lonesome eagle screeches as it circles the broken stump of the Washington Monument. Yawning, he lifts his loincloth and urinates on the wild roses beneath the balcony. Nothing like that first piss of the day to make a man feel like the commander in chief.

Having taken care of personal business, the President wanders back inside. The First Lady is still asleep, curled up within her own pile of skins next to the smoldering remains of last night's fire. "Geddupbich," he mutters, kicking her in the side. "Gogeddus sumfoo'."

"Fugyu. Lemmelone." She tries to retreat further beneath the squirrel hides, but then he kicks her again.

"Awright awright," she protests, squinting up at him. "Igetcha brek'fus."

"Damstrait. Move y'rass." He watches as she crawls out beneath the covers, and wonders if it's time to find another mate. Although she's barely fifteen years old, she's already given him two children–the first stillborn, the other severely retarded; he doesn't know it, but she's his half-sister, since they shared the same father but not the same mother –and she's no longer quite as attractive as she was when he captured her during a raid upon the Dems. Still, he considers as she shuffles out onto the balcony, she has all her fingers and toes, and not too many scabs. That counts for something.

While the First Lady answers her morning mail, the President walks across the moth-eaten rug that once bore the emblem of his office to a termite-ridden desk. Within a drawer are his totems of power. A bone knife, nine inches long and honed to a razor-sharp edge. A necktie—dark blue with red stripes, handmade countless years ago in Italy, now threadbare and bloodstained—which he carefully wraps around his head. And finally, the most holy of holies: a small enamel lapel pin, bearing the faded likeness of an American flag, that he kisses with chapped lips before affixing to his rabbit-skin vest. From beside the desk, he takes his spear, a steel rod with hide wrapped on one end, which an archeologist might have identified as having once belonged to the landing gear of the Apollo 11 lunar lander formerly displayed in the National Air and Space Museum.

The President came to possess these items the old-fashioned way. When he was twenty years old, he challenged the previous President to an election. The incumbent was a Dem, an old man of thirty-five, limbs weakened by scurvy and nearly blind in the left eye, yet nonetheless as dangerous as the alligators that lurk within the shallows of the Potomac. Yet his opponent had a very strong platform, consisting of a wooden club studded with rusty nails. The debate was held in the Mall, with both Dems and Pubs watching from either side; when the old man went down, his challenger allowed him the chance to deliver his closing remarks. They didn't last long, because by then the President was vomiting blood; the challenger offered rebuttal by cutting his throat, then carving open his chest, tearing out his heart, and devouring it within full view of the electorate. Following this, his party massacred the Dems, sending the survivors fleeing for the sanctity of Capitol Hill. A recount wasn't necessary.

Suitably attired, the President takes a moment to regard the faded and water stained portrait hanging lopsided upon the wall. An old, old man, with hair whiter than anyone he'd ever known, wearing dark clothes that looked frail and yet warm. Every morning since he'd won the right to sleep in this place, he'd wondered who this person was. Another President, no doubt, but how had he come here? Had he eaten his enemy's heart . . .?

From somewhere nearby came a faint feminine cry. The First Lady, her voice raised in either pain or delight. "Dammitbich!" The President storms out of the Oval Office, marches down a corridor of the West Wing. "Wachadoindere?"

He finds her in a nearby room, doubled over a broken couch. The Vice-President has mounted her from behind, his hairy butt trembling as he thrusts himself against her thighs. The President watches for a moment, annoyed by this breach of protocol, before he pulls the knife from his scabbard and, darting forward, shoves the blade deep within the other man's back. The Vice-President screams; blood gushes from his wound as he falls forward, pinning the First Lady against the couch. She's still whimpering as the President hauls him away from her. "Tolja t'get sumfoo'!" he snaps. "Nawdooit!"

She scampers away before he can strike her. The Vice-President flails helplessly upon the floor, a crimson froth around his mouth. The President kneels beside him, yanks his hair back to expose his throat. "Yerfired," he mutters. Then he accepts his resignation.

The rest of the White House staff is awake by then, the various aides and secretaries emerging from the offices and meeting rooms to cautiously peer around the door and through holes in the wall as the President takes what he wants from the Vice-President's corpse. No one looks at him until he's gone, then they fall upon the body, quarreling among one another for rights to his belongings.

The President doesn't care. He'd never liked the Veep anyway. Lack of party loyalty.

Breakfast is a rat, skinned and gutted, roasted on skewer and served medium-rare. Fine cuisine, although the President would have preferred squirrel this morning. He takes his morning repast in the Cabinet Room, surrounded by his senior staff picking through the leftovers of last night's state dinner. Barbequed opossum is pretty good, once you get past the rather oily aftertaste, and the maggots are sort of an appetizer. Mosquitoes and flies purr around them as they eat, and everyone laughs when the Secretary of Transportation breaks a rotted tooth upon a piece of bone.

A hollow, chopping sound from the room where he killed the Vice-President reminds the President of urgent business. The aides and secretaries will make the best of Veep's sudden departure, but cabinet-level officials deserve better compensation for their loyalty.

"Gottagetmofoo'," he growls, tossing ahead the rat skull from which he has just sucked the brains. "Gottafinsum." He glances at the Secretary of the Interior. "Yewno?"

The Secretary of the Interior considers this question for a moment. "Gatahyeggs reelgood, Prez. Gadowntodarivah, luk'roun, fin'sum. . ."

"Fugdat." This from the Secretary of Labor. "Gators hide

dernestsbedder." He spits out a piece of gristle, shakes his head. "Bil'mo bowts, go gatahhuntin' . . ."

"Nahway." The Secretary of Homeland Security farts luxuriously as he leans back against the wall. "Gatahs tacbowts, sink'um. Loosalottaguys . . ."

"Fuggum." Yet the President gets the drift of what he's saying. They can't continue to send people out on the river to hunt alligator; the Pubs don't have adequate craft for such an excursion, and the attrition factor is unacceptably high. As a result, quite a few tribesmen have crossed over to join the Dems, if only because they promise more food with less risk. "Goddanudda ideyah?"

"Hidoo, Prez." The Secretary of Defense idly pulls some lice from his beard. "Tacdahill."

Everyone stares at him in astonishment. "Yewgodda-beshiddinme," the Secretary of State mutters. "Dahill?"

"Sho'. Wynod?"

"Buddeygod . . ."

All at once, a loud *boom* from somewhere above: an airborne blast that shakes the decrepit building. Startled, everyone cringes, covering their heads as pieces of decayed plaster fall from the ceiling.

"Whaddahellizzat!" the Secretary of Defense yells.

"Cheezuz." The President gazes up at the ceiling, his eyes wide with amazement, "Datwas Cheezuz!"

"Datwazzunt Cheezuz." The Secretary of State scowls, shakes his head. "Datwasjusda boomboomding `gan."

The other cabinet members murmur in agreement. From time to time, they've heard these mysterious noises. They aren't caused by thunderstorms, because the weather has almost been calm when they've occurred, yet they've seen the strange white trails moving across the sky, led by tiny silver dots.

"No! Nonono!" The President is on his feet. "Boomboom-ding asine f'm Cheezuz!" He looks down at the others. "Wewuz talkinbout tacing Dems, an'den Cheezuz giffus asine . . .!"

"Datwuzzen. . ."

In three swift steps, the President is across the room. Grabbing the Secretary of State by his hair, he yanks his head back. Before the cabinet member can react, he feels the razor-sharp blade of the President's knife at his throat.

"Datwuz Cheezuz," the President hisses, his angry eyes boring into his own. "Sayidain'so."

The Secretary of State trembles, his forehead suddenly moist with sweat. "Hokay, hokay, prez," he whispers. "Dadwuz Cheezuz. . ."

"Sayidagin!" The knife bites into his skin, drawing a trickle of blood. "Sayidlowda!"

"Datwuz Cheezuz!" the Secretary yells in desperation, his eyes screwed up in pain. "Prez isrite! Datwuz Cheezuz!"

"Praysdaload," the Secretary of Labor quietly offers, his tone conciliatory. "Haymen."

"Haymen." The President stares at the Secretary of State for another moment before he withdraws his knife, then he turns to the others. "Gonnatac da Dems t'day."

"T'day?" The Secretary of Homeland Defense looks dubious. "Allahus?"

"Damstrait." The President lifts his knife. "Gedalla Pubs t'gedda. Gonnago tadahill. Kigsumass, geddusumfoo', mebbesum wimmin too. . ."

"Hoo-rah!" The Secretary of Defense is all for this. "Geddusum wimmin!"

"T'day?" Although humiliated, the Secretary of State remains cautious.

"T'day." The Prez doesn't look back at him as bends down to pick up his half-eaten rat. "Can'loose. Cheezuz onourside."

And then he finishes his breakfast. No sense in going into mid-term elections on an empty stomach.

⚓

By midafternoon, a small army has been mustered from

the urban wasteland surrounding the White House. Men and women, young and old, anyone able to carry a weapon and not too sick or frail to fight. War drums roust them from the ruins of the Old Exec and the Blair House, the half-collapsed high-rise of the National Press Building, the vast squatter camp of the Federal Triangle, the putrid underground warrens of the Metro stations. An army that's toothless, scrawny, cancerous, bowlegged and on the verge of starvation but an army nonetheless. A thousand points of light, lurching its way down Pennsylvania Avenue toward a mansion on the hill.

At the head of this faith-based initiative is the President. He rides into battle as a good commander-in-chief should, seated upon a litter carried by a half-dozen loyal Pubs. His spear is clasped in his right hand, his knife in his left. A silver platter, once presented to one of his predecessors as a gift from the ambassador of a country long since vanished, now hangs from his neck as a shield. The scalps of his vanquished foes are suspended from staffs carried by his honor guard, the Seecrit-Servis, and at the front of the procession is a warrior waving the last American flag flown from the White House roof before the coming of the ice.

As they approach Capitol Hill, a Dem sentry positioned on the roof of the National Gallery raises the alarm. One long, loud bellow from his horn before he's brought down by a Pub spear, but that's enough to let the Dems know that they're coming. By the time the Pubs reach the Mall, war drums are echoing off the vine-covered walls of the Smithsonian. From his litter, the President can see Dems scurrying for the safety of the crude barricades erected at the bottom of the hill, while short plumes of smoke rise from the shattered dome of the Capitol. All the same, though, he's satisfied. The Dems have been caught by surprise. The midterms will be short and swift. The polls predict a Pub victory.

Yet his troops have just skirted the wreckage of a Navy helicopter that went down at the intersection of Pennsylvania and 3rd during the evacuation, and have come within sight of the decapitated heads that Dems stuck on pikes alongside the Reflecting Pool, when the President hears an odd sound. A low, throbbing hum, sort of like that made by a bumble-bee, but louder, more metronomic. Looking around, he sees that others hear it, too. The litter-bearers nervously glance back and forth, and the mob behind him has become rest-less.

"Holdit!" He raises his staff, and the procession comes to a halt.

Now the hum is closer. Even the Dems pay attention. From on the other side of the barrier of rusting automo-biles, their war drums falter in their beat. Staring up at the Capitol, the President catches a glimpse of his arch-enemy. The Speaker of House stands at the top of the Capitol steps, wearing his war-bonnet of Pub scalps, surrounded by com-mittee chairmen. He's too far away for his expression to be discerned, yet it seems as if the Dem warlord is just as puz-zled as he is.

"Whuddafugizzat?" This from the Secretary of Defense, standing next to the litter along with the other cabinet members.

"Dunno." The President can't figure it out either, but he's not about to let it distract him. Raising his staff, he points it toward the Capitol. "Fohwahd . . .!"

"Ey! Lug!" The Secretary of the Interior points to the left. "Ovahdere!"

The President turns to behold a miracle.

A small round platform glides down 3rd Street, passing the burnt-out ruins of the Department of Labor. Levitating twenty feet above the weed-choked asphalt, lights flashing along its underside, it's held aloft by the humming sound. And standing upon it are a pair of figures . . .

"Cheezuz," the President mutters, his voice low with awe.

"Ifdats Cheezuz," the Secretary of Defense whispers, "whodat wiffem?"

"Dunno." The Secretary of the Interior shrugs. "Mebbe Cheezuz bruddah."

The visitors don't appear to be of this world. Dressed entirely in white, with hoods pulled up over their heads, they seem almost angelic. As the platform comes closer, the President sees not a face beneath the hoods, but only golden masks, devoid of any features yet reflecting the afternoon sun like gilded mirrors.

"Prays Cheezuz!" The President stands up on his litter, raises his hands. "Hescominta kigsumass!"

Not all of the Pubs are impressed, though. Someone in the mob hurls a spear at the platform. It falls short by a dozen feet, yet one of the figures immediately reacts. He raises his right hand; clasped within it is a short rod. There is the briefest glimpse of a beam of light, then the Pub who hurled the spear screams and collapses, a hole burned through the center of his chest.

"Holeecrap!" the Secretary of Defense shouts. "Cheezuz pizzed!"

"Fugdis!" the Secretary of the Interior yells. "Lesgedd-ouddahere!"

The Pubs panic. Screaming in terror, they turn and run back the way they came, stampeding across those behind them. The Seekrit-Servis hesitate for a moment, then they discard their staffs and bolt. Even the litter-bearers have had enough; the President is toppled from his perch as the men holding him aloft drop the litter and join the rest of the mob as they flee for their lives.

Dazed, the President clambers to his feet, looks around. Suddenly, he's alone. His Cabinet has abandoned him; knives and clubs are strewn all around, and the tattered flag lies crumpled in the street. Looking back over his shoulder, he sees his routed army in full retreat, already half a block away and getting smaller by the second.

Yet it scarcely matters, for the Dems are keeping their distance as well. Cowering behind the barricades, they watch in awestruck wonder as the platform slowly descends to the ground. As it glides closer, the President finds his knees quaking. For a moment he has an urge to make his own escape.

Yet he doesn't. Instead, he bends down, picks up flag that was left behind. Holding it aloft, he slowly approaches the platform. The low throb subsides as it settles upon the ground; the two figures silently watch as he comes closer.

"Howdee Cheezuz," he says, once he thinks he's close enough for them to hear him. "Imda Prez ovda Yewnited Staytes Uffa'merica."

The figures say nothing. He sees himself reflected in the mirrors of their faces, and suddenly feels very small and insignificant. At loss for words, he offers the flag. "Yewkin havedis, ifyewwan. Its rillyol', an . . ."

One of the figures raises a white-gloved hand, beckoning for silence. The President stops, watches as the other one reaches down to pick up a metal case. Its burnished aluminum surface catches the sun as he steps to the edge of the platform and offers it.

A gift. The President feels something catch in his throat. Putting down the flag, he walks forward to accept the offering. The case is heavier than it looks; he nearly drops it, but manages to keep it in his hands.

"Tankyew," he says softly. "Tankyew, Cheezuz. Yewdaman. Juswannasay . . ."

Again, the figure raises a hand. The President obediently falls quiet. Both figures return to the center of the platform. The throbbing sound resumes, and the President feels the hair rise on the nape of his neck. Then the platform lifts off once more. He watches as it ascends, then turns to go back the way it came, disappearing behind the half-collapsed hulks of government buildings.

By now, the Dems have gathered their courage. Hooting in glee upon finding their hated foe all by himself, they begin to climb across the barricades, their knives ready to add his head to the trophies surrounding the Reflecting Pool.

Yet the President is unafraid. He and he alone has been given the holy object. Raising it above him, he turns to face the Capitol.

"Lugwad Cheezus brung!" he shouts in victory. "Hegimme blessing! Imda Prez . . .!"

These are the final words of the last President of the United States.

⁂

The neutron bomb does little tertiary damage beyond the immediate radius of the blast zone. The President, of course, is instantly vaporized, as are the nearby Dems. The concussion topples a few structures already weakened by nature, but the Capitol itself remains intact. Yet every living creature within six miles of ground zero drops dead, killed by the massive pulse of ionizing radiation. In seconds, the ancient war between the Pubs and the Dems comes to a swift and bloodless conclusion.

Not long afterwards, men and women in spacecraft descend upon the ruins of Washington D.C. For many years now, they've awaited this moment, within the orbital colonies and lunar settlements where they've kept the flames of civilization alive; now they return to the ancestral lands of their forefathers, to lay claim to their common heritage. The old conflicts are over and done, a dark age best left in the past. The time has come to take the wounded Earth, heal it, slowly transform it back to place it had once been, before it fell prey to the whims of the arrogant, the misguided and the stupid.

The corpses of both Pubs and Dems are buried in a mass grave on the banks of the Potomac River. In time, cherry trees are planted on the site. In the many peaceful years to follow, their spring blossoms add a gentle fragrance to the air, rendering subtle beauty to a planet that, at long last, has become kinder and more gentle.

Introduction to Human Readable

Ernest Lilley

Cory is the embodiment of clever and inventive when it comes to visions of the future, and I really wanted a story from him. It just so happened that he had something that might fit . . . if I was interested in a novella rather than a short story and if I could share it with another publication. I hadn't planned on any novellas, but just one might add a nice contrast to the rest of the book and I was very intrigued by his sidelong glance at concepts like the Vingian Singularity and personal networks . . . but what really sold me was the viewpoint character and her story arc. The other publication wound up not having the right number of pages free or something and so I got to put "all original stories" back on the cover, but I expect you'll be seeing this again since it's too good a story to keep down.

HUMAN READABLE

CORY DOCTOROW

1. Nice networks don't go down

It was unthinkable that the invisible ants that governed all human endeavor should catastrophically fail, but fail they did, catastrophically, on the occasion of Trish's eighth date with Rainer. It took nineteen seconds for the cascade of errors to slow every car on the Interstate to a halt, to light up the dashboard with a grim xmastree of errors, to still the stereo and freeze the tickers of information and context that they had come to think of as the crawling embodiment of the colony that routed all the traffic that made up their universe.

"We are going to be: So. Late," Rainer said, and Trish swivelled in her seat to look at him. He was Fretting again, his forehead wrinkled and his hands clenched on the steering wheel. When they traded massages (third date) and she'd rubbed at his hands, she'd found them tensed into claws that crackled with knuckle-fluid when she bent each finger back and rubbed sandalwood-scented oil into it. He was mighty cute for a neurotic—at least he knew it when he was being nuts. Not that'd he'd stop being nuts, but he'd cheerfully admit it.

"We are not going to be late," she said. "We just need to manually route ourselves out of the dead spot and get back on the grid and we'll be on our way. We've got plenty of time."

"Dead spot?"

"Yes," she said. His forehead wrinkles were looking more Klingon by the second. "Dead spot." She forced a chuckle. "You didn't think that the whole world was down, did you?"

He relaxed his knuckles. "Course not," he said. "Dead spot. Probably ends up at the turn-off."

"Right," she said. "We need a map. I'm navigatrix. You're pilot. Tell me where your maps are, then get onto the shoulder and drive straight."

"Where my maps are? Jesus, what century do you live in? My maps are with the sextant and sundial, between my leeches and my obsidian sacrifice-knife."

She laughed. "OK, pal, I'll find a michelin, you drive. Every car has a couple maps. They self-assemble from happy meal boxes." She opened the glove compartment and started rooting through it while he pulled onto the shoulder and gunned the tiny two-seater along it.

"This is: So. Illegal," he said.

"Naw," she said. "I'm pretty sure you're allowed on the shoulder when the routing goes down. It's in the written-test manual. Learned it while I was helping my little cousin Leelee study. Aha!" she said, holding something up.

"You have a cousin named Leelee? That's uniquely horrible."

"Shut up," she said. "Look at this." It was an old-fashioned phone, of a certain handsome retro line that made it look like a dolphin fucking a silver dildo, the kind of thing marketed to old people who wanted a device with its affordances constrained to collapse the universe of all possible uses for things that fit into your hand into the much smaller universe of, say, a cell phone.

"Yeah, my mom left that behind a couple years ago. I looked everywhere for it but couldn't find it. She must've been snooping in the glove box. Serves her right. So what?"

"These things can unmesh and talk straight to a tower at a long distance, can't they?"

"I dunno, can they?"

"Oh yes, they can. Which means that they work in dead spots. So we can call and get directions."

"You think you're pretty smart, huh, dumpling?"

She put her finger to her temple and made an adorable frowny thinky face, and held it until he looked at her and laughed. They'd discovered their ability to make one another laugh when he'd farted while taking off his kilt (second date) and had reflexively swung the hem back to make it appear that his mighty gust was ruffling the pleats.

"What's your mom's number?" she said.

He recited it and she tapped it in.

"Hi there! This is Trish, Rainer's friend? We're on the way, but the, well the, but the—I mean to say, the grid's down or something. The car doesn't have any nav system, the dolby's out, the Interstate's a parking lot. . . . Oh, you too? God. Wonder if it's the whole country! So, we need directions from San Luis Obispo, to the cemetery, if possible."

[. . .]

"Why yes, it's venti nice to be meeting *you*," she said. "I've heard a lot about you, too. Yes, I'm giving directions; he's driving. Oh, that's so sweet of you. Yes, he *does* look like he's going to scrunch his forehead into his upper lip. I think it's cute, too. Right. Got it. Left, then right, then left, then a slight left, then up the hill. Got it. Whups! That's the duracell! Better go. Soon! Yes. Whoops."

"So?" he said.

"So, your mom sounds nice."

"You got the directions?"

"She gave me directions."

"So you know where we're going?"

"I don't have a single, solitary clue. Your mother gives *terrible* directions, darling. Pull off at the next exit and we'll buy a map."

"We are going to be: So. Late."

"But now *they know* we're late. We have an excuse. You: stop Fretting."

Once they were on the secondary roads, the creepiness of the highway full of stopped cars and crane-necked drivers gave way to a wind-washed soughing silence of waves and beach and palms. Trish rolled down the window and let the breeze kiss the sweat off her lip, watching the surfers wiping out in the curl as the car sped toward the boneyard.

"Are you *sure* this is the kind of thing you're supposed to bring a date to?"

"Yes," he said. "Don't Fret. That's my job."

"And you don't think it's even a *little* weird to take a girl to a cemetery on a date?"

"We're not *burying* anyone," he said. "It's just an unveiling."

"I still don't get that," she said. "I keep picturing your mom cutting a ribbon with a giant pair of gold scissors."

"Right, let's take it from the top," he said. "And you'd better not be getting me to talk to stop my Fretting, because appealing to my pedantic nature to distract me is a *very* cheap trick."

"I'm fluttering my eyelashes innocently," she said.

He laughed and stole a hand through the vent in her apron-trousers and over her thigh. "Achtung!" she said. "Eyes on road, hands on wheel, mind in gutter, *this instant!*" She put her hand over his and he put down the pedal. His hand felt nice there—too nice, for only eight dates and twenty-some phone calls and about 100 emails. She patted it again.

"This is kind of fun," he said, as they zipped past some surfer dudes staring glumly at their long-boards' displays, their perfect tits buoyant and colored like anodized aluminum with electric-tinted sun-paste.

"Ahem," Trish said, squeezing his hand tight enough to make his knuckles grind together. "You were about to explain tombstone-unveiling to me," she said. "When you got distracted by the athletic twinkies on the roadside. But I am sweet-natured and good and forgiving and so I will pretend not to have seen it and thus save us both the embarrassment of tearing out your Islets of Langerhans, all right?" She fluttered her eyes innocently in a way that she happened to know made him melt.

"Explaining! Yes! OK, remember, I'm not particularly Jewish. I mean, not that my parents are, either: they're just Orthodox. They don't believe in God or anything, they just like Biblical Law as a way of negotiating life. I renounced that when I dropped out of Yeshiva when I was 12, so I am not an authority on this subject."

"Let the record show that the witness declared his utter ignorance," she said. "But I don't get this atheist-Orthodox thing either—"

"Just think of them as Mennonites or something. They find the old ways to be a useful set of rules for navigating the universe's curves. God is irrelevant to the belief."

"So they don't believe in God, but they pray to him?"

"Yeah," he said. The surfers were all coming in now, jiggling their boards and rebooting them and staring ruefully at the radical cutback off the lip, dude, gnarly, as they plodded up the beach. "The ritual is the important part. Thinking good thoughts. Having right mind.

"It's good advice, most of it. It doesn't matter where it comes from or how it got there. What matters is that if you follow the Law, you get to where you're going, in good time, with little pain. You don't know why or how, but you do."

"It's like following the ants," she said, watching the stop-and-go traffic in the other direction. "Don't know why they tell us to go where they do, but they do, and it works."

"Well, I guess," he said, using the tone of voice that told her that he was avoiding telling her how wrong she was. She smiled.

"*Anyway.* The thing about Jews—ethnic Jews, cultural Jews, forget the religion here—is that we're pretty much on the melodramatic end of the grieving scale. We like to weep and tear at our hair and throw ourselves on top of the coffins, right? So there's like 5,000 years of this, and during that time, a bunch of social scientists—Rabbinical scholars—have developed a highly evolved protocol for ensuring that you grieve your dead enough that you don't feel haunted by guilt for having failed to honor them, but not grieving so much that you become a drag on the tribe.

"When someone dies, you bury him right away, usually within 24 hours. This means that you spend an entire day running around like your ass was on fire, calling everyone, getting the word out, booking last-minute travel, ordering in from the caterers, picking out a box, fielding consoling phone-calls, getting the rabbi on the phone, booking the limo, so much crap that you can't spare even a second to fall to pieces. And then you bury him, and while you're at it, your family extrudes a volunteer to go over to your house and take all the cushions off of one of the sofas, hang sheets over all the mirrors, and set out enough food to feed the entire state, along with an urn of Starbucks the size of an oil-drum.

"Before the service starts, the rabbi gives you a razor-blade and you slash a hole in your lapel, so that you've got the rent in your heart hanging out there in plain sight, and once you get back home, you spend *seven days* grieving. You pray three times a day with a quorum of ten men, facing east and singing the Kaddish, this really, really depressing song-prayer-dirge that's specially engineered to worm its way into the melancholy receptors of the Semitic hindbrain and make you feel really, really, really miserable. Other people come over and cook for you, all three meals. You don't see yourself in the mirrors, you don't sit on cushions, and you don't do anything *except mourn* for a whole week.

"Then it's over. You take a walk, leaving by one door and coming back in by the other. You put the mourning behind you and start your new life without your dear departed. You've given over your whole life for a whole week, done nothing but mourn, and you're completely sick of it by then, so you're almost glad to be done.

"Then, six months or a year later, usually just before Jewish New Year's, which is in the fall, you have a tombstone erected at the gravesite. The stone-cutters tie a white cloth around it, and everyone gathers there, and there's a sermon, and that dirge again, and more prayer, and everyone has a good hard cry as the scabs you've accumulated are ripped away and all your pain comes back fresh and scalding, and you feel it all again in one hot second, and realize with a guilty start that you *have* been neglecting the memory of the loved one, which is to say that you've gotten on with your life even though his is over, which is to say that you've done perfectly healthy, normal stuff, but you feel totally, completely overwhelmed with guilt and love, which are kind of flipsides of the same emotion—"

"You don't believe that, do you?" She held her breath.

"Well, kind of. Not that they *should be*, but hell they *are*, most of the time, then."

"Good thing we're not in love, then, right?" she said, in reference to their sixth date, when they'd decided that they would hold off on any declarations of love for at least an entire year, since they were most often moved to utter the Three Words of Significance when they were besotted with e.g. post-orgasmic brain juice or a couple of cocktails.

"Yes, counsellor."

She shook her head. He *knew* she was an academic, not a practicing lawyer, but he loved to tease her about it, ever since she'd revealed (after the third date, on the phone) that she'd spent about ten seconds in private practice after she'd worked for her congressman and before she'd joined the faculty at UCLA.

"You're out of order," she said.

"This whole damned car is out of order!" he said. "So that's the ritual. You *said* you wanted to meet the parents and sisters and aunts and grandmothers and cousins and uncles and nephews and in-laws the next time we all got together. This is it."

"Right," she said. "I asked for this." And she had, of course. Hadn't asked for the graveside elements, but she'd been curious to meet this big sprawling enterprise of a family that he was always nattering on about. This seemed as good an occasion as any. "So," she said. "Is this a traditional date among Your People?"

He chuckled. "Yes, this is Yom Shiksa, the ritual bringing of the gentile woman to the family so that she may become the subject of intense, relentless scrutiny and speculation."

She started to laugh, then saw that the tractors were stilled in the fields they were passing, that a train was stopped in its tracks, that the surfers were unable to get their roll-cage dune buggies to take to the road.

"You all right, babe?" he said, after a couple minutes of this.

"Just wondering about the dead spot," she said. "I wish we knew what had happened."

"Nothing too bad, I'm sure," he said. "It's all self-healing. I'm sure we'll be back online soon enough."

✦

They rolled into the parking lot for his family's *shul*'s section of the giant graveyard a few minutes after 1 p.m., just over an hour late, along with the majority of the other attendees, all of whom had had to navigate manually.

"Where are your sisters?" Rainer's mother said, even before he'd kissed her cheek.

Rainer screwed his face up in a scowl and dug in his pocket for a yarmulke. "Do I know? Stuck in traffic, Ma. The grid's down everywhere."

Trish watched this bemusedly, in her cool loose cotton apron-trousers and blouse. She scuffed her toe conspicuously and Rainer turned to her, and it was as though he'd forgotten she was there. She felt a second's irritation, then a wave of sympathy as she saw the spasm of anxiety cross his face. He was nervous about her meeting his family, and nervous about who would arrive when, and nervous about where his sisters were with their enormous families and meek husbands, trapped somewhere on southern California's squillion-mile freeway network.

"Ma," he said. "This is my friend, Trish."

"Pleased to meet you, Mrs. Feinstein," Trish said. The old woman was remarkably well preserved, her soft skin glowing with heat-flush, her thick hair caught in a tight bun and covered with a little scarf that reminded Trish of Rainer's yarmulke. She wondered if she should be wearing one, too. Mrs. Feinstein's eyes flicked quickly to her shoes, up her legs and boobs, to her face and hair, and then back to her face. She opened her arms and drew Trish into a hug that smelled of good, subtle perfume, though Trish knew so little about scent that she couldn't have said which.

"Call me Reba, darling," she said. "It's so good of you to come."

And then she was off, hustling to corral a wayward knot of horseplay-aged cousins, stopping to shake hands with the deceased great-uncle's poker buddies in their old-man pants, golf shirts and knit yarmulkes bobby-pinned to their thinning hair.

Trish took stock. Looked like every other graveyard she'd been in, which wasn't that many. At 35, she'd been to half a dozen family funerals, a couple of college buddies who OD'ed or cracked up their cars, and one favorite poli-sci teacher's service, so she was hardly an expert on bone-yards, but something was amiss.

"What's with the pebbles on the headstones?" she whispered to Rainer, who was scanning the road for signs of his sisters.

"Huh? Oh. You drop those on the monument when you visit the grave, as a sign that someone's been there."

"Oh," she said, and began to cast about for a pebble she could put on his great-uncle's headstone once it was unveiled. There were none to be found. The ground had been picked completely clean. Looking at the thousands and thousands of ranged marble headstones, each topped with a cairn of stones—and not just stones, either, toys and seashells and small sculptures, she saw now—and she understood why.

"What are you doing?" Rainer asked. He might have been irritated, or just nervous. It was hard to tell when he was Fretting, and he was clearly going coo-coo for coco-puffs.

"Looking for pebbles," she said.

He said [fuck] very quietly. "I meant to bring some. Damnit. I've got twenty relatives buried here and we're going to go past every single tombstone before we get to leave and I don't have a single rock."

"Can you leave toys or other stuff, like on those stones?"

"Yeah," he said. "I suppose. If I had other stuff."

She opened her purse and pulled out the dolphin-dildo cellphone. "You still need this?" she said.

He smiled and his forehead uncreased. "You're a genius," he said.

She set it down on the pavement and brought her heel down on it hard, breaking it into dozens of fragments. "All the pebbles we'll ever need," she said, picking them up and handing them to Rainer.

He put his arm around her shoulders and squeezed. "I'm awfully fond of you, Counsellor," he said, kissing her earlobe. His breath tickled her ear and made her think of the crazy animal new-relationship-energy sex they'd had the night before; she was still limping, and so was he and she shivered.

"You too, steaky paste," she said. "Now, introduce me to all of your relatives."

"Introduce you?" He groaned. "You don't think I remember all of their names, do you?"

❦

Afterward, they formed a long convoy back to the nearest family member's house, a great aunt? a second cousin?

Rainer was vague, navigating by keeping everyone in sight, snaking along the traffic jam that appeared to have engulfed the entire state, if not the whole coast.

"You made that law, yes? We've all heard about you." This was the sixth time someone had said this to her since they'd arrived and Rainer had made her a plate of blintzes, smoked salmon, fresh bagels, boiled eggs, and baby greens salad with raspberry dressing, then had been spirited away into an endless round of cheek-pinching and intense questioning. She'd been left on her own, and after having a couple of grave conversations with small children about the merits of different toys, she'd been latched upon by one of the Relatives and passed from hand to hand.

"I was involved in it, but I didn't write the law," she said.

"Look at you, so modest, you're blushing!" the Relative said. She reached out to steady a cut-glass vase as it wobbled in the wake of two small boys playing keep-away with a third's yarlmulke, and Trish realized that this was probably the hostess.

"This place is just supercalifragilistic," she said, with an economical gesture at the tasteful Danish furnishings, the paper books in a handsome oak bookcase, the pretty garden out one side window and the ocean out the back window.

"Thank you," the great-aunt said. "My Benny loved it here." She misted up. Trish finally added two and two, remembered the BENJAMIN chiseled into the marble headstone, and the blank spot on the other half of the tombstone, realized that this wasn't just the hostess, this was the *widow*, and felt about for a thing to say.

"It was a beautiful ceremony," she said. She had a couple napkins tucked in the waistband of her pants, and without thinking, she extracted one and folded an angle into it, reaching for the corner of the great-aunt's eye. "Look up," she said, and blotted the tear before it could draw a line of mascara down the widow's cheek.

The old woman smiled a well-preserved smile that reminded Trish of Rainer's mom. "You're a sweet girl," she said. "Me, I'm not so good with names, and so I've forgotten yours."

"I'm Trish," Trish said, bemusedly. Rainer's grammar got yiddishized when he wasn't paying attention, and she adored the contrast between its shtetl credibility and his witty, smooth public banter persona. It had attuned her to little phrases like, "Me, I'm not so good."

The widow shook her hand. "I'm Dorothy. It's a pleasure to make your acquaintance. Would you like to come out to the garden with me?"

❧

Once they were seated, young male Relatives materialized and set up shade-umbrellas and brought out trays of iced juice.

"They're not after the inheritance, you know," the old woman said with a snort. "Their parents are *very* well-off. They don't need from money. They just adore me because I've spoiled them rotten since they were babies and I'd take them swimming and to Disneyland."

"You have a beautiful family," Trish said.

"Do you have a big family, too?" The old woman put on a pair of enormous sunglasses and sipped at her pink grapefruit juice.

"Not like this one," she said. There were a couple hundred people in the house, and Rainer had spent the whole car-ride back from the cemetery Fretting about all the relations who *hadn't* made it.

"Oh, this one! Well, this is a special case. This family accumulates other families. My Benny had a small family, and when he married me, they just joined us. All the high holidays, we ate here, or at my parents' place, God rest them. Your family is in DC?"

"All over."

"But you're from DC, no?"

"Not really. I grew up in Chicago and Seattle."

"But you made that law—"

"I really didn't, honestly! I was clerking for a Supreme Court judge when the case was heard, and I wrote his dissenting opinion, and when we lost, I quit and went to work for a PAC that was agitating for copyright reform to accommodate free expression, and then when Senator Sandollar got voted in and they started the Intellectual Property committee and made her chairman, I joined her staff as a policy wonk. So I worked on it, along with a couple thousand other people, not counting the millions who contributed to the campaign and the people who knocked on doors and so on."

"How old are you, darling?"

"Thirty-five," she said.

"At thirty-five, I was having babies. You, listen to you. Listen to what you've *accomplished*! I'm proud just to *listen* to you. Rainer is lucky to have you. You two will get married?"

Trish squirmed and felt her face grow hot. Neither of them really believed in marriage. Whenever anyone brought the subject up around Rainer, he'd grimace and say, "Are you kidding? It'd make my mother *far* too happy; she'd keel over from joy."

There was some kind of disturbance down the beach, one that had been growing steadily over the past several minutes, and now the Relatives were all turning their attention that way, to a couple of small boys in miniature suits who were ruining the shine on their shoes running in the sand like lunatics.

Something in the way they were running, the distant expressions she couldn't quite make out on their faces. It made her think back to high-school, to working as a beach lifeguard on Lake Michigan in the summers, and before she knew what she was doing, she'd kicked off her shoes and was running for the shore, her legs flashing immodestly through the vents in her apron-trousers.

She was still yards away from the hissing surf when she began to assess the situation. There was the small boy, bobbing in the ocean, where the undertow had spit him up after sucking him under. There was the swimmer, unconscious on the beach, face down. Couldn't tell if his chest was moving, but the small boy was in a suit, not swimtrunks like the swimmer, and that meant that he was part of Rainer's Family, which she had begun (on the eighth date, no less!) to think of as her own, and so she had him as her primary target before she reached the sea.

She didn't bother finicking with the buttons on her top, just grabbed her collar and yanked, leaving her in a bra that revealed less than some bikinis she owned, but did so through a cunning arrangement of lace, mesh, and structural engineering that was probably illegal in Texas. She undid the bows on each hip holding up her pants and stepped out of them, leaving behind a very small pair of white panties whose primary design consideration had been to avoid showing lines through thin trousers, with modest coverage of all her nethers coming in a distant second.

She plunged into the water without hesitation, moving swiftly but surely, taking care to keep her feet dug in against the undertow as she waded out toward the young boy. She was a strong swimmer, but the water was shockingly cold after the heat of the garden and the buzzing afternoon and it sucked at her calves and legs like a jacuzzi intake. Her breath roared in her ears as she rode the swells, and then she was soaked by a succession of breakers, and then she had the boy's little hand.

She hauled him to her, seeing that he was only five or six, and that his pouting lips were alarmingly blue and that his skin was as pale as cream. She scooped the water out of his mouth, hooked her arm around his neck and tilted his head back and began to slosh back toward shore. When she was waist-deep—immodestly revealed in a bra that she was quite certain had gone completely transparent—she pinched his nose and blew into his mouth, not quite getting her mouth out of the way before he vomited up a gush of salt-water, blintzes, diet coke, and bile. She spat and wished that she could duck her head and get a mouthful of ocean to rinse with, but she couldn't without dunking the boy, too, so she hauled him up out of the water and handed him to the Relative who was standing with his arms on the shore, his fine leather shoes soaked with cold seawater.

She looked for the swimmer, and saw that he was still face down in the sand. "You, you and you," she said, pointing at three young cousins whose wide eyes were flicking from her boobs to her crotch—white underwear, Christ, why white underwear today?—to the boy on the sand, who was mobbed now with Relatives whose hubbub had reached deafening proportions, "Go to the house, find an old-fashioned phone and call emergency services. Tell them where we are, and that we have two drowning victims, one a child, neither breathing. What are you going to do?"

The tallest of the three managed to make eye-contact long enough to say, "Find a cell-phone, call emergency, tell them where we are, two drownings, not breathing."

"Right," she said. "Come back when you're done and tell me that it's done."

"You, you," she said, picking out two tall uncles who looked like they'd worked out or played sports before they found whatever careers had paid for the nice suits they were wearing, "Carry him here and lay him down on his side."

She looked for Rainer and found his ass sticking out of the scrum around the boy. She snagged him by the belt and dragged him back. "Rainer," she shouted. His forehead was scrunched, but he was clear-eyed and grim and looked like he was listening to her, which she found very pleasing. "You need to get everyone back at least five steps from that kid, and make them quiet down," she said.

"Right," he said, and took off his jacket and handed it to her.

"Hold it yourself," she snapped, "I've got things to do."

"It's to wear," he said.

She surprised herself with a grin. "Thanks,"

The Relatives were murmuring, or crying, or bickering, but Rainer *hollered*. "LISTEN UP," he said. "All of you get over there by that rock, NOW, or my girlfriend won't be able to save Jory's life. GO!"

And they went, amazingly, crushing back so quickly they looked like a receding tide. The tall uncles deposited the swimmer in the sand between them, and she checked his breathing and saw that it was good.

"Turn him on his side and tell me if he starts to choke," she said, and turned to the little boy, struggling to remember her rescue breathing.

<hr>

She got the boy breathing and ended up with more puke on her face, on Rainer's jacket, in her hair. His pulse was thready but there. She turned to the swimmer and saw that he was a muscular surfer dude in board shorts with a couple of bitchin tatts and a decent body-paint job. He was breathing, too, but his heart was erratic as hell. She pressed two fingers to his throat.

"What happened?" she said. "Who saw it happen?"

One of the aunts stepped forward and said, "My son says they were playing—"

She held up her hand. "Where's your son?" she said.

"He's back at the house," the aunt said, startling back.

"Send someone for him, then tell me what happened."

The aunt looked like she'd been slapped, but the other Relatives were staring at her and so she had to talk, and then the boy arrived and he told it again and it was pretty much the same story, but she was able to get more details, as she began to examine both the boy and the surfer's bodies for cuts, bruises, breaks and punctures. She gave the boy's clothes the same treatment she'd given her own, gently but forcefully tearing them off, using a seashell to start the tears at first, then a pocket-knife that someone put in her hand.

The story was that the kids had been playing when they'd seen the surfer floating in the breakers, and they'd dared each other to fish him out, and the undertow had sucked them out to sea. One had gotten away, the other had ended out beyond the waves, and meanwhile, the surfer had beached himself on his own.

"Right," she said. "Blankets and pillows. Elevate their feet and wrap them up good." She stood up and staggered a step or two before Rainer caught her, and the crowd made a noise that was at once approving and scandalized.

"Get me to the sea," she said. "I need to soak my head."

So he walked her into the water, he still in his suit-pants and dress shirt and tie, and held onto her while she dunked her head and swirled a mouthful of salt water in her mouth.

"Where are the fucking paramedics?" she said, as she sloshed back out with him.

"There," he said, and pointed at the horizon, where a Coast Guard clipper was zooming for the shore. "The cell-phone was dead, so I fired up a couple flares. You didn't hear them?"

"No," she said. He could have set off a cannon and she wouldn't have noticed it.

She got back to the shore just in time to see the surfer convulse. She was on him in a second, kneeling at his side, doing airway-breathing-circulation checks, finding no pulse, and slamming him onto his back and beginning CPR.

Some time later, she was lifted off him and two para-medics went to work on him. Someone put a robe over her shoulders and a cup of juice in her hands. She dropped the juice in the sand and sticky liquid and beach sand covered her legs, which she realized now that she hadn't depilated in a week, and that made her realize that she'd spent a pretty crucial amount of time prancing around naked in front of her date's family, and that that was probably not on the timetable until the fifteenth date at *least*.

She looked up at Rainer, who was still in his shoes and as she was in bare feet loomed over her. "God," she said, "Rainer—"

He kissed her. "I love you, Patricia," he said.

"Ooh," she said, with a weak smile. "You're breaking the rules!"

"Can you let it go this once?"

She made her scrunchy thinky face and then nodded. "Just don't make a habit of it, you lunk."

<hr />

It would have been perfect if only the surfer hadn't died.

They didn't get home until well after midnight. Parts of LA appeared to be on fire as they inched their way along the freeway. It was weird to see LA at this speed. They were used to clipping along at 60 or 70—over 80 if the traffic was light—flying over the freeway so fast that the scenery was just a blur. Only the year before, the *New Yorker* had run a 40-page paen to LA, a public apology declaring it the most livable city in America, now that it had licked its traffic problems. It balanced lots of personal space with thorough urbanization and urbanity. It was why they both lived there.

Now they seemed to have traveled back 50 years in time, to the bad old traffic-jam and smog days. Looters danced below, torching stores, and the traffic moved so slowly that some people were apparently abandoning their cars to *walk* home which made the traffic even worse. The smoke from the fires turned the sunset into a watercolor of reds and mustards and golds; tones that had blown away with the smog when the last gas-sucking Detroitmobile was retired for a plastic Nickle-Metal Hydride jellybean, and all the lanes were repainted to cut them in half.

It was nightmarish. When they got off the ramp at Studio City, they found homeless guys directing traffic with gas-tubes they'd torn out of the bus-shelters. The tubes glowed in the presence of microwave radio-frequency radiation, and as each of the trillions of invisible ants in the system attempted to connect with its neighbors and get the traffic set to rights again, the RF noise made the tubes glow like sodium lamps.

They coasted into Trish's driveway and collapsed in her living room.

"You were *wonderful*, darling," Rainer said, peeling off the tracksuit that one of his cousins had scrounged from the gym-bag in her trunk and donated to Trish. Her skin was gritted with sand and streaked with stripes of sunburn.

"God," Trish said, lolling back on the sofa, just letting him gently brush away the sand and rub lotion into her skin. "You spoil me," she said.

"You're unspoilable," he said. "Wonderful girl. You saved their lives," he said.

"What a fucking day," she said. "You think that my lifeguard training made up for my scandalous undergarments in your family's minds?"

He snorted and she felt his breath tickle the fine hairs on her tummy. "You're kidding. My mom told me that if I didn't marry you, she'd have me killed and then fix you up with someone else from the family, told me it was my duty to see to it that you didn't get away, just in case someone else fell in the ocean."

He looked around at the blank walls. "Creepy not to have any news at all," he said.

"There's a TV in the garage," she said. "Or maybe the attic. You could find it and plug it in and find out that no one else knows what's going on, if you feel like it."

"Or I could escort you to the bathtub and we could scrub each other clean and then I could give you a massage," he said.

"Yes, or you could do that."

"Where did you say the television was?" he said.

"You are going to be: In. So. Much. Trouble." She twined her fingers in his hair and pulled him up to kiss her.

2. Progress pilgrims

It took three days for even the thinnest crawls to return to the walls. In the meantime, people dug out old one-to-many devices like radios and televisions and set them up on their lawns so they could keep track of the aftermath of The Downtime.

He slept over those three nights, because no one was going anywhere, anyway, and they had a running argument over how many dates this counted as, but truth be told, they had a wonderful time, making omelettes for one-another, washing each other's backs in the shower, stealing moments of sex in the living room at two in the afternoon without worrying about being interrupted by a chime, ringer, bell or vibe.

When they weren't enjoying each other, they took coolers of fizzy drinks onto the lawn and watched the neighbor's TV set and saw the pundits describing The Downtime. The news-shows were having a drunken ball with this one: as the only game in town, they were free to bring a level of craft to their newsmongering that hadn't been seen since Trish's parents' day, when news-networks turned catastrophes into light operas, complete with soundtracks, brand-identities, logo-marks and intermissions where buffoons worked the audience for laughs.

"Oh, she's your favorite, isn't she?" Trish asked, goosing Rainer's bicep and taking a sip of his peach ginger-ade. The pundit had been in heavy rotation since the TV went back on the air. She was a Norwegian academic mathematician who wrote books of popular philosophy. She was a collection of trademark affectations: a jacket with built-up shoulders, a monocle, a string tie, nipple tassles, and tattooed cross-hatching on her face that made her look like a woodcut of a Victorian counting-house clerk. Rainer loathed her, she'd been on the committee to which he'd defended his Philosophy of Networks thesis, and she'd busted his balls so hard that they still ached a decade later when he saw her on the tube.

The pundit explained the packet-switching, using trains versus automobiles as a metaphor: "In a circuit uniwerse, every communication gets its own dedicated line, like a train on a track. Ven I vant to talk to you, ve build a circuit —a train track—betveen our dewices. No one else can use those tracks, even if ve're not talking. But packet-svitching is like a freevay. Ve break the information up into packets and ve give every packet its own little car, and it finds its own vay to the other end. If vun car doesn't arrive, ve make a copy of its information and send it again. The cars have brakes and steering veels, and so they can all share the same road vithout too much trouble."

Rainer grit his teeth and hissed at the set. "She's faking the accent," he said. "She thinks that Americans believe that anyone with a European accent is smarter than we are. She can pronounce vee and doubleyou perfectly well when she wants to—she speaks better English than I do! Besides, *she stole that line from me*," he said, "from my *thesis*," he said, his face scrunching up again.

"Shh, shh," Trish said, laughing at him. He wasn't really angry-angry, she knew. Just a little stir crazy. He was a networking guy—he should have been out there trying to make the network go again, but he was on sabbatical and no one at UCLA wanted to hear from him just then.

And then the pundit was off onto ants—networks modelled on ant-colonies that use virtual phermomenes to explore all possible routes in realtime and emerge a solutions to the problem of getting everything, everywhere, in shortest time. Rainer kept barking at the TV, and Trish knew he was doing it to entertain her as much as for any reason, so she laughed more and egged him on.

The TV cut back to the news-dude, who was a very cuddly ewok who'd made his name hosting a wheel-of-fortune, jumping up and down and squeaking excitedly and adorably whenever a contestant won the grand prize, his fur-plugs quivering. He cupped his paws to his cheeks and grinned.

"But ants aren't perfect, are they?" the ewok said.

"He's feeding her!" Rainer said. "She's going to go off on her stupid walking-in-circles bit—"

"The thing about using wirtual ants to map out the vorld and make routing recommendations is that ve can't really tell the difference betveen a good solution and a bad vun, without trying it. Sometimes, ants end up valking in circles, reinforcing their scent, until they starve to death. Ve might find that our cars tell us that the best vay from San Francisco to San Jose is via a 1500 mile detour to Las Wegas. It may be true—if all the traffic everyvhere else is bad enough, that might be the fastest vay, but it may just be the ants going in circles."

"God, talk about taking a metaphor too far," he said. Trish thought that Rainer was perfectly happy to think about the ants as ants, except when someone raised a point like this, but she didn't see any reason to raise that point just then.

The ewok turned to the camera: "One scientist says we *should* expect more Downtimes to come. When we come back from this break, we'll talk to a University of Waterloo researcher who claims that this is just the first of many more Downtimes to come."

The screen cut over to a beautiful, operatic advertise-ment for some Brazilian brand of coca-cola, wittily written, brilliantly shot, with an original score by a woman who'd won three grammies at the Independent Music Awards in Kamchatka the year before. They watched it with mild attention, and Trish absently fished another bottle out of the cooler and chewed the lid off with her side-molars.

She looked at Rainer. He was gripping the armrests of his inflatable chair tightly, dimpling the hard plastic. She held the bottle to his lips and he took it, then she rubbed at his shoulders while he took a swallow.

"Let's go back inside and play," she said. "They won't have anything new to tell us for days."

The crawls were alive the next morning, exuberantly tracking across the walls and over the mirror and down the stairs. They picked out the important ones and trailed them to convenient spots with a fingertip and devoured them, reading interesting bits aloud to one another.

Soon the crawls had been tamed and only a few personal messages remained. Trish dragged hers over to the tabletop, next to her cereal bowl, and opened them up while she ate. Outside, she could hear the whisper of cars speeding down the road, and she supposed with a mingling of regret and relief that she should probably go into her office.

She opened her personal mail. It had been three days since she'd read it, but for all that, a surprisingly small amount had accumulated. Of course—everyone else had been without connectivity, too. This was mostly stuff from the east coast and Europe, people who'd been awake for a couple hours.

She read, filed and forwarded, tapping out the occasional one-word answer to simple questions or bouncing back messages with a form letter.

Then she came to the note from the Coast Guard medic. He didn't mince words. It was in the first sentence: the surfer dude she'd rescued had had a second cardiac arrest on the boat. They'd tried what they could, but he hadn't recovered. He was a freak statistic of The Downtime, another person who'd lost his life when the ants spazzed out. They'd recovered his board and found its black-box. The accelerometer and GPS recorded the spill he'd taken after the loss of climate and wave-condition data from the other surfers strung out on the coast. He'd stayed up for about ten seconds before going under.

She stared numbly at the note, the spoon halfway to her mouth, and then she dropped the spoon into the bowl, not noticing that it splashed milk down her blouse.

She got up from the table and went into the kitchen. Rainer was there, in a change of clothes they'd bought from a mom-n-pop gap at the mall on the corner that had been taking IOUs from anyone who could show a driver's license with a local address. She grabbed his wrist, making him slosh starbucks down his front, she took the cup out of his hand and set it down on the counter, then put her arms around his chest and hugged him. He didn't protest or ask any questions, he just put his arms around her and hugged back.

Eventually, she cried. Then she told him what she was crying about. She let him tell her that she was a hero, that she'd saved Jory's life and almost saved the surfer's life, and she let him tell her that it wasn't her fault for sloshing into the ocean to rinse off the barf, and she let him tell her that he loved her, and she cried until she thought she was cried out, and then she started again.

He took her upstairs and he lay her down on the bed. He undressed her, and she let him. He put her in fluffy jammies, and she let him. He wiped away her makeup and her hot tears with a cool face cloth, and she let him. He took her hand and ran his fingers over her fingernails, squeezing each one a little, the way she liked, and she let him.

"You're going to have a nice lie-down for a couple hours, and I'm going to be right beside you. I'll call the department secretary and tell him you're taking a personal day and will be in tomorrow. Then we're going to go see Jory and his family, so that you can see the boy whose life you saved, and then we are going to go for a walk in the hills, and then I'm going to put you to bed. When you get up in the morning, you can make an appointment to see a grief counsellor or not. Today, I'm in charge, all right?"

Her heart swelled with love and she felt a tear slip down her cheek. "Rainer," she said, "you're a wonder."

"You inspire me, darling," he said, and kissed her eyelids shut.

Their thirty-fifth date was their last.

"You're going back to Washington," he said, when he saw the boxes in her office.

"Yes," she said.

He stood in the doorway of her office. Trish was painfully aware of the other faculty members in the corridor watching him. Their romance was no secret, of course. Everyone in the law department knew about him, all the network engineers knew about her, and they both took a substantial amount of ribbing about "mixed marriages" and "interfaith dating."

Trish realized with a pang that it was likely that everyone in the law department knew that she'd decided to go back to the Hill but that he'd only suspected it until this instant.

"Well, good for you," he said, putting on a brave face that was belied by the Fret wrinkles in his forehead.

"I'm sorry," she said. "I should have told you once I decided, but I didn't want to do it over the phone—"

"I'm glad you didn't," he said, holding up his hand. "Do you want to come out for dinner with me anyway?"

She gestured at the half-packed office. "The movers are coming in the morning."

"Well then, do you suppose you could use some help? I could get some burger king or taco bell."

She looked at him for a long moment, swallowing the knob in her throat. "That would be lovely. Mexican. I mean, 'taco bell,'" she said. "Thank you."

He let her pay for it. "You're making the big bucks now," he said. And he was a surprisingly conscientious packer, padding her framed pictures carefully and wrapping her knick-knacks in individual sheets of spun fiber.

"Well then," he said, once he'd finished writing out a description of his latest box's contents on its outside, "you always told me that Hill Rats were Hill Rats for life, I suppose."

"Yeah," she said. She knew she should explain, but they'd had the argument about it three times since the new

PAC had contacted her and offered her the executive director position. The explanation wouldn't get any better now that she'd made up her mind.

The new PAC, The Association for a Human-Readable World, was the brainchild of some people she'd worked with while she was on the Hill. They'd asked her to hire a team, to scout an office, and then to camp out in the offices of various important committee chairmen until they passed a law limiting the scope of emergent networking meshes. The Europeans had enacted legislation requiring cops, hydroelectric agencies, banks, hospitals and aviation authorities to use "interrogatable" networks within ten days of The Downtime. With fifteen thousand dead in Western Europe alone, with Florence in flames and Amsterdam under two meters of water, it was an easy call. The US had scoffed at them and pointed to the economic efficiencies of a self-governing network, but the people who were funding Human-Readable World wanted to know where old concepts like "transparency" and "accountability" and "consent of the governed" fit in when the world's essential infrastructure was being managed by nonsentient ant-colony simulations.

<hr />

"Be gentle with us, OK?" he said.

"Oh, I wish I had your confidence in my abilities," she said, sucking on her big-gulp of coke.

He put down his food and looked hard at her. He stared longer than was polite, even for (ex-) lovers, and she began to squirm.

"What?" she said.

"You're not putting me on. Amazing. Patricia Lourdes McCavity, you have felled an empire and you are setting yourself up to fell another—and it's one that I'm pretty heavily invested in, both professionally and financially."

"Come on," she said. "I'm good, but I'm not superwoman. I was part of a team."

"I've read your briefs. Position papers. Opinions. Speeches. Hell, your press releases. They were the most cogent, convincing explanations for intellectual property reform I'd ever read. You weren't the judge, but you were his clerk. You weren't the committee chairman, but you were her head staffer. Taco Bell underestimated you. Coke underestimated you. Starbucks underestimated you. Disney underestimated you. Vivendi and Sony underestimated you. Now you're running your own organization, and it's pointed at me, and I'm scared shitless, you want to know the truth. I'm not underestimating you." He'd drawn his dark eyebrows together while he spoke, and lowered his head, so that he was looking up at her from under his brow, looking intense as the day they'd met, when he was delivering a brilliant lecture on ant-colony optimization to a large lay audience at the law-school, fielding the Q&A with such convulsive humor and scalding lucidity that he'd melted her heart.

She felt herself blushing, then wondered if she was flushing. She still loved him and still craved the feeling of his skin on hers, wanted nothing more than another lost weekend with him, taking turns being the strong one and being the one who surrendered, soothing each other and spoiling each other. Thinking of that first meeting brought back all those feelings with keen intensity that made her breasts ache and her hands flutter on the box she was eating off.

"Rainer," she began, then stopped. She took a couple deep breaths. "I'm not gunning for you, you know. You and I want the same thing: a world that we can be proud to live in. Your family's company has contributed more to the public good than any of us can really appreciate—"

He blushed now, too. She never talked about his father's role in the earliest build-outs of ant-based emergent routing algorithms, about the family fortune that he'd amassed through the company that bore his name still, 30 years after he'd stepped down as Chairman of the Board. Rainer was a genius in his own right, she knew, and his own contributions to the field were as important as his father's, but he was haunted by the idea that his esteem in the field was due more to his surname than his research. He waved his hands at her and she waved hers back.

"Shush. I'm trying to explain something to you. Between your father and you, the world has increased its capacity and improved its quality of life by an order of magnitude. You've beaten back Malthus for at least another century. That makes you heroes.

"But your field has been co-opted by corrupt interests. When you study the distributions, you can see it clearly: the rich and the powerful get to their destinations more quickly; the poor are routed through franchise ghettoes and onto toll-roads; the more important you are, the fewer number of connections you have to make when you fly, the better the chance that you'll get a kidney when you need it. The evidence is there for anyone to see, if only you look. We need standards for this—we need to be able to interrogate the system and find out why it does what it does. That's an achievable goal, and a modest one: we're just asking for the same checks and balances that we rely on in the real world."

He looked away and set down his taco. "Trish, I have a lot of respect for you. Please remember that when I tell you this. You are talking nonsense. The network is, by definition, above corruption. You simply can't direct it to give your cronies a better deal than the rest of the world. The system is too complex to game. Its behavior can't *be predicted*—how could it possibly be *guided*? Statistics can be manipulated to 'prove' anything, but everyone who has any clue about this understands that this is just paranoid raving—"

She narrowed her eyes and sucked in a breath, and he clamped his lips shut, breathed heavily through his nose, and went on.

"Sorry. It's just wrong, is all. Science isn't like law. You deal with shades of grey all the time, make compromises, and seek out balance. I'm talking about mathematical truths here, not human-created political constructs.

There's no one to compromise *with*, a human-readable emergent network just doesn't exist. Can't exist. It doesn't make sense to say it. It's like asking for me to make Pi equal three. Pi *means* something, and what it means *isn't* three. Emergent networks *mean* not human readable. "

She looked at him, and he looked at her, and they looked at each other. She felt a sad smile in the corners of her lips, and saw one tug at his, and then they both broke out in grins.

"We're going to be seeing a lot of each other," she said.

"Oh yes, we are," he said.

"Across a committee room."

"A podium."

"On talk-shows."

"Opposite sides."

"Right."

"No fighting dirty, OK?" he said, raising his eyebrows and showing her his big brown eyes. She snorted.

"Give me a hug and go home," she said. "I'll see you at the hearings when they introduce my bill."

He hugged her, and she smelled him, thinking, *this is the last time I'll smell this smell.*

"Rainer," she said, holding him at arm's length.

"Yes?" he said.

"I'm going to call you, when I have questions about ant-colony optimization, all right?"

He looked at her.

"I need the best expertise I can get. It's in your interest to see to it that I'm well-informed."

Slowly, he nodded. "Yes, you're right. I'd like that. I'll call you when I have questions about policy, all right?"

"You're on," she said, and they hugged again, fiercely.

Once he was gone, she permitted herself the briefest of tears. She knew that she was right and that she was going to make a fool out of him, but she didn't want to think of that right then. She felt the place behind her ear where he'd kissed her before going home and looked around her office, five years of her life in thirty banker's boxes ready to be shipped across the country tomorrow, according to a route that would be governed from moment to moment by invisible, notional, *ridiculous* insects.

She ate more taco bell. The logo was a pretty one, really, and now that it had been adopted by every mom-and-pop burrito joint in the world, they'd really levelled the playing field. She thought about the old Taco Bell mystery-meat and plastic cheese and took a bite of the ground beef and sharp Monterey Jack that had come from her favorite little place on the corner, and permitted herself to believe, for a second, anyway, that she'd made that possible.

She was going to kick ant ass on the Hill.

3. Conflict of Insect

Trish gathered her staff in the board room and wrote the following in glowing letters on the wall with her fingertip, leaving the text in her expressive schoolmarm's handwriting rather than converting it to some sterile font: "First they ignore you. Then they laugh at you. Then they fight you. Then you win."

Her staff, all five of them, chuckled softly. "Recognize it?" she asked, looking round at them.

"Pee-Wee Herman?" said the grassroots guy, who was so young it ached to look at him, but who could fire a cannonload of email into any congressional office on 12 hours' notice. He never stopped joking.

The lawyer cocked an eyebrow at him and stroked her moustache, a distinctive gesture that you could see in any number of courtv archives of famous civil-rights battles, typically just before she unloaded both barrels at the jury-box and set one or another of her many precedents. "It's Martin Luther King, right?"

"Close," Trish said.

"Geronimo," guessed the paralegal, who probably

wasn't going to work out after all, being something of a giant flake who spent more time on the phone to her girl-friend than filing papers and looking up precedents.

"Nope," Trish said, looking at the other two staffers—the office manager and the media guy—who shrugged and shook their heads. "It's Gandhi," she said.

They all went, "Ohhhh," except the grassroots guy, who crossed to the wall and used his fingertip to add, "And then they assassinate you."

"I'm too tough to die," the lawyer said. "And you're all too young. So I think we're safe."

"OK," Trish said. "This is an official pep talk. They're playing dirty now. Last night, my car tried to take me to Arlington via Detroit. My email is arriving on a 72 hour time-delay. My phone doesn't ring, or it rings all night long. I've had to switch it off.

"But what all of this means is that I've got more unin-terrupted work-time than ever and I'm getting reacquaint-ed with my bicycle."

"Every number I call rings at my ex-girlfriend's place," the grassroots guy said. "I think we're going to get back together!"

"That's the right attitude, boy-o," the lawyer said. "When life gives you SARS, make sarsaparilla. I appear to be unable to access any of my personal files, and any case law I query shows up one sentence at a time. I've discovered that the Georgetown University law library makes a very nice latte and serves a terrific high tea, and I've set Giselle to work on refiling and cross-indexing twenty years' worth of yellow pads that had previously sat moldering in a storage locker that I was paying far too much for."

"Which has given Giselle a rare opportunity to explore the rich civil rights history that you embody," Trish said, looking pointedly at the paralegal. "But I suspect that she could use a hand, possibly from a grad student or two who could get some credit for this. Let's ask around at George-town, OK?"

The lawyer nodded. The office manager pointed out that their bill-payments were going astray after they'd been dispatched to their suppliers but before they were debited from their—dwindling—account, which meant that they were getting a couple days' worth of free cash-flow. Only the media guy was glum, since he couldn't field, make or review calls or press releases, which made him pretty useless indeed.

"Right," she said, and scribbled something on one of the steno pads she'd bought for everyone when their email started going down three times a day. "This guy owes me from back in the copyright wars, I fed him some good stories that he used to launch his career. He was the ABNBC Washington bureau chief until last year and now he's teaching J-School at Columbia. Take the afternoon train to Manhattan and bring him back with you tonight. Don't take no for an answer. Tell him to bring his three most promising protégés, and tell him that they'll have all the access they need to produce an entire series on the campaign. Sleeping on our sofas. Following us to the toilet. Everything on the record. Do-able?"

"It's do-able," the media guy said. "I'm on it."

Once they'd all cleared out, the lawyer knocked on her door. "You going to be all right?" she asked.

Trish waved her hands at the piles of briefing books, red-lined hardcopies, marked-up magazine articles and memos from her Board of Directors. "Of course!" she said. She shook her head. "Probably. We never thought we'd get this far, remember? All this psy-ops shit they're pulling, it's just more proof that we're on the right track. No one should be able to do this. It's the opposite of democracy. It's the opposite of civil discourse."

The lawyer smoothed her moustache. "Right on," she said. "You've should be proud. This is a hell of a fight, and I'm glad to be part of it. You know we'd follow you into the sun, right?"

Trish fluttered her hands. "God, don't give me that kind of responsibility."

"All right then, into the ocean. We're making this happen, is what's important."

"Thanks, babe," Trish said. She put on a brave smile until the lawyer had backed out of the office, then stared down at her calendar and looked at her morning schedule. Three congressional staffers, a committee co-chair, an ACLU researcher, and the head of the newly formed Emergent Network Suppliers' Industry Association—a man she had last seen in her office at UCLA, backing away from a long and melancholy hug.

❦

When he rang off the phone and joined her, finally, she straightened out her smart cardigan and said, "Rainer, you're certainly looking . . . well."

". . . funded," he finished, with a small smile. The Emergent Network Suppliers' Industry Association's new offices were in a nice Federal Revival building off Dupont Circle, with lots of stained glass that nicely set off the sculptural and understated furniture. "It's not as grand as appearances suggest, Trish. We got it for a song from the receivers in the Church of Scientology's bankruptcy, furnishings included. It *is* nice though. Don't you think?"

"It's lovely," she said. Around her, staffers bustled past in good suits and good shoes and smart haircuts. "Hard to believe you only set up shop a week ago," she said.

"It came furnished, remember," he said.

"Oh yes, so you said," she said, watching a kid who looked like he'd gone tops in his class at the Naval Academy put his ankles up on the plasticized return beside his desk and tilt his chair, throwing his head back with wild laughter at whatever it was some other Hill Rat (in her mind, it was a key Congressman's aide—some old frat buddy of Mr Navy 2048) was saying at the phone's other end.

She looked back and Rainer and saw that he was staring where she had.

"Well, it's a far cry from academic research," he said.

"I know you'll be very good at it. You can explain things without making it seem like an explanation. The first lesson I ever learned on the Hill was, 'If you're explaining—'"

"'—you're losing,'" he said. "Yeah, I've heard that. Well, you're the old hand here, I'm just learning as I go. Trying not to make too many mistakes and to learn from the ones I do make."

"Do you want some free advice, Rainer?"

He sat down in one of the chairs, which bulged and sloshed as it conformed itself to his back and butt. He patted the upholstered jelly beside him. "You may always assume that I would be immensely grateful for your advice, Trish," he said.

She sat down and crossed her legs, letting her sensible shoe hang loose. "Right. DC is a *busy* place. In academic circles, in tech circles, you might get together to feel out your opponent, or to make someone's acquaintance, or to see an old friend. You might get together to enjoy the company of another human being.

"We do that in DC, *after* working hours. Strictly evenings and weekends. When you schedule a meeting during office hours, it has to have a purpose. Even if it appears to have no purpose, it has a purpose. There's a protocol to meetings, a secret language, that's known to every Hill Rat and written nowhere. What time you have the meeting, who's there, who's invited, who knows it, how long you schedule, whether you cater: they all say little things about the purpose of the meeting. Even if you have no reason to call the meeting, one will be read into it.

"If this was any other city in the world, it would make perfect sense for you to look me up once you got to DC. We're still friends, I still think about you from time to time, but here in DC, you calling me over for a meeting, this kind of meeting, at this time of day, it means you're looking to parley. You want to strike a deal before my bill goes to the committee. I don't know how well you know the Hill, so I don't

want to impute any motives to you. But if you took a meeting like this with anyone else, that's what they'd assume."

Rainer's forehead crinkled.

"No Fretting," she said. Then she smiled a sad smile.
"Oh, Fret if you want. You're a big boy."

He twiddled his thumbs, caught himself at it, and folded his hands in his lap. "Huh," he said. "Well. I *did* want to
talk to you because it's been a while and because we meant
a lot to each other. I *also* wanted to talk to you about the bill,
because that's what I'm here to do, at a pretty decent salary.
I *also* wanted to see you because I had an idea that you'd be
different here in your native habitat, and well, that's true."

She refused to let that make her self-conscious. Of
course she was different, but it wasn't geographic. The last
time they'd seen each other, they were lovers and friends.
Now they were ex-lovers who were being paid to accomplish
opposing, mutually exclusive objectives. She knew that
there was a certain power in not saying anything, so she
wrapped herself in silence and waited for him to say something. She didn't have to wait long.

"Your bill is going to committee?"

"Well, I certainly hope so," she said. "That's what I'm here
for, after all. The discussion draft has been circulating for a
week, and we're confident we'll see it introduced and assigned to committee by the end of this week. That's what
we're told, anyway. It's got strong bipartisan support. Selling
Congress on the importance of human-generated governance
is pretty easy. Wouldn't want to be in your shoes."

He grinned. "You're trying to psych me out."

"Maybe," she said, grinning back. "But that's nothing
compared to the psych job that we've been getting down at
my office." She told him about the phone weirdness, the
oddball traffic-management. "Someone on your side has a
funny sense of humor."

His smile faded. "You're still trying to fake me out," he
said. "If you're seeing corruption in the net, it's because
you're looking so hard, you can't help but find it. You're

reading malice into accident. Dead spots aren't personal, you know. This is a law of nature—the networks emerge solutions, they're the best they can come up with. If you don't like the results, talk to nature, not me."

She shrugged. "Whatever, Rainer. I know what's happening. You'll believe what you want to believe." She pursed her lips and made an effort at controlling her irritation. "It's really happening, and it's not helping your side. If you know who's responsible, you might let him know that the dirty tricks are what convinced Senator Beauchamp's staff to green-light the bill. Conspiracy is supposed to be beneath the surface. It doesn't look so good when it's exposed to fresh air and sunshine."

"You've got to be kidding," he said. "Doesn't matter, I suppose. All right, message received. If I happen to run into someone who I think should hear it, I'll be sure to pass it on, OK?"

"That's all I ask," she said.

"You want to talk about the bill now?"

"Have you seen the discussion draft?"

He squirmed. "No," he admitted. "I didn't know it existed until just now."

"I'd offer to send you a copy, but I expect it would take a week to arrive, if it ever did. Why don't you ask that guy," she gestured at the Navy man, "to get you a copy? He looks like he knows his way around. And then drop by my office if you want to chat about it."

She stood up and tugged at her cardigan again. "It's been very nice seeing you," she said. She picked up her coat and her mitts. "Good luck settling in."

He gave her a hug, which felt weird, hugging was strictly west-of-the-Mississippi, and she broke it off firmly and showed her to the door. The first snows were coming in, and the steps were slightly icy, so she maneuvered them slowly, carefully. When she reached the road, he was no longer in the doorway. He was standing right behind her, breath coming out in foggy huffs.

"Trish," he said, then stopped. His arms dropped to his sides and his shoulders slumped.

"Rainer," she said, keeping her voice calm and neutral.

"God," he said. "God. How'd this happen, Trish? Look, I've never been happy the way I was with you. I haven't been that happy since. God, Trish—"

"Rainer," she said again, taking one of his hands, firmly, motherly. "Rainer. Stop it. You're here to do a job, and your job requires that you and I keep it on a professional level. It doesn't matter how it happened. . . ." But it did, didn't it? She'd left him to come east and do something he thought of as wrong-headed and backwards and superstitious. But she'd left him, not the other way around. And he'd never recovered, though she'd built herself a new life here. It wasn't a contest (but she was winning anyway). "It doesn't matter. We respect each other. That's enough."

He deflated and she said, "Oh, come here," and gave him a long and soulful hug, right there on the street, knowing that she was giving the hug and he was taking it. Then she let him go, spun him round, and gave him a little push back toward his office.

By the time she reached the corner and looked back over her shoulder, he was nowhere to be seen.

<hr/>

That afternoon, her phone started ringing normally, with actual people on the other end. Her outbound calls were connected. Her email was delivered. Her car got her home in record time. She sighed as she eased it into her driveway and carried her briefcase inside and poured herself a very small glass of Irish whisky so rare that it had been known to make grown men weep. Normally, she saved it for celebrations, but if she was celebrating something, she was damned if she knew what it was.

Her phone rang as she was licking the last few drops of liquor from the little glass. It was the lawyer, with news.

"I just stopped by the office and found a messenger on the doorstep. He had hard-copy of a press-release from Senator Beauchamp's office. They're introducing the bill in the morning. Congrats, kid, you did it."

Trish set the glass down and said [whoopee] very quietly and very emphatically.

"You're durned tootin'," the lawyer said. "And double for me."

Of course, it wasn't over by a long shot. Getting a bill introduced was not the same as getting it through committee. Getting it through committee was not the same as getting it passed in the Senate, and getting it passed in the Senate was not the same as getting it passed in the House, and then who the hell knew what the hereditary Chimp-in-Chief in the Oval Office would do when it was passed through the bars of his cage with his morning banana.

But she had ridden back into town less than a year before, and she had gone from nothing to this. The ACLU was supporting the bill, and EFF, EPIC, all the old civ-lib mafia had opened their arms to her. She poured herself one more very small whisky, gave herself a fragrant bath and put herself to bed, grinning like a fool.

"There are four news-crews, six print reporters, and a couple of others here to see you," the office-manager said. The office phones were out again, but that hadn't stopped a fair number of determined people from figuring out that they could actually move their physical being from one part of Washington to another and have a real, old-fashioned face-to-face. The lawyer and she had each taken a dozen press "calls" that morning, with their embedded reporters from Columbia J-School perched obtrusively in the corners of their offices, taking copious notes and filming constantly.

"Others?"

"A mixed bag. Some Hill people, some I'm not sure about."

Trish stood and stretched out her back, listening to it pop. She usually worked in bursts, typing or talking for an hour, then taking a little walk to gather her thoughts and touch base with her co-workers. Today, she'd been glued to her seat from 7 a.m. to after lunchtime, and her back and butt were shrieking at her.

She walked into the front area, trailed by her reporter. She recognized some of the journos and some of the Congressional staffers, and a local rep from a European Privacy think-tank in Brussels, and—Rainer.

He was turned out in a very natty suit and a homburg, a fashion that had recently come back to DC, and she knew that he'd been put together by a personal shopper. Her own Board had suggested to her, matter-of-factly, that she should get one of her own once the bill cleared committee, since she'd be doing tons of press and as sharp a dresser as she fancied herself, she was no pro. Her prodigious talents, they assured her, lay elsewhere.

He took her hand with both of his and gave her a long, intense hand shake that drew stares from the journos and the think-tank man.

"Nice to see you again, Ms. McCavity," he said, somberly.

"A pleasure as always, Mr. Feinstein," she said.

"I'm sorry to drop in on you unannounced," he said, "but I hoped that I could have just a moment of your time." Belatedly, he remembered to take off his silly hat and then he fumbled with the right way to hold it, settling for dropping it to his waist and upending it. She thought he looked like a panhandler in a Charlie Chaplin movie and she suppressed a smile. His curly hair had been gelled into a careful configuration that reminded her of the glossy ringlets of a black poodle.

"I suppose we can do that," she said. She turned to her other visitors. "Who's got a 3 p.m. deadline?" she said. Two of the print-reporters held up their hands. "You then you," she said. "Who's got a 5 p.m. filing deadline? 6 p.m.? 10 p.m.?" She triaged them all, promised to meet the think-tank man for dinner at an Ethiopian place in Adams-Morgan, and led Rainer into her office and closed the door.

He looked at her embedded reporter and cocked his head.

"Sorry, Rainer," she said. "I have a shadow for the duration. Just pretend he isn't here. You don't mind, do you dear?" she said to the reporter, who was very young and very bright and missed nothing. He shook his head and made some notes.

"The bill's dead," Rainer said, after he'd sat down.

"Oh really?" she said.

"Just heard from Senator Rittenhouse, personally. He takes the position that this should be in Commerce, not Judiciary, and is calling hearings to make that happen."

Rittenhouse was another powerful committee chairman, and this wasn't good news. What's more, he was in the pocket of the network operators and had been for a decade, so much so that editorialists and talk-radio types called him "The Senator from The Internet."

Still, it wasn't catastrophic. "That's interesting," she said, "but it's a far cry from killing the bill. It's pretty standard, in fact. Just slows things down." She smiled at him. He was just a kid sometimes, so out of his depth here. He reminded her of the Relatives she'd met that day, the little boys in their miniature suits running on the beach.

He shifted in his seat and fondled his hat-brim. "Well, I guess we'll see. My press-liaison has set up a post-mortem debate on one of the news-networks tonight, and I thought you might want to represent the other side?"

She smiled again. He was twice the rhetorician that she was, but he had no idea how to play the game. She'd have to be careful to bruise, not break him.

⁂

"We, as a society, make trade-offs all the time," Rainer

said. He was wearing a different suit this evening, something that Trish had to admit looked damned good on the
studio monitors (better than her frumpy blouse and wool
winter-weight trousers). "We trade a little bit of privacy for
a little bit of security when we show identification before
going into a federal building—"

The ewok held up his paw. "But how much should we
be willing to trade, Ms. McCavity?"

She looked into the camera, keeping her eyes still, the
way she'd been told to if she didn't want to appear touret-
tic. "Wickett, when Franklin said, 'Those willing to give up
a little liberty for a little security deserve neither security
nor liberty,' he wasn't spouting empty rhetoric, he was laying the groundwork for this enduring democratic experiment that we all love. Look, we're not opposed to the use of
autonomous networks for *some* applications, even *most*
applications, with appropriate safeguards and checks and
balances. No nation on earth has the reliance that we do on
these networks. Are they an appropriate way of advising
you on the best way to get to the mall on a busy Saturday?
Absolutely, provided that everyone gets the best advice the
system can give, regardless of economic status or influence.
But should they be used to figure out whom the FBI should
open an investigation into? Absolutely not. We use judges
and grand juries and evidence to establish the sufficiency
of a request to investigate a private citizen who is considered innocent until proven guilty. We learned that lesson
the hard way, during the War on Terrorism and the
Ashcroft witch-hunts. Should we trade grand juries and
judges for ant-colonies? Do you want the warrant for your
wiretap issued by an accountable human being or by a simulated ant-hill?"

The ewok turned to the camera. "Both sides make a
compelling case. What do you think? When we come back,
we'll take your calls and questions." The lights dimmed and
it adjusted its collar and cracked its hairy knuckles on the
table before it. Ever since it had made the move to a pbs, it

had been grooming its fur ever-more conservatively and trying out a series of waistcoats and short pants. It turned to her and stared at her with its saucer-sized black button eyes. "You know, I just wanted to say thanks—I had self-identified as an ewok since I was five years old, but Lucasfilm just wouldn't license the surgery, so I went through every day feeling like a stranger in my body. It wasn't until your law got enacted that I was able to find a doctor who'd do it without permission."

She shook its paw. "It wasn't my law, but I helped. I'm glad it helped you out." She unconsciously wiped her palm on her thigh as the ewok turned to his make-up boy and let him comb out its cheeks. She stared at Rainer, who wasn't looking good. She'd had him on the ropes since their opening remarks, and the ewok kept interrupting him to let her rebut—and now she knew why.

Rainer had his phone clamped to his head, and he was nodding vigorously and drumming his fingers. He was sweating, and it was making his hair come un-coiffed. Trish's own phone buzzed and she looked down at in surprise. It was her voice-mail, coming back to life again. It had started when she got to the studio—when she got within a few yards of Rainer, she realized. Messages coming in. She'd transcribed a dozen in the green-room before they'd dragged her into makeup.

The studio lights blinked and Rainer popped the phone back into his pocket and the ewok turned to look back into the camera, examining the ticker scrolling past his prompter. He introduced them again, then turned to Trish.

"Ms. McCavity, Alberto in San Juan writes in wanting to know what changes we should institute in the networks."

She said, "It's not my place to say what technical changes the networks need to have. That's where experts like Mr. Feinstein come in. We'd ask the administrative branch to solicit comments from people like him to figure out exactly what technical changes could be made to allow us to remain competitive without giving up our fundamental liberties in order to beat the occasional traffic jam."

"Mr. Feinstein?"

He grinned and leaned forward. "It's interesting that Ms. McCavity should disavow any technical expertise, since that's what we've been saying all along. If she's getting stuck in traffic, it's because there's a *lot* of traffic. The antnets route *five thousand percent more traffic* than our nation's highways ever accommodated without them, and they've increased the miles-per-hour-per-capita-per-linear-mile by *six thousand, four hundred percent.* You're stuck in traffic? Fine. I get stuck sometimes too. But for every hour you spend stuck today, you're saving *hundreds* of hours relative to the time your parents spent in transit.

"The other side of this debate are asking for something impossible: they want us to modify the structure of the network, which is a technical construct, built out of bits and equations, to accommodate a philosophical objective. They assert that this is possible, but it's like listening to someone assert that our democracy would be better served if we had less gravity, or if two plus two equalled five. Whether or not that's true, it's not reasonable to ask for it."

The ewok turned to her.

She said, "Well, we've heard a great deal about the impossibility of building democratic fundamentals into the network, but nothing about the possibilities. This hard, no-compromise line is belied by the fact that we know that the rich and powerful manipulate the network to their own advantage, something that statistics have proven out—"

"See, this is *exactly* how these Human-Readable types do it, it's how their media-training goes. They are here to ask for changes to *technical* specifications, but they disavow any technical knowledge, and when they're called on this, they spout dubious 'statistics' that 'prove' that up is down, black is white, and that millionaires can get to the movies in half the time that paupers can. The Emergent

Network Suppliers' Industry Association represents the foremost experts in this field, but you don't need to be an expert to know that these networks *work*. The ants take us where we want to go, in the shortest time, with the highest reliability. Anyone who doubts that can dig out her map and compass and sextant and try to navigate the world without their assistance, the way they do in Europe."

Her mouth was open. *Media training?* Where did he get this business about *media training?* "I'm not sure where Mr. Feinstein gets his information about my media training from, but personally, I'd rather talk about networks." She paused. "Let's talk about Europe, where they *have* found ways of creating transparency and accountability for these 'unregulatable' algorithms, where the sky *hasn't* fallen and the final trump hasn't sounded. What do they know that we don't?"

"What indeed?" the ewok said, breaking in and giving her the last word again. "More of your questions after this break."

They got in their cars together after they'd scrubbed off their makeup and shaken paws with the ewok, riding down in the elevator shoulder to shoulder, slumped and sweaty and exhausted. They didn't speak, and the silence might have been mistaken for companionable by someone who didn't know any better.

They got off at the same floor in the parking garage and turned in the same direction, and Trish spied his car, parked next to hers, the last two on the floor. Quickening her step, she opened her door and turned the car on, backing up so that she was right behind Rainer.

He backed out slowly, looking at her quizzically in his rearview, but she refused to meet his eye, and when he pulled out, she rode his bumper.

"Sweet fancy Moses," she breathed, as the traffic parted before them, allowing them to scythe through the streets, onto the Beltway. She hung grimly onto his bumper, cutting off cars that tried to shift into her lane. Moving this fast after so much time stuck on the roads, it felt like flying. She laughed and then got a devilish idea.

Spotting a gap in the passing lane, she zipped ahead of Rainer and swerved back into his lane so that she was in the lead. As though a door had slammed shut, the traffic congealed before them into a clot as thick as an aneurysm. She hissed out a note of satisfaction, then waited patiently while Rainer laboriously passed her again, and the traffic melted away once more.

It was tempting not to get off at her exit, but she had to get some sleep, and so she reluctantly changed lanes. There wasn't much traffic on the road, but every traffic light glowed vindictive red all the way to her house.

The Chairman of her Board messengered over a hand-written note of congratulations that was on her doorstep. Beneath it was a note from Rainer's great-aunt, with the best wishes of his mother in neat pen beneath it. She read its kind words as she boiled the kettle, and put it into her pile of correspondence to answer. Rainer's great-aunt wanted to know if she had met a nice boy in DC yet, but she didn't come right out and say it, too subtle for that. The women in Rainer's family got all the subtlety, and they recognized their own kind. It was why she and the old lady kept writing to each other; that and so that the Relatives could reassure themselves that someone in full possession of life-guardly skills and a level head was watching out for Rainer's interests.

This business of hand-written, hand-delivered notes and letters was actually kind of charming, she thought as she put her feet up on her coffee table and opened up her flask of very special Irish whisky again.

⚜

She and Rainer went head to head in half a dozen more skirmishes that month—her phone popping back to life every time she got within shouting distance of him. The on-again/off-again hearings in both Judiciary and Commerce never quite materialized.

She was better at playing the game, but he was a fast learner, and he had much deeper pockets and working network infrastructure. Her Board approved her renting out an empty suite of offices below their office and converting them to bedrooms for her staff for days when their cars couldn't get them home. They secretly borrowed elderly network appliances from relatives or bought them in the dollar-a-pound bin at the Salvation Army, but always, within a few hours of being in the possession of someone in the employ of the Association for a Human-Readable World, the devices would seize up and lose their routes to the network. Their offices started to fill up with dead soldiers, abandoned network boxes that no one could get online.

The embedded journalists went home after the second week. Their own gear was seizing up, too, as though the curse of the Association for a Human-Readable World was rubbing off on them. They vowed to return when things got interesting again, but they were of no use to anyone without working cameras, mics, and notepads.

Christmas came and went, and New Year's, and then February arrived and the city turned to ice and slush and perpetual twilight. The paralegal quit—she needed a job where the phones worked so that she could call her girlfriend. The media guy took a series of "personal days" and she wasn't sure if he'd show up again, but it didn't matter, because the press had stopped calling them.

Then came the second Downtime.

It struck during morning rush-hour on Valentine's Day, a Monday, and it juddered the whole country to a halt for eight long days. The hospitals overflowed and doctors used motorized scooters to go from one place to another, unable to spread their expertise around with telemedicine. Firemen perished in blazes. Cops arrived too late at crime-scenes. Grocery stores didn't get their resupplies, and schools dug out old chalkboards and taught the few students who lived close enough to walk. Fed cops of all description went berserk, and could be seen walking briskly from one federal building to another, their faces grim.

And suddenly, miraculously, every journalist, policy-wonk, staffer, advisor, clerk and cop in DC wanted to have a chat with the Association for a Human-Readable World.

⚜

She hired three more people that week, and borrowed four more from fellow-traveller organizations. Paying their salaries for the next four weeks would bottom out the group's finances, but she knew that this was now or never, and the Board backed her, after some nail-biting debate.

Rainer showed up on the fourth day of the Downtime, and she found him standing, bewildered, in the hustle of her office as her staffers penned notes on steno pads to their contacts on the Hill and handed them to waiting bicycle couriers in space-program warmgear that swathed them from fingertips to eyeballs. She plucked him out of the bustle and brought him back to her office.

"I've got a hell of a nerve," he said, sitting in her guest-chair.

"Really?" she said. "I hadn't noticed."

"Well, I haven't been showing it off. But I'm about to. I need advice. My office is falling apart. You've been living with no communications and no travel for a year now, you know how to make it work. We're completely lost. I've come to throw myself on your mercy." He looked up at her with his big brown eyes, and then they crumpled shut as he made his Fretting face.

"You're playing me, Rainer," she said. "And it won't work. Whatever I feel for you, I've got a job to do, and if this Downtime tells us anything, it's that I'm doing the right thing, and you're doing the wrong thing."

He hung his head. He wasn't even the slightest bit natty that day. She supposed that his personal assistant was stuck in Falls Church or Baltimore or somewhere, unable to get into the city. Judging from the slush and road-salt on his shoes, he must have walked the two miles between their offices.

"What's more, I don't have any advice to give you, in particular. We're not faring well here because we're doing something differently—we're faring well because we're doing what we've been at all along, because of a network outage that you claim is impossible, is a figment of our imagination. Those bike messengers: we've been their best customers for months now. Everyone else is begging for service from them, but they're always here when we need them. We've got beds and changes of clothes and toilet-kits in the offices downstairs. We've been living through a Downtime for a couple of quarters now—we've hardly noticed the change. If you want to cope as well as we are, well, you can go back in time, rent out spare offices to house your staff, establish a good working relationship with a bike-messenger company, learn to navigate the Metro and the freeways by map, and all the other things we've done here."

He looked defeated. He began to stand, to turn, to leave.

"Rainer," she said.

He paused.

"Close the door and sit down," she said.

He did, looking at her with so much hope that it made her eyes water.

"Here's my offer," she said. "You and I will lock ourselves in this office with the last draft of my bill. My staff will run interference for me with the Judiciary committee, and we will draft a version of my bill that we can both live with. We will jointly take it to Senators Beauchamp and Rittenhouse, with our blessings, and ask them to expedite it through *both* committees. Every Congress-critter on the Hill is sitting around with his thumb up his ass until the lights come back on. We can get this voted in by Tuesday."

He stared down at his hands. "I can't do it," he said. "My *job* is *not to compromise.* I just can't do it."

"Come on, Rainer, think outside the box for a minute here." Her heart was pounding. This could really be it. This could be the solution she'd been waiting for. "Even if the bill passes, there's going to be a long deliberation over the contours of the regulation, probably at the FCC. You'll be able to work on the bureau staffers and at the expert agencies, take ex-parte meetings and lobby on behalf of your employers. It's all we've ever asked for: an expert discussion where the public interest gets a hearing alongside of private enterprise and government."

But he was shaking his head, standing up to go. "You're probably right, Trish," he said. "I don't know. What I know is, I can't do what you're asking of me. They'd just fire me."

"If the Downtime continues, they won't be *able* to fire you; they won't even know what you're up to until it's too late. And then they'll make the best that they can out of it. No one is better qualified to represent your side in the administrative agencies."

He put his ridiculous hat on and wrapped his scarf around his neck, and they looked each other in the eyes for a long moment. She waited for the involuntary smile that looking into his eyes inevitably evoked, but it didn't come.

"I don't understand you, Trish. You won this incredible victory for cooperation, for collective ownership of our intellectual infrastructure. Ant-networks demand the same cooperation from the nodes, that my phone pass your car's messages to his desk. Let's just set aside the professional politics for a second. Just you and me. Tell me: how can you *not* support this?" He looked at her out from under his brows, staring intensely. He swallowed and said, "It was the surfer, wasn't it?"

"What?" she said.

"The one who died. That's why you're doing this. You want to make up for him—"

She couldn't believe he'd said it. Taken such a cheap shot. "I'm surprised you didn't save that one for television, Rainer. Jesus. No, I'm doing this because it's *right*. In case you haven't noticed, your self-healing, uncorruptable network is *down*. People are suffering. The economy is tanking. The death toll is mounting. You won't even bend one *inch*, one *tenth of an inch*, because you're worried about losing your job."

"Trish," he said, "I'm sorry, I didn't mean—"

Her office door opened and there stood her embedded journalist. "I just got in from Manhattan," he said. "Can I set up in that corner there again?"

"Be my guest," she said, grateful for the distraction. Rainer looked at her, forehead scrunched, and then he left.

⚜

"It's a good thing you're not over him," the lawyer said, pouring her another victory whisky. The bill had passed the House with only one opposing and two abstentions, and had squeaked through the Senate by five seats, at five minutes to midnight on the eighth day of the Downtime. They were halfway to the bar (where the office manager had been feeding twenties to the bartender to stay open) when the grid came back up, crawls springing to life on every surface and cars suddenly zipping forward in the characteristic high-speed ballet of efficiently routed traffic. They'd laughed themselves stupid all the way to the bar and after a brief but intense negotiation between the lawyer and the barman, he'd produced a bottle of Irish that was nearly half as good as the stuff Trish kept at home.

"I'm going to pretend you didn't say that," Trish said, sipping tenderly at the booze.

"Come on, girl," the lawyer said, twirling her moustache. "Be serious. You two had so much sexual energy in that room, it's a wonder you didn't make the bulbs explode. It's how you got inside each other's heads. You weren't selling the committee, you were selling *him*, and that's what made you so effective. We're going to need that again at the FCC, too, so no getting over him until after then."

Trish drank her whisky. She didn't know what to say
that. He'd looked ten years older tonight, in the corridors,
whispering to his committee members, to his staffers, his
face drooping and wilted. She supposed she didn't look any
better. It had been, what, three days? since she'd had more
than an hour's sleep.

"I don't get it," she said. "How could he be so dumb? I
mean, it's obvious that the system is being gamed. Obvious
that we're being targeted through it. Yet he sits there,
insisting that white is black, that up is down, that the
network is autonomous and immune to all corruption."

"It's like a religion for them," the lawyer said. "It doesn't
need explaining. It's just right-living. It's the Law."

Trish thought back to the ceremony in the graveyard,
the dirge and the prayers to a god no one believed in. Had
Rainer really renounced his faith when he dropped out of
Yeshiva?

"Here's to a human-readable world," Trish said, raising
her glass. Around her, the staffers and borrowed staffers
and hangers-on and even the barman raised their glasses
and cheered. It was warm and the feeling swelled in her
tummy and up her chest and through her face and she
burst out in what felt like the biggest smile of her life.

She'd learned a long time ago never to send email while
drunk, but it had been too much last night.

"What if, Rainer, what if—what if the reason for the
Downtimes is that someone is manipulating the network
and that's breaking it. Did you ever wonder about that?
Maybe the network *is* as good as you say it is—until
someone screws it up by trying to get preferential treatment
for his pals.

"Wouldn't that be a kick in the teeth? We get five
squillion percent increases in across-the-board routing -
efficiency, but in the end, it's never enough for people

who can't be happy unless they're happier than someone else.

"The thing that saves the human race, but if we adopt it, it will destroy us. Irony sucks."

She'd signed it "Love," but even drunk, she'd had the sense to take that out before sending it. Saying "Love" would have been no more appropriate than saying, "You know, I *did* save your cousin's life." She'd called in no favors, she'd run no blackmail, and she'd won anyway.

He rang her doorbell at 5 a.m. She was barely able to drag herself out of bed.

"I figured you'd be getting up to deal with the press soon," he said, and she groaned. He was right. She'd earned some time off, but it'd be a month before she could take it. Too much press to do. She appreciated anew how much work it must have taken to be any of her old bosses from the copyright wars: the judge, the senator, the executive director of the PAC.

She was in her robe, and he was in jeans and a UCLA sweatshirt. He didn't have any gel in his hair, which was matted down by the knit cap he'd been wearing. He looked adorable.

"They fired me this morning," he said.

"Oh, hon—" she said.

"I would have quit," he said. "I'm outmatched."

She felt herself blush. Or was she flushing? She was suddenly aware of his smell, the boy smell, the smell that she could smell in his chest, in his scalp, in his tummy, lower . . . She straightened up and led him into the living room and started the coffee-maker going.

"When do you fly back, then?" she said.

He looked at her, smiling. "I don't know," he said. "I haven't booked a ticket."

She felt an answering smile at the corners of her mouth and turned into the fridge to fetch out some gourmet MREs. "Bacon and eggs or pancakes?" she said, then laughed. "I guess bacon is out," she said.

"Oh, I'm willing to bet that that bacon hasn't been anywhere near a pig," he said, "but I'll have the pancakes, if you don't mind."

She set everything to perking and went into the bedroom to pull on something smart and camera-friendly, but everything was in the hamper, so she settled for jeans and a decent shirt from last-year's wardrobe.

When she opened the door, he was standing right there, taller than her. "I think you're right," he said. "About the network. It's the best explanation I've heard so far."

She wrapped herself in silence again, waited for him to say more.

"You see, the *true*, neutral network is immune to corrupting influences and favoritism. So the existence of corruption and favoritism means that what we've got *isn't* a true network. Which means you're right! We need to have hearing to get to the bottom of this, so that we can build the true network." He smiled bravely. "I thought maybe you could use an expert in your corner who'd say that in a hearing?"

"Thanks," she said, and slipped under his arm and back into the kitchen. Suddenly, she wanted very much to be back at her office, back with her staff, talking to reporters and overseeing a million details. "I'll think about it."

"I'm giving up my apartment at the end of the month—next Monday. I won't be able to afford it without the Association's salary," he said.

Her place was big. A bedroom, a home office, a living room and a dining room. It was a serious deal for DC, even outside the Beltway. It could easily accommodate a second person, even if they weren't sleeping together.

Her office—her staff—the press—the bill—her Board.

"Well," she said, "I've got to get going. I'll shower at the office. Got to get there in time to catch the Euro press-calls. Let me put your breakfast in a bag, OK?"

He looked whipsawed. "Uh, OK. Can I give you a ride?"

"No, I'll need my car this afternoon. Thanks, though."

She kept her voice light, didn't meet his eyes. Kept thinking: her office—her staff—the bill.

"Well," he said. He turned for the door. Stopped. She tensed. He turned back to her. "Trish," he said.

"It's OK," she said. "It's OK. We just have religious differences, is all."

She slipped past him and into her car, and left him standing in her driveway. As she asked the car to plot a route for her back to the Hill, she dug through her purse for a pocket-knife. At the next red light, she took her lapel and slashed at it, opening a rent in her shirt that reflected a little of what her heart was feeling. It made her feel a little better to do it.

— For Alice

INTRODUCTION TO SHOPPING AT THE MALL
Ernest Lilley

I like everything in here, but I'll admit this is one of my favorites, so I saved it for last. Canadian writer Jim Gardner pays tribute to an SF classic in this thoroughly modern tale of the future of capitalism and the fate of the nation. One of the ironies about the future is that it's something those things you can affect, but you may not be able to stick around and see how things turned out. In its slightly warped way, this is one of the more hopeful futures I had a chance to glimpse, and I hope you like it as much as I do.

Shopping at the Mall

James Alan Gardner

When the U.S. self-destructed, nobody noticed at first. We'd developed a knack for ignoring whatever the Americans did.

Then China mentioned that the U.S. had stopped paying for all those T-shirts and fishing rods. It wasn't the first time this had happened, but it did catch a bit of attention. Next, Canada noticed that all the American TV stations were stuck on auto-loop, playing the same shows over and over again every four hours. It wasn't the first time *that* had happened either, but put the two things together and it made people wonder. A few months later, Mexico finally got curious enough to peek across the border only to discover that every man, woman, and child in the U.S. was dead. A coroner from Brussels ruled it mass suicide, even though he admitted he and his staff of three had cut corners in the investigation. "But I'm sure," he said, "it was suicide-ish," and the rest of the world accepted that.

The U.S.A., characteristically believing itself immortal, hadn't left a will. Everybody asked, "Who gets America's stuff?" But there was only one sensible answer: it had to be sold to cover the country's debts. Anything left over . . . but that was a guaranteed laugh-line at any comedy club in the world. Considering the size of American debts, *nothing* would be left over. For decades, the U.S. had had practically no income—just the royalty money that people paid to listen to Elvis and watch *Die Hard 2*.

Still, as one of the many professional liquidators hired

to sell the assets of the deceased, I wanted to get as much as possible. I had an easier job than some; my loathsome competitor, Guillermo Singh, got assigned downtown Detroit (heh), but I was picked to auction off the District of Columbia.

My first step, of course, was to scope out the property. I brought along my family. They like taking part in my work, even when they don't understand what I'm selling.

"Washington, D.C.," said my wife Rei. "Is that the place with the cowboys?"

"Well," I said, "some were cowboy-ish."

My son Ivan asked, "Is the United States the one where they say, 'Pip pip cheerio?'"

"No, dear," said Rei, "United States is the one that called itself a melted pot."

Note to self: before auctioning the place off, I had to enhance Washington's brand identity

It was local spring, rife with cherry blossoms and pandas shuffling in mating dances. Sometime during the twenty-first century, the city administration had noticed (a) a plunge in tourism, and (b) the extinction of most indigenous wildlife due to the Indigenous Wildlife Support Act. The mayor had decided to kill two birds with one stone by bioengineering pandas from the National Zoo, producing breeds that filled every ecological niche. This was the basis for a PR campaign aimed at drawing in tourists: WASHINGTON —COME FOR THE PANDAS, STAY FOR THE FUN!!

The campaign was no more successful than its predecessor (WE LEGISLATE EXCITEMENT!) or its follow-on (PURSUE THE HAPPINESS!!!) but the pandas had thrived: black-and-white squirrel pandas sitting on their haunches up in the trees; black-and-white rat pandas roaming the back streets in search of bamboo-filled dumpsters; black-and-white bat pandas fluttering around at sunset; black-and-white orca pandas hunting black-and-white penguin pandas just beyond the dikes that kept the city from being flooded. My daughter Shwaanzee was particularly taken with the fuzzy black-and-white caterpillars that would soon become panda butterflies. I left her and the rest of the family in one of the panda-filled parks while I scouted the rest of the city.

I was pleased to see the former owners hadn't trashed the place on their way out. The property wasn't clean, but it was clean-ish, and it had a lot of older buildings that looked vaguely familiar. I like that when I'm selling a city. Generic homes and office towers are practically worthless; you just send in wrecker robots to clear the land, and maybe after the property is sold, you can re-use some of the construction materials when you "build to suit." But I thought Washington's vintage architecture might do well with antique collectors . . . and anyway, in the liquidation business, we love the phrase "as is."

※

While robots created a catalog of what the city contained, I got down to the most important part of my job: marketing. Good liquidators don't just list what they have for sale; they figure out a hook that tells buyers, "This one is special."

After all, I was competing with every other liquidator flogging parcels of the U.S., some of whom had really *interesting* property to push. Whoever got to sell Hollywood was sitting on a goldmine—equal only to Memphis and the still-radioactive ruins of Redmond. In the coming months, there'd be thousands of auctions across the country, and I didn't want mine to be outshone by Missoula (JUST AS WILD AS YOU THINK!) or Nantucket (EVERY WORD OF THE LIMERICK IS TRUE!).

So I had to spin my sale to capture the public's imagination—maybe not the *whole* public but a niche that would buy what I had to sell.

"How about history buffs?" Rei suggested that night at the supper table. "Can you pretend that Washington has historical significance?"

"Every city has *some* historical significance," I replied. "For Washington, you can say 'Dickens slept here.' But history buffs are quirky. At an auction last week, one of Gandhi's breechcloths went for more than a million, but his glasses didn't get an opening bid." I shook my head. "You can never tell what history buffs will be keen on. By sheer luck, you might have something that appeals to them . . . but then you don't have to advertise because they'll line up at your door without prompting." I pondered for a second, then added, "On the other hand, people who only *think* they're history buffs . . ."

Rei laughed. "You've thought of something clever?"

"Well," I said, "clever-ish.

Brand Identity #1: History Land

My knowledge of Washington history came from reading a single encyclopedia entry. That put me ahead of almost everyone on the planet, but I thought I should learn more. That's why I invited my old friend Omar to visit. He'd been my roommate at the Sorbonne. Since Omar was a history major, I liked to ask for his advice on any job where I wanted to glorify the past.

By the time Omar arrived, my family had settled into the city's presidential palace (or whatever it was called). It was the only place in town with anything close to a modern comm connection . . . and that was stashed down in the basement, in an unmarked room filled with outmoded surveillance equipment. My son Ivan thought the room had been used by American intelligence agents furtively spying on the rest of the world. I was more inclined to think El

Presidente snuck in here for virtual full-bodies, but I didn't say that in front of the boy. Anyway, the comm link allowed the kids to go to school and my wife (who writes pop songs) to access her music synthies back home, so we were set up just fine. (The palace was infested with panda mice, but Shwaanzee befriended a stray panda cat that was doing his best to rectify the situation.)

As soon as Omar's body stabilized after transmission, he suggested we go for a walk. We strolled down what he called the Mall—a longish green-space with a local god's temple on one end, a big domed building on the other (probably a college, though it only had two lecture halls), and a huge phallic symbol in the middle. Shwaanzee (who's always had a schoolgirl crush on Omar) asked eagerly, "So did any history happen here?"

"No," said Omar, "this is more a commemoration of history that happened elsewhere."

Shwaanzee pointed to the phallic symbol. "So what does that commemorate?"

Ivan snickered. Rei glared at him and his sister. "That's enough of *that*."

"But," Ivan insisted, "I bet you could sell that, umm, thing for lots of money. Couldn't you, dad?"

I nodded. There's always a market for oversized erotica, especially from little-known cultures. I'd never worried about selling that particular item; it was everything else that bothered me.

"So could we say," I asked Omar, "that this city is like a historical theme park? The kind of park with exhibits commemorating the Siege of Sevastopol and the birth of Pablo Neruda?"

"I suppose so. Except that the events memorialized here aren't so famous."

"Like what?" I asked.

Omar pointed at monuments and named names. The rest of us stared blankly. Even Shwaanzee, who usually hangs on Omar's every word, glazed over after a few seconds.

But maybe, I thought, we can still pull this off. Some-times you can create an "emperor's new clothes" effect: you set up a sale and advertise it as if any fashionable person should recognize what you're hawking. Gauche nouveau riche trend-seekers rush to buy because they don't want to admit they've never heard of the stuff.

It was worth a shot. And I didn't have any better ideas.

Thus was born: HISTORY LAND—REVEALING THE SECRETS "THEY" DON'T WANT YOU TO KNOW. It seemed like a promising approach: breezily admitting that Washingtonian lore might be obscure, but not because it was boring or unimportant. Word about these events had been *suppressed*. By means of this auction, cognoscenti could pierce the veil of lies and discover awful truths.

Or something like that. It never pays to be specific when invoking an air of conspiracy.

In the week preceding that first auction, my whole fam-ily had fun writing catalog entries for things we didn't understand. *What is the meaning of the strange Ellipse inscribed on an otherwise normal lawn? Why monuments to Vietnam and Korea thousands of kilometers from Asia? And what hideous secret does the eye-in-the-pyramid seal . . .* nah, that one crossed the line. Everyone would think we'd mocked up that seal ourselves to create an air of cheap mystery. I sent Ivan with nano stone-eaters to erase that symbol on all the buildings where it appeared. Otherwise, it would damage our credibility.

Came the day of the auction. Turnout was good . . . but I'd been monitoring similar sales-events across the U.S. and turnout had been good at every one. People were curious to see America. Unfortunately, big crowds didn't guarantee big business. Proceeds at other sales had been poor. People said, "Everything's so run down . . . and so *ordinary*."

Which was true. American cities like Albany or

Albuquerque were no different from cities anywhere else in the world. They had the same coffee shops as Bangkok or Brasilia. They had the same shopping malls as Stockholm or Soweto. The only difference was that the U.S. versions were usually old and seedy, unlike their fresher, better-kept relatives out in the real world.

I told myself I'd do better with Washington than the people liquidating other cities. D.C.'s run-of-the-mill properties were nothing to crow about, but HISTORY LAND had promise . . . provided naïve customers would swallow hooks like THE NATIONAL PORTRAIT GALLERY: WHO ARE ALL THESE PEOPLE AND WHY HAVE YOU NEVER HEARD OF THEM? WHAT TERRIBLE TRUTHS DID THESE SEEKERS DISCOVER THAT THEY HAD TO BE ERASED FROM PUBLIC CONSCIOUSNESS?

That particular line worked—I sold the entire gallery to a Jakarta bio-industrialist who said, "My trophy husband is interested in shit like that." But it was one of my few successes. People looked but didn't buy. Many just fed the panda pigeons, or drank beer and ate hot dogs in the hospitality tents. At the end of the day, I still had most of my big-ticket items on hand.

"The thing is, dad," Ivan said that night at supper, "nobody really *likes* history. Especially history that happened to other people."

I had to admit he was right.

❧

Don't think I was discouraged. I'd never expected to unload the entire city in a single sale. Significant estates almost always need several kicks at the can, each spun for a different class of buyer: first the idle rich, then professional dealers, then weekend bargain-hunters, and so on down to Portobello Road hoi polloi.

So around the dinner table in the presidential palace, I asked my family and Omar if they had any new ideas.

"What about democracy?" Omar asked.

"What about it?" I replied.

"Americans considered Washington a symbol of democracy. They were very big on freedom. They thought they'd invented it."

"No way," said Ivan. "Athens invented democracy."

Shwaanzee told him, "You think you're so smart. If Uncle Omar says Americans invented democracy, they did."

"They didn't," Omar said. "Neither did Athens. But Americans were the first to make a fetish out of it."

"What's a fetish?" asked Shwaanzee.

"Eat your dinner," said Rei.

"But you can sell fetishes for lots of money," said Ivan. "Can't you, dad?"

"What have you been telling that boy?" Rei asked me.

"He must have eavesdropped when I was selling off Brisbane." I turned quickly to Omar. "But I'm sure you meant 'fetish' metaphorically, right?"

"Well," said Omar, "metaphoric-ish. With Americans and liberty, take nothing for granted."

"Liberty is good," said Shwaanzee. "Isn't it, Uncle Omar?" Before Omar could answer, Shwaanzee added, "For the next sale, we should do whatever Uncle Omar says. Cuz he's *smart.*"

Omar looked embarrassed. Rei and I gave him reassuring looks. "We know he's smart, honey," I told Shwaanzee. "And who knows? This democracy angle might work. Everybody takes it for granted nowadays, but once upon a time, most countries were run by kings and dictators." I turned to Rei and Omar. "If we could sell the idea that Washington was an important step forward from the bad old days . . . with the Revolution and all . . ."

"The Revolution!" Ivan said. "Is this where they guillotined people?"

"Different revolution," Omar told him. "And Washington D.C. wasn't part of America's revolution either. The city wasn't founded till a few years after the fighting ended."

"But its attitude is revolution-ish," I said. "Down with

the Fat Cats. Down with The Man. Down with unjust taxes and power to the people!"

"Are you and I talking about the same Washington?" Omar asked.

I smiled. "We've proved straight history doesn't work. Now we're going for High Concept."

Brand Identity #2: Liberty Land

A guillotine fit just fine in the rotunda of that college at the end of the Mall. Rei said it was the perfect setting. And Ivan and Shwaanzee put up memorials of other famous revolutions all around the place . . . like a giant mural of Mao's Long March hung across the pillars in front of the Supreme Court, and statues of Pancho Villa and Emiliano Zapata in the gap where the National Portrait Gallery used to be.

These decorations were only intended to create an ambience—what Omar called "the *aroma* of freedom." We didn't want to state explicitly that Washington had been involved with any of these revolutions (though Omar said there were a few in Latin America we'd be safe in mentioning). Our plan was simply to evoke a general aura of rebelliousness: that in-your-face take-no-crap crush-your-enemies sense of pugnacious entitlement that practically *screamed*, "Washington."

The slogan for this sale was LIBERTY LAND: BUY INTO THE FREEDOM! (We'd discussed FREEDOM FOR SALE AT REASONABLE PRICES, ALL THE FREEDOM MONEY CAN BUY, and GIVE ME LIBERTY OR GIVE ME DEALS! but those didn't test well with focus groups.) To stay with the theme, we piped appropriate music through loudspeakers across the entire district—the Internationale, La Marseillaise, Tubthumping, and a lot of other defiant tunes that no doubt got Washingtonian hearts pumping back in the old days. We even adjusted the menus in the hospitality tents: Democracy Dogs, Independence Ale, and Anarchy Apple Pie.[1]

---

[1] Yes, I avoided the obvious joke. Give me *some* credit. *The Author*

In short, we'd changed demographics: from stuffed-shirt history lovers to down-and-dirty 18-to-49's.

Rei said, "This is shaping up more like a party than a sale."

I told her, "The customers we want to attract don't know the difference."

⋆⋅⋆⋅⋆

It was a much wilder day than the first—several fights, people dancing naked in the reflecting pools, and a lot of shameless drunkenness. Most of our murals got defaced, and the Zapata statue was pushed over by a young inebriate who got creeped out because its eyes seemed to follow him.

Luckily, no one damaged the actual Washington merchandise. Unluckily, the reason was that people didn't take much notice of it. *Everyone* has an opinion, good or bad, about Emiliano Zapata. But who cares about unknowns like that god with the beard on the oversized throne? Kids stayed well back from that guy's statue because they thought he looked scary. Adults argued (idly) whether it was Zeus or an unknown local deity. But nobody showed any profitable interest in the god-statue, and nobody wanted to spend real money to take it off my hands.

(Okay, one of my pre-marriage girlfriends offered a few bucks for the statue as a mercy bid. Rei told her thanks but no thanks.)

Even so, the sale wasn't a total loss. Get a bunch of 18-to-49's drunk, play earsplitting music, and it's amazing what junk you can sell. Some of those dioramas at the Museum of Natural History went for *serious* cash. But once again, I was left with a disappointing amount of stock when we closed for the night.

Omar said, "I guess the connection between Washington and liberty is stretched pretty thin these days."

Ivan said, "But we got a really good price for the guillotine."

＊＊＊＊＊

That night in bed, Rei said, "I think it's like hot dogs."

"Excuse me?" I said, a little louder than I planned.

She gave me a mock slap. "No really. Somebody must have invented hot dogs, right? Maybe Omar even knows who and when. But that's just a piece of trivia. Just the name of somebody who happened to have a wiener and a bread-roll, and who put the two together. Now that people everywhere eat hot dogs, we're happy they were invented, but we don't much care who did it. We've moved on."

I said, "This is a metaphor, right? Not some obscure wifely hint that you want me to get you a snack?"

"It would be different if the inventor had kept making hot dogs," Rei said. "Because it's interesting to compare different brands of hot dogs and evaluate which brand is best. But if you just invent hot dogs and think that's enough—if your big claim to fame is that you once made a single hot dog, but then you got out of the business—and meanwhile everybody else is learning to make hot dogs too, and you're just pissing them off by saying, 'Those aren't the right kind of hot dogs' . . . well, the day finally comes when everybody in the world is eating hot dogs without even thinking about it, and you've won, you've *won*, except you don't know it because you're locked in your room, sulking."

I got out of bed. "So how many hot dogs do you want me to bring?"

Rei said, "Is there anything left of that apple pie?"

Brand Identity #3: Sentimentality Land

"So," I said at breakfast, "it's time for the lowest common denominator."

"Which is?" Omar asked.

"We started with history—that's brainy and upper-class. Then we went with revolution—that grabs the middle class, because it lets them fantasize about breaking things and having ideals. So the next targets down are the plebes. Any ideas how to rope them in?"

"Sentimentality and brutality?" Ivan suggested—making me proud that the boy actually *listened* to his old man.

"And how do we achieve those goals?" I asked.

"The Big Lie," Ivan and Shwaanzee recited in unison.

I gave them each an extra slice of toast.

"What would the Big Lie be in this case?" Omar asked.

"Hot dogs," said Rei.

We all looked at her.

"Hot dogs," she repeated. "We say they were invented at the Hirshhorn."

"That's definitely a big lie," Omar observed.

"But we haven't sold the Hirshhorn yet, have we?" Rei said. "So we link it to hot dogs. Some hot-dog-loving guy who's made a fortune in plumbing equipment will buy the place for his son's sixth birthday . . . just to impress all the other kids by telling them, 'This is where the hot-dog was born.'"

Omar snorted. "I suppose you'll say baseball was invented in that park near the river . . . and jazz in the Kennedy Center. The original monster truck competition was held in Dupont Circle and that crappy little airplane in the Smithsonian was the first to cross the Atlantic."

Rei said, "Speak slower, I'm writing these down."

"But . . ."

"It's all about sentimentality," I said, interrupting. "The warm fuzziness loved by people everywhere. There must be a million kitschy things whose origins have been forgotten. Snow domes. Beauty pageants. Chocolate bars. Coke. We tell the world they all started here, and peg their beginnings to the merchandise we still need to sell."

"But it's not true," Omar said. "With a little research, I

could likely find the real stories of where those things started . . ."

"So could anybody else," I told him. "Everyone's got smart data agents that can run through the search engines till something turns up. But that's not the point. When your lies are outrageous enough, the public will play along. People *love* snake oil salesmen—the more brazen the better. When they get home, they show off the snake oil they bought and everyone has a good laugh."

Ivan said, "It's called marketing, Uncle Omar. Everybody does it. Well . . . everybody-ish."

I gave the boy another slice of toast.

<hr />

We called it BELIEVE IT OR NOT: LOST SECRETS OF THE INSCRUTABLE WEST. We were shameless. Every building in the district was the site of some world-first, and every statue acquired an impressive background. The stories didn't have to make sense; we didn't try to link them with known history or even the limits of physics. For example, Omar invented a wonderful tale about that bearded god at the end of the Mall—that he'd been a giant lumberjack who could split logs with a single blow of his ax, that he'd dug huge rivers and canyons, that he'd had a pet ox named Ulysses and a dog named Jefferson Davis . . . all kinds of things like that. Shwaanzee said it was the best story she'd heard in her life. Omar mumbled that he'd borrowed bits of it, but Shwaanzee told him he'd borrowed exactly the right things. He was the smartest man *ever*.

I only wish Omar's smartness had been given a chance. That slimy Guillermo Singh—the one selling off downtown Detroit—must have been spying on us while we discussed our strategy. I suppose he bugged our home with some kind of nano-surveillance; it was just his style never to play fair. So the day before we were ready to announce our own sale, he announced his . . . stealing every one of our ideas. He claimed baseball had been invented in some crappy Detroit stadium, not to mention the hot dog, the chocolate bar, monster trucks, and all the rest.

I was so mad I called him to give him a piece of my mind. He just laughed. "Detroit invented unfair competition too," he told me. "But cheer up. When I rake in a fortune, you and your nice little family can be proud of how well your ideas worked. Isn't creativity supposed to be its own reward?"

I got pretty creative calling him bad names, but it wasn't rewarding at all.

⌐═╤╤╤╤═⌐

That night's supper was the glummest we'd ever eaten. I admit I felt defeated. Oh, we'd still clear out Washington eventually, but with no marketing hook to catch the public's attention, I'd just be nickel-and-diming the inventory. That's no way to live.

Rei tried pitching new ideas. Maybe it was just my mood, but everything she suggested only depressed me more. Shwaanzee wanted to go ahead with our sale anyway, but it would never have worked. Ivan wanted to tell the whole world what a bad person Guillermo Singh was, and how he'd stolen our inspirations. But I was certain Singh would produce some convincing story, maybe even with evidence and witnesses, to make it look like he'd thought of everything himself. When he played dirty tricks, he was thorough.

At the end of the meal, Omar said, "Enough is enough. We need cheering up. How's about we take a trip out of the city? Just to get away for a while."

"Where?" Shwaanzee asked.

"I've got a confession," Omar said. "When you invited me to Washington, you know the first thing that went through my mind? I said, 'Washington, wow! This is my chance to see Dulles airport.'"

"What?"

"Dulles airport. It's not right in D.C., but it's only short way outside. I've always been interested in Dulles because it's where *Die Hard 2* took place."

"Excuse me?" I said. "I thought *Die Hard 2* was just in some made-up place."

"The story is made up but the place is real. There are even some shots of D.C. in the background. Probably just stock footage, but still . . ."

"You mean," I said, "we've been straining our brains to invent a marketing hook when we could just say *Die Hard 2* and the whole damned world would come slobbering to own anything even vaguely connected with the greatest cinematic achievement of all time?"

✦

We made a fortune. An *obscene* fortune. Guillermo Singh could have his silly hot dogs and unfair competition.

Of course, most of our sales revenue went to the U.S.A.'s creditors. But we still got to keep our percentage— enough to set the family up for life, with plenty left over to indulge our whims.

Like buying the presidential palace. The kids had got used to living there. They liked it. So did Rei and I. And the house had enough space that Omar could visit anytime he wanted to.

Just this evening, Omar, Rei and I stood on the balcony watching Shwaanzee ride her panda pony around the rose garden while Ivan haltingly worked his way through *Love Me Tender*. (He's learning to play the guitar). Panda crickets chirped on the lawn while panda gulls circled against the reddening sunset sky.

"It's lovely, isn't it?" Rei said, putting her arm around me. "I had reservations when we first came here. The very thought of coming to America—it scared me. Americans scared me, even if they were gone. They were just so insistent on being foreign. But now . . . I guess we've all become Americans, haven't we?"

"Well," I said, putting one arm around her and the other around Omar, "American-ish."

A Word about WSFA

The Washington Science Fiction Association (WSFA) was started in 1947 by seven science fiction fans who met at that year's Philadelphia Worldcon. Many WSFAns are active in convention-fandom and we helped run the 1998 Baltimore Worldcon and are planning a bid for D.C. for 2011. We ran the DC area science fiction convention Disclave from 1950 to 1997, and now have run Capclave every year since 2001.

Capclave 2005 will be held October 14-16 at the Hilton Washington Silver Spring with guests of honor Howard Waldrop, Patrick Nielsen Hayden, and Teresa Nielsen Hayden. For more information see www.capclave.org.

Our magazine, *The WSFA Journal,* was started in 1965 and has been published regularly (except for a three year gap) ever since. The Journal includes minutes of our meetings, book and movie reviews, humor, science-fiction stories, and the occasional odd article. Over 30 years of the Journal's archives are available at our website: www.wsfa.org.

WSFA Press began in 1989 and published collections of short stories by Disclave Guests of Honor for four years. Books included: *Father of Stones* by Lucius Shepard (1989), *Through Darkest Resnick With Gun and Camera* by Mike Resnick (1990), *Edges of Things* by Lewis Shiner (1991), *Home by the Sea* by Pat Cadigan (1992). These books were produced by Mike Walsh who has since launched his own publishing empire, Old Earth Books. *Future Washington* is the first WSFA Press book in 13 years but we have plans to produce more.

The Association meets on the first and third Friday of every month at the homes of its members. First Friday is traditionally in Virginia, and Third Friday in Maryland, to accommodate folks on either side of the District. We plan conventions and special events, conduct club business, discuss ways of promoting SF in the D.C. area, and yes, sometimes even talk about science fiction.

You can visit our website (http://www.wsfa.org) and come by in October for Capclave . . . if you happen to be in Washington in the future.

— Sam Lubell , President, 2005

FUTURE WASHINGTON

2005

Future Washington edited by Ernest Lilly was published by Washington Science Fiction Association, Inc., 10404 43rd Avenue, Beltsville, Maryland, 20705 One thousand, two hundred copies have been printed by Thomson-Shore, Inc. One thousand in paperback, and two hundred hardcovers. The typeset is Bookman, Adobe Woodtype Ornaments 2 and Freshbot, printed on 60# Joy White Offset. The hardcovers' binding cloth is Pearl Linen. Print Production by Garcia Publishing Services, Woodstock, Illinois.